3/13

FALSE FRONT

FALSE FRONT

Diane Fanning

This first world edition published 2012
in Great Britain and in the USA by
SEVERN HOUSE PUBLISHERS LTD of
9–15 High Street, Sutton, Surrey, England, SM1 1DF.

British Library Cataloguing in Publication Data

Fanning, Diane.
  False front. – (A Lucinda Pierce mystery)
  1. Pierce, Lucinda (Fictitious character)–Fiction.
  2. Women detectives–Fiction. 3. Detective and mystery
  stories.
  I. Title II. Series
  813.6-dc23

ISBN-13: 978-0-7278-8127-4 (cased)

All Severn House titles are printed on acid-free paper.

Severn House Publishers support The Forest Stewardship Council [FSC],
the leading international forest certification organisation. All our titles that
are printed on Greenpeace-approved FSC-certified paper carry the FSC logo.

Typeset by Palimpsest Book Production Ltd.,
Falkirk, Stirlingshire, Scotland.
Printed and bound in Great Britain by
MPG Books Ltd., Bodmin, Cornwall.

Dedicated to the real Lara Quivey
And to the seekers of justice at the Downstate Illinois Innocence Project

ONE

'It's not a suicide,' a voice shouted from the doorway.

Homicide Lieutenant Lucinda Pierce ignored the noise and focused on absorbing the scene around her. To the left, against the wall, a black lacquer table with curved legs bore a large white and red vase containing a greenhouseful of red roses and white lilies. The petals appeared to be as soft as chamois. The floral arrangement overwhelmed the residential space in its size and expense – more suited to a hotel lobby or the entrance of a too-pricey restaurant.

A field of stark white marble veined with black stretched beneath Lucinda's feet. The stone led to two broad steps stretching wall-to-wall. It, too, seemed too much – too grand for a place called home. Beyond the marble flooring, wide heart of pine planks led into an expansive living room populated by white and red chairs and sofas and black lacquer tables. The room ended with floor-to-ceiling glass that bowed out toward the James River as if yearning to set sail.

Directly in front of her, right above the marble steps, an arched walkway, like a bridge over a small stream, spanned from one side of the second floor to the other – the top railing of black lacquer supported by the warm tones of aged pine spindles. Near the center of the walkway, a wooden chair with an upholstered seat pushed against the rail. Attached to the railing, a thick yellow rope formed a dense knot, suspending the body of a middle-aged woman.

'Someone murdered my wife,' the voice from the doorway said. Lucinda assumed it was the voice of Frank Eagleton, the male resident of the home.

Lucinda turned around and faced him. A tall, well-built man in a charcoal suit, striped tie and Italian loafers leaned into the room between the two uniformed officers blocking his access. A very good but still perceptible hairpiece perched on the top of his head. Deep-set blue eyes flashed, his full, lower lip stuck out in defiance. He gave the appearance of a man who was unused to being ignored.

Turning to Sergeant Robin Colter, Lucinda whispered, 'Get the husband away from the doorway. Do it nicely. But make sure the uniforms keep him outside on the premises.' Lucinda returned to her examination. Below the woman's feet, the bright red soles of a pair of Louboutin black spiked heels slashed across the white marble like a fresh wound.

The deceased, presumably Candace Eagleton – the only female living at this address – wore a black pencil skirt and a stark white silk blouse. Around her neck, a light green stone pendant hung from a gold chain. The same stone was in her earrings and on the ring finger of her right hand. Was the way she was dressed telling? Was she on her way out? Did she dress like that around the house, or did she put on a favorite outfit to commit suicide?

Was there significance to the display of the body? No one opening the door could miss her. The high-vaulted ceilings in the foyer seemed to press down, forcing all eyes in the direction of the deceased woman. Beyond the elevated walkway, the ceilings soared up again in the sun-drenched room beyond. Was that her last moment of theatre? Did she want to make sure her husband noticed her at last? Or was her prominent location an arrogant slap from a killer?

'Money can't buy you love.'

Lucinda grinned and turned toward the sound of the familiar gruff voice of the coroner. 'Doc Sam! Is that what you think this is all about – love?'

'Of course. She either felt unloved and, thus, ended her miserable existence, or she was unloved and that person snatched her life away. Love or the lack of it is a backdrop to every story.' The word love sounded incongruous falling off the lips of an old curmudgeon with a balding head of wispy hair and rumpled clothes.

'Are you becoming a romantic in your old age?'

'I'm not too old to show up at yet another of your crime scenes, Pierce,' he said as he tugged on a Tyvec suit and booties.

'True. But love, Doc Sam?' The eyebrow above her good eye arched nearly to her hairline.

'I'm not getting senile, if that's what you think. Blame my granddaughter. She keeps telling me about my lack of faith in humankind and my permanent state of surly cynicism – she actually used that phrase; just fifteen years old and she threw "surly cynicism" at me. Anyway, she nags me to look for the positive, look for the silver lining, look for the love.'

'And you're actually listening and following her advice?'

'She's my granddaughter, Pierce. My only granddaughter. I'm trying but *your* surly cynicism doesn't make it easy.'

Lucinda laughed and faced the body presumed to be Candace Eagleton once again. 'The husband says it's not a suicide.'

'And that surprises you, Pierce? What family does believe a loved one could take their own life?'

'Not surprised at his comment but I am surprised at how perfect the scene looks.'

Doc Sam stepped up to the woman's feet and looked up at her hands. 'Appears to be some dirt under her fingernails.'

'That seems out of character. Looks like a fresh manicure and a pedicure. Look at her. Look around you. This is a woman who takes great care with appearances.'

'Hmm,' Doc Sam said. 'That could explain the perfectly composed suicide scene.'

'Perhaps. But who is the most likely suspect when a woman dies violently in her own home?'

'The husband.'

'Most definitely, Doc. So why would the most likely suspect direct us away from a suicide conclusion?'

'Playing head games with the dumb cops?'

'Most possibly. I hope you can provide some answers for me,' Lucinda said. 'Make sure the hands are bagged before you move the body.'

'Do I tell you how to do your job, Lieutenant?' Doc Sam growled.

Lucinda rolled her eyes. 'Yes, you do. All the time.' She walked away and headed up the stairs.

Doc Sam called after her, 'Do you ever listen?'

Lucinda simply smiled as she stepped onto the walkway. She turned right and entered a symphony of rose and white in a spacious master suite as expansive as some homes. The room smelled softly of refined femininity – a quiet marriage of timid lilies highlighted by demure vanilla. The rose color in the carpet and the draperies was the shade of a soft blush. In a corner, an old child's rocking chair held an antique doll with blonde ringlets, dressed in an outfit that nearly matched the bedspread.

A coved ceiling rose above a four-poster bed covered with a lacy white spread sprinkled with tiny pink roses. The head of the bed was mounded high with decorative pillows in all shapes and shades of rose and pink. In the sitting area, two dark rose chaises sat before the window like two beach chairs facing the sea, the view of the river serene and magical. Between the chaises, a table, draped to the floor in white, bore a bud vase with a singular red rose.

Lucinda stepped into the master bathroom with its floor of white marble and its walls of white, pink and clear glass tiles. The dark rose surface of the vanity stretched long with two basins of translucent white on its surface. A large spa tub with a dozen jets was surrounded by green, growing plants and windows. A separate shower with sprays jutting from three walls stood beside the tub. The water closet was discreetly concealed behind a chest-high wall.

A door led to a walk-in closet with built-in drawers, shelves and hanging bars. She walked through an expansive selection of women's clothing and shoes before exiting out of the other door and back into the bedroom. Not one square inch of space – not one single item – gave the impression that any man had ever walked through the doorway into this female sanctuary. Had she ever shared this room with her husband?

Lucinda emerged from there into the harsh reality of a crime scene. The body no longer hung from the railing but rested on an open body bag, hands bagged, head tilted to one side. She moved on to the other side of the walkway and entered a room that could not have been more different from the one she left.

It was a second master suite, a bit smaller than the room across the walkway but certainly of a sufficiently elegant size. A bold bed frame of rough timber supported a king-sized mattress covered with a dark plaid spread that rose up in a hump at the end of the bed. A pile of decorative pillows formed a mountain on the window seat. A rustic nightstand bore a lamp made from deer antler, an alarm clock and two hand weights.

The draperies around the window of the sitting area matched the plaid of the bedspread. A chair and a recliner upholstered in dark green leather with brass brads sat at broad angles in front of the window. A primitive bent twig table sat betwixt them – a bottle of Jack Daniels, an ice bucket and two glasses on its surface.

Through the doorway to the bathroom, Lucinda spotted a slate-tiled walk-in shower big enough to sluice down a whole football team. A small walk-in Jacuzzi sat in a corner, flanked by windows. Rustic wood formed the vanity, its surface covered with a thick pane of glass. Two copper basins sat on top of that. Behind a chest-high wall were a urinal and a water closet.

Through the closet door, Lucinda found the same meticulous, personalized attention to detail in the storage design. This closet, however, was filled with male clothing exclusively. There was even an alcove built to the correct dimensions to hold a pair of the waist-high waders that trout fishermen wear. The door on the other side opened into the bedroom. It seemed apparent that the couple had not shared a bedroom. Did that mean they had not shared a sex life?

Lucinda went back downstairs and scanned the front yard until she caught Robin Colter's eye. She raised her chin and Robin cut off her conversation with a patrolman and came inside. 'Is the husband in the back of a car?' Lucinda asked.

'Yes. He threatened to leave since no one would listen to him. He tried to barrel his way through the officers at the front door. We ended up putting him in cuffs to get him in the patrol vehicle. Once there, though, he calmed down. I took off the cuffs and he swore he would not attempt to leave the car until the detective in charge talked to him. He even said he was willing to spend the night there if he had to do so, as if it was his idea to climb into the car.'

'Makes you wonder if he bullied his wife, too,' Lucinda said.

'He does seem used to getting what he wants, when he wants it. The last time I talked to him, he was demanding a timetable. He said he didn't mind waiting, but he needed some parameters.'

Their conversation was interrupted by Doc Sam. 'Pierce, you better take a look at this.' He held up a clear plastic sleeve with an open piece of paper inside it.

> ~~Dear~~ Frank,
> *You have taken my heart, crushed it, stomped on it and pulverized it. You have destroyed my ability to love. I suspect that, if we remained together, it would only be a matter of time before you take my life.*
>
> *I have been working to obtain an independent source of income because once I leave, I will not want to be connected to you in any way. If you are reading this note, that means I have secured the revenue I need. All that remains is the division of the estate.*
>
> *Since the house was built with the money I brought to the marriage, it seems right that I remain in it. However, if you want the house, you can have it. If you want to sell the house, we can do it. I simply want out.*

Your betrayed wife and the debased mother of your children,
        Candace

Lucinda read the letter out loud and handed it back to Doc Sam. 'Perhaps the husband is right after all. Someone did murder his wife.' She looked out to the patrol car holding the husband, raised her hand and pointed her finger like a gun. 'Tag, you're it, Frank Eagleton.'

TWO

F BI Special Agent in Charge Jake Lovett sat at his desk studying the man across from him. Behind him, the blinds were drawn to eliminate the distraction of the cityscape from his visitor. A long bookcase ran from wall-to-wall below the window. Stacks of files with protruding multicolored Post-it notes littered the top of it. An open laptop sat on the right-hand side of his desk, a telephone, framed photograph of his parents and a bobbing woodpecker on the left. In front of him a legal pad and pen lay waiting.

In the chair opposite the agent, a man shifted from side to side as he twisted a baseball cap in his hands. He covered his balding head in a peculiar comb-over style reminiscent of Donald Trump. Jake wondered how anyone could look at the financial mogul on television and think, 'Hey, that's just the look for me.' He appeared to be about fifty – a worn-out fifty – with bags under his eyes, large pores across his nose and gray bristles sprinkled along his jawline, giving the appearance that he shaved in the dark.

'Nothing you are saying is making much sense,' Jake said. 'As I said, without your name, the nature of the crime and the identity of the person who is threatening you, I don't know what I can possibly do to help you.'

'You have to help me or I'm a dead man,' the man pleaded.

'I appreciate that you have concerns about your personal safety but you still have told me nothing that explains why you are here at the FBI instead of a local law enforcement office.'

'I did. I told you. There's a federal connection.'

'Yes, you did say that. But you have given me no indication of how there is a federal connection. Does it involve a federal employee?'

'I don't know if that's the correct way to put it or not but maybe.'

'Did the crime happen on federal property?'

'I don't know. There was one meeting at the Lincoln Memorial. Does that count?'

'It might if I knew what happened at the monument.'

The man exhaled loudly. 'I can't tell you until I know I won't be prosecuted.'

'So you were involved in a crime that might be a federal crime?'

'Actually, there are two crimes,' he said and flashed a grin.

'Two crimes? Are either of them federal?'

'I'm not sure. I don't think the first one is but I might be wrong about the property lines when it comes to my part of the thing. And the second one, well, I thought it might be because someone who might become a federal employee is involved.'

Jake bent his head down and scratched the nape of his neck. 'We are going nowhere here. I think this is a waste of time. You told me that it was a matter of national security. You told me it involved a high-level person in the government. You told me it could damage the President of the United States. But since you walked into my office you have told me nothing to substantiate those claims. I believe it's time you left,' Jake said as he rose to his feet.

The man jumped up. 'No. No. You can't send me out there without protection. I was followed here. I know it. If I walk out that door I'm a dead man. They'll know I've been in your office.'

'Sir, please.' Jake placed a hand on the man's shoulder and applied minimum pressure to maneuver him towards the door. 'You go on home and think about this a little more. If you decide to be more forthcoming with your information, you are more than welcome to return.'

The man dropped to the floor, crossed his legs, and wrapped a hand around the arm of the chair. 'No. No. You can't make me. I'll tell you everything. But I have to have some guarantees. I have to know you will keep me safe. I have to know I won't be prosecuted.'

Jake was now convinced he had a nutcase in his office. 'OK, sir. Calm down.' He leaned back against his desk and crossed his arms. 'You've gotta spill something if you want my help. Explain what you said about the property lines.'

'I'm not sure whether the body was buried inside the Thomas Jefferson National Forest or just outside of it.'

'Body? Are you saying someone was murdered?'

'Yeah. But I didn't do that. I just dug the hole and helped throw it in.'

'Who was murdered?'

'I'm not sure. The body was wrapped in a blanket. The only thing that I could see was a little bit of hair that stuck out at one end. Looked like a woman's hair.'

'When did this happen?'

'Oh, 'bout thirty years ago.'

'Thirty years ago?'

'Yep. But that's just the first crime I know about.'

'What's the second crime?' Jake asked.

'A death threat.'

'To you?'

'Now why would I threaten myself?'

Jake shook his head. 'So you made the death threat?'

'Sort of.'

'Sort of? What the heck does that mean?'

'I said the words the other person standing next to me told me to say.'

'Who was standing next to you?'

The man sighed. 'C'mon, man. Aren't you paying any attention? The individual who killed that woman thirty years ago.'

'OK. So who did you threaten?'

'It was that person's threat really . . .'

'Right. Who was threatened?'

'A woman.'

'Oh, for God's sake! What woman?' Jake said, leaning forward with his hands on his hips.

'I don't know.' The man shrugged.

'You don't know? You—' An incoming call interrupted Jake. He lifted the receiver and said, 'Lovett.'

'OK. Face recognition software gave us some possibilities and we narrowed it down from there. We believe you are speaking to Charles David Rowland, currently residing in Norfolk, Virginia, previously a resident of Trenton, New Jersey. A lot of arrests. No felony convictions.'

'Thank you,' Jake said and disconnected the call. 'Why don't you get up off the floor, Mr Rowland, and have a seat in the chair.'

The man started to rise with a smile on his face but froze in place halfway in his ascent. His smile disintegrated as he said, 'Excuse me?'

'Drop the act, Mr Rowland. How long since you've paid a visit to Trenton?'

The man rose to his full height and took two steps backward.

'Sir, have a seat.'

'You'll regret this,' he said and bolted for the door.

Jake followed him into the hall but saw no sign of him. He opened the door to the stairwell but heard no sound of footsteps. He looked at the elevator. The screen indicated that it had stopped one floor below him. He stabbed at the button and swore under his breath as it continued its descent.

Jake pulled out his cell and called down to the security desk in the lobby. The officer answered but had difficulty understanding him because of the high level of noise. 'What is going on down there?' Jake screamed into the mouthpiece.

'Senator Fowler and a flock of media,' the officer shouted back.

'Stop the man coming off the elevator. He's about—'

'What?'

Jake looked at the digital screen. The elevator was already on the ground floor. 'The man coming out of the elevator—'

'What about him?'

'Stop him, damn it.'

'The guy in the ball cap?'

'Yes.'

'He's already gone.'

Jake disconnected from the call. He rushed back into his office and pulled up the blinds. He thought he saw a glimpse of someone dart behind the building next door but wasn't sure if it was Rowland. He slumped down in his chair and picked up the receiver on his desk and dialed the local police department to request a BOLO (Be On the Look-Out) for Charles David Rowland.

He didn't know what Rowland's game was but his curiosity had been piqued. It might be inconsequential but then again, the mention of the President raised the stakes. The man's talk of the White House occupant threw the investigation into Secret Service territory. He made a note to call and brief them on his strange encounter after he filed a report for his own agency.

THREE

Lucinda sent Robin to inform Eagleton that he was being transported to the justice center downtown. She stood in the doorway to watch his reaction. Robin opened the back door of the vehicle and leaned forward. A moment later she staggered backward as Eagleton erupted from the car. A patrolman rushed over and helped Robin get him cuffed once again and shoved back inside. Lucinda could hear the bellows of Eagleton's voice but could not decipher the words.

She went upstairs again. If there was dirt under Candace's fingernails – if she was murdered – there should be signs of a struggle somewhere. She'd seen nothing obvious on her last examination. This time, she'd look closer. Her nose nearly pressed against the outside frame of the door, she peered at every inch up one side and down the other.

Moving inside the room, she repeated the process. Midway down the unhinged side, she saw light scratch marks in the paint on the wall and tiny grooves in the woodwork. She stuck a red sticker next to the barely perceptible scars.

She got down on her hands and knees and crawled across the bedroom floor. When she reached the wall, she turned around, moved over a foot, and headed back in the opposite direction. She repeated this process several times until she reached the bottom of the bed. She ran her finger around the indentation that circled one leg, and then crawled forward until she reached the second one. There her finger hit a small, solid object. The shadows of the bed covering made it necessary to pull out her flashlight to see what her finger found.

She saw one green stone bead and then another. How long had they rested there? Had it been days, weeks, months? Or did they land there earlier that day? The stones appeared to match the jewelry the victim was wearing when she was found. Had she worn a bracelet that morning? Was it broken by force when someone attacked her? Did the perp try to pick up all the pieces and missed these two? Or was it all just a coincidence? Lucinda's nose involuntarily crinkled with distaste at the latter possibility.

Lucinda continued her search of the floor. She was still on all fours when she heard Marguerite Spellman call her name. Lucinda leaned back on her heels and spotted the forensic specialist standing in the door frame, her hands gloved, her body covered in a blue Tyvec suit from the booties on her feet to the hood over her head.

'Glad to see you, Spellman,' Lucinda said.

'Have you found anything?' Marguerite asked.

'Take a step inside and look at the spot on and near the frame that I marked. What does it look like to you?'

Marguerite peered at it without saying a word. She pulled a portable light and a magnifying glass out of her kit bag. She examined the area even more closely. 'Possibly fingernail scratches but it could have been caused by something else.'

'There is some sort of dirt under the victim's fingernails,' Lucinda said.

'Hmm.'

'Could she have grabbed there when someone extracted her from the room?'

'Maybe,' Marguerite said. 'I'd have to compare the paint and the debris under her nails.' She pulled out a camera and added a macrolens before shooting a close-up of the area in question. She swabbed the damaged area and then collected paint samples. While she worked, Lucinda returned to her examination of the floor.

Marguerite packed away the samples and asked, 'Anything else?'

'Yes,' Lucinda said as she crawled back to the bedpost leg where she found the beads. 'Take a look at these.'

Marguerite lowered herself to the floor and followed the beam of Lucinda's flashlight. 'No way to tell how long they've been there.'

'No, not really,' Lucinda admitted. 'They appear to match the other jewelry the victim wore but I won't know for sure until we collect them. I wanted an in situ shot first.'

'Not going to be easy,' Marguerite said. 'I'll do my best.' She slid under the bed with her photographic equipment and took shots from several angles. She then retrieved and bagged the stones.

Lucinda completed her examination of the bedroom floor. 'I moved slowly and looked very carefully, Spellman. If there is anything else to find in this carpet, it's going to take someone with more than one eye to find it.'

'I imagine you would have seen anything that's there, Lieutenant.

But I'll assign the tech with the youngest and sharpest pair of eyes to repeat the scan just to be sure.'

'Good. Your team's all here?'

'Sure is.'

'OK. I'll leave it all up to you, then,' Lucinda said. 'I need to get down to the justice center to talk to the husband.'

'You think he did it?'

'Don't know but I sure wouldn't place a bet on his innocence.'

As Lucinda drove downtown, she hoped she wouldn't have to cancel her dinner date with Jake that evening but knew she probably would. It happened too often. Either she had an investigation that interrupted their plans or he did. They rarely seemed to catch a demanding case at the same time. They more often came one after another, sometimes making it impossible for them to get together for days or even weeks. But the first hours of any murder investigation mattered too much and at this point, she knew she couldn't break for a moment until she at least knew whether she was looking at a homicide or a suicide.

She called the morgue and asked for Doc Sam. She was told he was in the middle of an autopsy. She was pleased to learn he was working on her victim – if that's what she was. An answer to that big question should be forthcoming in no time.

Back at the justice center, she went straight to the basement to check on the doctor's progress before going upstairs to grill Frank Eagleton. She pulled on a gown and head gear but held her hands behind her back rather than glove-up. She didn't think she'd be there long.

'Got anything for me, Doc?'

Doc Sam growled and said, 'You know I can't form conclusions until I complete the job and as you can see I'm elbow-deep in it now.'

Lucinda stifled a grin at his literal use of the hackneyed phrase. 'Yes, sir, Doctor. I know that but I thought you might be willing to share your brilliant observations.'

He glared at her over the tops of his glasses. 'You need to display more respect for your elders, Pierce.'

'Sir, you know—'

'Don't start, Pierce. I cleaned out under her fingernails and sent the sample upstairs to the lab for the witch that runs the place to examine. She'll be giving you the official report on that.'

Lucinda grinned at his description of Audrey Ringo, the head of the forensics lab. 'What did the sample look like?' Lucinda asked.

'You know I can't tell anything just by looking at it.'

'You didn't—'

'Yes, I did. I popped it under the microscope to give it a quick look before sending it to Audrey. It appears to be skin cells, paint chips and threads of some fiber or another. But I can't swear to any of that because I didn't test it. As you well know, that's not my job. This is my job,' he said, pointing both hands at the body on the stainless steel slab. 'Now, will you let me get back to it?'

'Certainly, you old curmudgeon. I'll send Colter down to observe. I've got to talk to the husband.'

'Curmudgeon, Pierce? Now that was uncalled for . . .'

'I know, Doc. But sometimes I simply lose control. And "curmudgeon" sorta rolls across the tongue and tickles the palate, doesn't it?'

'Get out of here, Pierce.'

Lucinda chuckled while she slipped out of the surgical garments and hopped in the elevator to go to her office. When she walked into the reception area, she heard pounding and a loud voice drifting down the hall. 'Let me out of here. Where is that damned detective? Why is this door locked? I demand my freedom.'

'Oh, good grief,' Lucinda said with a sigh.

Kristen, the department's petite and, in Lucinda's estimation, far too perky secretary and receptionist was still new enough to be amused by the behavior of visitors in the interrogation room. She laughed, tilted her head, tossing her shoulder-length brown hair off to one side and said, 'Yes. We've tried to ply him with hospitality. We offered him coffee, soda, water. Sergeant Colter even offered to run out and get him a sandwich if he would only settle down. But he refused it all – obviously preferring to pound and shout than to indulge in food or drink. Seems like it's time for a lion tamer – got your whip and chair?'

As if in response, Eagleton let out a particularly loud and feral bellow that Lucinda thought she could feel in the soles of her feet. 'This is ridiculous!' she spat out as she marched down the hall. She landed a fist on the reinforced glass window. 'Cut it out!'

He responded with more pounding. 'I demand . . .' he shouted.

'Sit down, Mr Eagleton!'

'I demand—'

'No one gives a damn about your demands. Sit your ass down in that chair if you want me to talk to you.'

Eagleton stopped pounding and pulled back his head as if in shock that she'd spoken to him that way. But he didn't move away from the door.

'I am serious, Mr Eagleton. Stop this childish display and sit in that chair now or I'll rustle up a couple beefy cops who will cuff you, shackle you and muscle you down to a holding cell where you can cool your jets for a while.' Lucinda glared through the window.

A look of defiance crossed Eagleton's face. Then his shoulders slumped and he turned, crossed the room and sat in the chair. He lifted both hands and raised his shoulders in a shrug.

Lucinda opened the door far enough to stick her head through. 'Now, you just sit there quietly, like a good boy, and I'll be back in a few minutes.'

Eagleton rose from the chair and started to bluster.

'Sit, Mr Eagleton. Sit.'

His eyes formed slits and his lips curled up as he lowered himself into the chair.

Lucinda sighed and went to her office. She sent an email to the records department requesting any priors on Frank Eagleton and another to Lara Quivey in Research asking for an instant background report on him. She went to the kitchen to get a cup of coffee. By the time she returned she had a response to her first query, indicating that Eagleton had no record. While she was reading it, the message from Lara arrived in her inbox. She printed it out and read it while she walked back down the hall. As she learned about his background of wealth and privilege, she was surprised that he hadn't demanded an attorney already and feared he would do just that when she asked her first question.

FOUR

Lucinda sat down across from Eagleton and tried to hold his gaze, but in less than ten seconds he turned away. 'I'm not a cat, Lieutenant. I don't enjoy staring contests.'

Instead of responding, she kept her eyes on his averted face.

Finally, he turned back towards her and raised his eyebrows. 'When did you last see your wife, Mr Eagleton?'

'This morning, when I went to work.'

'What time was that?'

'Seven fifteen, seven thirty.'

'Was she wearing the same clothing as she was when we arrived at your home?'

'No, Lieutenant,' he smirked. 'She was wearing a towel. I stuck my head into her room and asked her if she planned on being home all day.'

'And why did you and your wife have separate bedrooms?'

'It was her decision, Lieutenant. Not mine.'

'Why the separate rooms, Mr Eagleton?'

'As I said, it wasn't my idea.'

'That didn't answer my question.'

'I liked sharing a bed with my wife. She might have been getting older but I still appreciated her body and the comfort of her warm presence next to me at night. I haven't slept all that well since she moved across the hall.'

'One more time, Mr Eagleton: why did the two of you not share a bedroom?'

He slapped his hands on the table. 'Simple, Lieutenant. She was really pissed off.'

Lucinda clenched her jaw. 'And why was she pissed off, sir?'

Eagleton sighed. 'Someone told her I was having an affair with my secretary.'

'Were you?'

'Was I what?'

'Don't be obtuse, Mr Eagleton. Were you having an affair?'

He blew air out of loose lips, making them vibrate against each other. 'Yes,' he said. 'It didn't mean anything. It was just recreational. Stress relief. It didn't mean I didn't still love my wife.'

'Did you, Mr Eagleton? Did you still love your wife?'

'Of course I did. She's the mother of my children. She helped me build my business. She helped make me a success.'

'That sounds like gratitude, not love.'

'You're not married, are you, Lieutenant?'

'Please answer the question.'

Eagleton leaned forward with his elbows on the table. 'Gratitude is one of the building blocks of lasting love, Lieutenant.'

'Nice philosophy, Mr Eagleton,' she said as her lips involuntarily formed a sneer. 'And you demonstrate your gratitude to your wife by climbing into bed with someone else?'

'That had nothing to do with my wife.'

'Is that how your lover saw it?'

'Lieutenant, I did not lie to that girl. I told her from the start that I would never leave my wife. I told her I was just looking for good times and relaxation.'

'Really? And how did she react to that?'

'She stood up on the bed, stark naked, her legs spread, straddling my waist and said, 'Good. Just consider me your new therapist.'

Lucinda looked at the sparkle in Eagleton's eyes and recoiled from it. His wife's death didn't seem to sully the pleasure of his illicit memories one little bit. 'Back to the last time you saw your wife: what did she say? Was she going to be home all day?'

'She said, "Maybe." She said, "A client is meeting me here at the house at nine. If it goes well we may go to lunch after our meeting."'

'Did she tell you who that client was? For that matter, what did your wife do for her clients? What kind of service did she provide?'

'No. I have no idea. She told me nothing. She used to do public relations work but that was ages ago. So I asked her, "Client? What kind of client? You don't have a job."'

'And her answer?' Lucinda asked.

'All she said was, "See Frank, you know nothing about me. You hardly know I am alive." I said, "You never told me you had a job." And she said, "You never asked. Now will you please leave so I can get dressed?" And that pissed me off.'

'Why?'

'We've been married all these years,' he said, his voice rising. 'I've seen her starkers more times than I've had a beer. And I have to leave for her to get dressed?'

'How much did it piss you off, Mr Eagleton?'

'Enough to make me stalk out without saying "goodbye."'

'Is that what you did, Mr Eagleton?'

'That's what I said, isn't it?'

'No. It isn't, sir. You said that it made you angry enough to stalk out of the room, not that you did stalk out of the room.'

Eagleton popped to his feet. 'Now you are playing word games?'

'I'm not playing any games. I do not think the death of your wife is a game, do you?'

'Don't be ridiculous.'

'Please sit down, Mr Eagleton. And try to control your temper.'

He glared at her and lowered down into the chair.

'Thank you,' Lucinda said. 'Now, did it piss you off enough to make you attack your wife?'

'What? I've never raised a hand to that woman.'

'Did you fake her suicide to cover up your crime?'

Eagleton shot to his feet again. Veins pounded in his forehead and neck. His face flushed red. 'What's wrong with you? I'm the one who told you it was not a suicide. Remember?'

'Clever ruse, don't you think?'

Eagleton stepped up to the side of the table, his hands clenched by his sides. 'How dare you?'

'Mr Eagleton, don't make me restrain you. Get back on your side of the table and sit down.'

He sucked a deep breath in through his nose, making his chest heave. A look of distaste curled his lips. 'You sicken me,' he said as he took a step back. 'I've told you I loved my wife,' he said as he slid back into his seat.

'You also told me you were having a cheap affair with one of your employees. I can't quite fit those two concepts into one bucket.'

'I never said "cheap."'

'So you were in love with this girl?'

'No. It was sex – just sex.'

'You know we will have to speak with her?'

Eagleton rolled his eyes. 'Yes. Not the happiest realization I've had today.'

'What was that?'

'What was what?' Eagleton asked.

'Your happiest realization this morning. What was that? Learning you're now a widower?'

'Goddammit!' he said, slapping his hand on the table. 'I'm talking to you for one reason and one reason only. My wife did not commit suicide. She wouldn't. That means someone killed her. I want that bastard locked up.'

'Did your wife have any enemies?'

'Only perceived ones.'

'What does that mean?'

'Sometimes she acted like I was the enemy but that was nothing new. From time to time, she'd get all paranoid that I was plotting to leave her. She'd get the children to question me. But I knew she couldn't help herself. She had a pathological poor sense of self-worth. Then, when she got that note telling her about the girl a year and a half ago, she focused her paranoia on her. She saw the girl as her enemy. But she wasn't. She had no plans to take her place. She was just – just – just . . .'

'Just what, Mr Eagleton?'

'Just there.'

'And what is this young woman's name?'

'April,' Eagleton said.

'April what?'

'April Flowers.'

'What's her real name, Mr Eagleton?'

'That's it.'

'Really?'

'Call personnel. They'll tell you. Her parents were idiots. That is not my fault.'

'Isn't that supposed to be "April Showers?"'

'As I said: her parents are idiots. Now what are you doing to find whoever killed my wife?'

'We're doing a lot, Mr Eagleton. This is just part of it. We've obtained a search warrant and are going through your home looking for any little bit of forensic evidence. We've also gotten search warrants for all the home computers. But most importantly, Mr Eagleton, the autopsy being performed on your wife's body should tell us if this is a homicide or a suicide. I am most interested in what was under your wife's fingernails. If you did attack your wife, there is a strong possibility we will find your DNA there. We will know then that you did, in fact, attack your wife.'

Eagleton propped his elbows on the table and rested his forehead in his palms as he sighed. Raising his head, he said, 'What can I do to get you to stop wasting time on me and go find her killer?'

'For starters, you can give me an address for April Flowers.'

'I don't know her mailing address but she lives in Commonwealth Towers, Apartment 712. You don't seriously think that little twit had anything to do with my wife's murder, do you?'

'Mr Eagleton, do you know what the two most likely scenarios are in this situation?'

'No, Lieutenant.'

'The first most common result is that the autopsy report will confirm a suicide—'

'But, I told you . . .'

Lucinda raised her hands. 'I know, Mr Eagleton. But something else is very common – probably the vast majority of family members of suicides have at least a short period of time when they deny the possibility. You would not be the first.'

'OK. OK. What is the other scenario?'

'That would be you, Mr Eagleton.'

'Back to that again.'

'Yes, sir. When a person is murdered in their own home, the most frequent perpetrator is the spouse or significant other.'

'So there's nothing I can do?'

'Yes, there is. You can continue to be cooperative. You can call me if you think of anything that might be significant. And you can wait with some degree of patience until we learn how your wife died.'

'Meanwhile, whoever killed her just sits out there and gloats.'

'I have no leads to a possible suspect other than you, at this point, Mr Eagleton, and you have not been able to offer any possibilities except perhaps for your love interest . . .'

'I do not love that girl.'

'You said. We will see if her view of the relationship matches yours. I'll be talking to her – so you see, at this point, you are not the only suspect. Hopefully, the forensic analysis will lead us to others if neither of you are guilty.'

'How about if I take a lie detector test?'

'That might be appropriate later on. But not now – not while we still don't know if we have a homicide or not.'

'Like I said: nothing I can do until you're done screwing around.'

'You can call it what you want, but what we are trying to do is to determine what happened to your wife, Mr Eagleton. I would think that's what you would want.'

Eagleton rose to his feet. 'I suppose this means I am not under arrest?'

'No, sir, you are not.'

'Good. While you're spinning your wheels, I'm going to get my own investigation going.'

'I must warn you not to obstruct our investigation, Mr Eagleton.

You'd be best served leaving those matters to us. And please do not inform Miss Flowers that I intend to visit.'

Eagleton walked to the door and turned to face her. 'You ever hear the expression "you get what you pay for?"'

'Certainly,' Lucinda said with a nod.

'I look at you and what do I see – a one-eyed, scarred woman with a chip on her shoulder paid a government employee salary. No offense, but I am able to hire a private investigator with at least as much experience as you, who earns in a month what you make in a year – and he has both eyes. Who do you think I'll trust?'

'Whomever you've bought and paid for, Mr Eagleton.'

He jerked open the door, spun around and said, 'Damn you, Lieutenant,' before he walked out of the room.

Self-consciously, Lucinda brought one hand to her prosthetic eye and ran her fingers down the craters of scar tissue on that side of her face. 'Damn me, indeed,' she said to the empty room.

FIVE

Lucinda's cell vibrated in her pocket. She picked it up and said, 'What've you got, Doc Sam?'

'C'mon down here and I'll show you,' he said and disconnected the call.

Lucinda walked down two flights of stairs and into the morgue.

'She definitely died from hanging,' he said as she entered the room.

'Suicide?'

'Nah, look at this . . .' He pointed to Candace's neck.

'What am I seeing, Doc?' Lucinda asked.

'Abrasions on the skin caused by the rope. Instead of a simple line that pulls up behind the ears, there are multiple fainter lines around the deep indentation that is the apparent one caused by the drop of the body. Almost as if she made a few false attempts before she succeeded. And I don't think that's possible.'

'I don't understand,' Lucinda said.

'If I had to guess, I'd say that someone tortured her before they killed her.'

'Torture?'

'Think of it like you would manual strangulation. Remember that guy up in Arlington? He'd choke the women until they passed out. When they revived, he'd do it again. Over and over.'

'Yes, I read about him.'

'It looks like someone jerked her up by her neck several times before sending her over that railing to finish it. But then again, it could just be an odd suicide. Not really sure yet.'

Lucinda sighed. 'Do you think you'll be able to make a determination?'

'Don't know. Maybe when Audrey the lab tyrant gets me an analysis of what was under her fingernails. Maybe when I get the toxicology report. Maybe never.'

'What about the time of death?'

'I can give you a range but it overlaps both the time the husband said he was at home and most of the time he said that he was absent from the home.'

Lucinda turned on her heels and walked out without a word. She was churning with frustration. If there was an answer, he would find it. Wouldn't he? And if he didn't, where did that leave them? A possible killer who could never be prosecuted? A suicide her husband would not understand or accept? Or was there even a worse possibility that she could not yet begin to imagine?

Lucinda walked under the unnatural glow of mercury lights shining down on the sidewalk. She pulled open a tall glass door and strode up to the desk in the lobby of the high-rise apartment building. She flipped out her badge and said, 'I am here to speak to April Flowers.'

A bone-thin, male receptionist with pitch-black hair and cold blue eyes gave her an appraising look. He reached forward to a panel of buttons.

'I'd rather you didn't do that. Why don't you just give me access to her floor?'

The young man's mouth formed an exaggerated O. 'My, my,' he said. 'Sounds serious.'

Lucinda flashed a grim smile and waited.

He fidgeted in silence for a moment and then said, 'OK. I wouldn't want to interfere with police business.' He started around the counter and stopped. 'Maybe I should call the manager first?'

Lucinda folded her arms across her chest. 'You are incapable of

making a simple decision on your own? How often do you call
the manager? Every evening? Do you ever worry about being too
much of a nuisance? Has the manager ever expressed displeasure
over your inability to think for yourself?'

He flushed red. 'That was totally uncalled for, Officer. I was just
thinking aloud.'

'Lieutenant,' Lucinda corrected.

'Whatever! Follow me,' he said as he swung around the counter
and headed for the elevator. When the doors opened, he scanned
the identity card on the lanyard around his neck and hit the button
for the tenth floor.

Lucinda stepped inside the lift and asked, 'Apartment number?'

'Ten-ten.'

As the doors started to close he stuck his face close to the dimin-
ishing gap. 'If she's not home, you are not authorized to go inside
her unit.'

Reaching the hallway, Lucinda looked up and down its length at
the rough concrete walls, shiny concrete floor, industrial hardware
– typical new construction for the current hip residential spot in
downtown. She turned right and walked half the length in that
direction before arriving at the door marked '1010.'

She listened for a moment but could hear no sound from the
apartment. She pressed the door buzzer and thought she heard
the whispery sound of slippers slipping across the concrete floor
inside. Metal slid softly and an eye appeared in the peephole.
Lucinda held up her badge.

The door opened a crack. 'Yes, may I help you?'

'April Flowers?'

'Yes?'

Lucinda held her badge toward the crack in the door as she tried
to get a good look at the woman on the other side. She couldn't
see much but a bowed head with long, shiny blonde hair hanging
down straight as a plumb line, obscuring her features. 'Lieutenant
Pierce. Homicide. I need to talk to you about a friend of yours.'

'I have a dead friend?'

'I think not. Please may I come in?' Lucinda asked.

April shut the door, disconnected the chain and reopened the
door, inviting Lucinda inside. She was shorter than Lucinda but
average in stature for a woman. Her thinness, though, made her
appear tiny – small enough to be blown away by a baby's breath.

She led Lucinda past the kitchen and into the living room. The end wall was all glass with a view over the downtown area including the lush Robert E. Lee Gardens in Stonewall Jackson Park. Ironically, the street renamed in honor of Martin Luther King, Jr bordered one side of the open green space. Only in Virginia, Lucinda thought.

As they sat down across from one another, Lucinda asked, 'Do you know Frank Eagleton?'

'Yes, he's my boss.'

'Is that all? Just your boss?'

'What do you mean?' she asked, tilting her head to the side and widening her dark brown eyes.

'Are you or have you ever been romantically involved with Mr Eagleton?'

'Romantically? No. He's old enough to be my father.'

'OK. Are you sexually involved with Mr Eagleton?'

'Involved? What do you mean, involved?' April asked.

Lucinda leaned forward, resting her elbows on her knees. 'Have you ever engaged in sexual intercourse with Mr Eagleton or performed any other act that could be construed to be sexual in nature?'

'Me? Mr Eagleton?'

'Miss Flowers, please stop playing coy.'

April straightened her posture and folded her hands in a demure bundle on her lap. 'Whatever do you mean, ma'am?'

'I mean, miss, that Mr Eagleton already admitted to screwing around with you. Your avoidance of the question is annoying.'

'Mr Eagleton . . .' April pursed her lips and ran her tongue across them. 'I can't imagine what would have made Mr Eagleton say that.'

'Do you know Candace Eagleton?'

'Of course. She's come into the office on several occasions. I haven't seen her recently, though.'

'Really? Are you sure you didn't pay her a visit this morning?'

'Why would I do that? Did something happen to Mrs Eagleton?'

'Please answer the question, Miss Flowers. Did you go to the Eagleton home this morning?'

'I was at work this morning,' April said.

'Have you ever been in the Eagleton home? Think before you answer, Miss Flowers. If we find your fingerprints in that house after you've denied being there, you will regret it.'

April rose to her feet and walked over to the exterior wall, leaning her forehead against the glass. She spun around and said, 'You can't tell Candace.'

'Tell Candace what?'

'You have to promise,' April said and bit lightly on her lower lip.

'I promise I will not say a word to Candace Eagleton.'

April sighed, walked back to her chair and flopped into it. 'I did go there a couple of times. Once we made love in Candace's bed. I know that was wrong – on so many levels. I just hate that woman for making it difficult for Frank and me to be together.'

'You two had plans?'

'Of course. We wanted to spend the rest of our lives together.'

'But Candace was in the way?'

'She knew about our affair but she still didn't let him go.'

'Did Candace tell you that?' Lucinda asked.

'Oh, no. I didn't talk to Candace about that.'

'Is that what Frank told you, then?'

'He didn't have to tell me. I knew he loved me. We were soul-mates. I knew his heart's desires without asking.'

'Interesting, Miss Flowers. Mr Eagleton seems totally unaware that your relationship was anything but recreational.'

April furrowed her brow. 'What do you mean by that?'

'Mr Eagleton made it clear to me that he had no intention of leaving his wife. He said he loved her. He said you were simply a convenience. A sexual outlet.'

'How dare you!'

Lucinda threw up her hands. 'These are not my words, Miss Flowers. They came from the mouth of your sexual partner.'

'You are lying. The moment Candace is out of the picture, we'll be flying off to Reno to get married.'

'Did Frank tell you that?'

'Not in so many words.'

'So when you found out your little fantasies about Frank Eagleton would never come true, because he would not leave his wife, you did the only other thing you could do, didn't you?'

'What?'

'You killed Candace Eagleton, didn't you?'

'Killed? What are you talking about? She's dead?'

'Did Frank help you kill her?'

'No. What are you saying?'

'So you did it on your own?'

'I didn't say that. I didn't do that. Whatever Frank did, he did it on his own. I had nothing to do with it.'

'You think Frank killed his wife?'

'I don't know. He didn't talk to me about it. He grumbled about her from time to time but when I pressed him he would not explain his complaints. He would not answer my questions.'

'You think Frank is capable of committing murder?'

'I think Frank can do anything he sets his mind to. He is a powerful and persistent man. I've seen him destroy other people – not physically but financially, emotionally – just because they were in his way. He is heartless. You see how he betrayed me.'

'And you want to spend the rest of your life with this man?'

'Not anymore. He has trivialized our relationship.'

'That bothers you more than the fact that he is a suspect in the death of his wife?'

'Well, if he did it for love – if he did it for me – it wouldn't be right but I could understand. I could forgive him,' she said in a whisper.

'I doubt if Candace Eagleton would if she could. And if he is responsible, the State of Virginia won't be so gracious either. And that goes for you as well, Miss Flowers. If we learn you played any small role in that woman's death – even simply that you possessed foreknowledge of the crime – there will be no forgiveness for you either.'

'I've done nothing wrong,' she said, her lips forming a pout.

'Let's not exaggerate, Miss Flowers.'

'Well, consenting adults and all that – maybe you are not sophisticated enough to understand.'

Lucinda laughed at that statement coming from a young secretary in her early twenties. 'Fine, Miss Flowers. Here's my card. If you think of any odd, unusual or unexpected behavior by Mr Eagleton, please give me a call. Maybe when you grow up a bit, your moral compass won't wobble so badly.'

'What?'

Lucinda shook her head and left the apartment. April shouted down the hall, 'What do you mean?'

SIX

Jake walked into his Spartan apartment, wondering once again why he wasn't more motivated to make the space more personal – more like home. It was a perfectly good unit with a lot of potential but it felt like a way station. A place to sleep, work and waste time. He didn't feel as if he lived here. One more time, he promised himself that he'd spend the weekend getting some of his belongings out of storage.

He grabbed a beer and the stack of mail he picked up at his box on his way inside. He set aside a telephone bill, tossed the junk mail in the recycling bin and placed the latest issue of *Sports Illustrated* beside his recliner. All that remained was a small envelope addressed to him in careful block printing. The return address made him smile – it was a note from Charley Spencer.

He pulled out a thank-you card. Inside it was filled with labored cursive writing. It was obvious Charley had taken great care to make her words neat and legible. A faint scent hit his nose. He pulled the card up to his nose and sniffed – lavender. He chuckled.

She thanked him for talking to her class on career day. *Everybody said you were cool. They thought I was lying when I said I knew an FBI agent – now they believe me.* She signed it: *Your best friend's best friend, Charley Spencer.*

He used a magnet to pin the note to the refrigerator, wondering when he'd be able to show it to Lucinda. When she cancelled their dinner dates, he didn't like it but he understood. Hot on the trail of a new investigation, she might not even give him a passing thought. That's always the way it was with her. And, he had to admit, he was just the same. It made it difficult to build a relationship. He thought again about suggesting that they live together on a trial basis.

Even if they called it a trial, he knew it would be more than that. It would be a test drive on an obstacle course – a reckless leap into commitment. Should he ask? Was he ready? Was she ready? He shook his head, deciding not to decide once again.

He grabbed another Dos Equis from the refrigerator and sat

down to read his magazine. By the time Lucinda called just before eleven that night, Jake was lost in a dream. 'Lovett,' he said, struggling to take the sound of sleep out of his voice.

'I'm sorry, Jake. You said to call when I was finished for the night – I didn't mean to wake you.'

'Good thing you called. If I'd slept in this position in the chair tonight, my neck would have been as tight and unmovable as a vault.'

'Interesting analogy. Are you working a bank robbery?'

'I wish. I'm spending most of my time with homeland security nonsense.'

'Nonsense?'

'I don't believe half of our agency's press releases. I don't think it's diligence and hard work that's spared this country from another terrorist attack. I think it's plain dumb luck.'

'Really?'

'In my opinion, the only terrorist plots we've uncovered and stopped have been the ones that never had a chance of succeeding in the first place. Anyway, enough about the boring mundane chores of a Special Agent in Charge. What's going on with that suspicious death you caught this morning?'

'Not much. Every time I think I'm going to get an answer, I get more questions. We don't have anything solid to determine if it's homicide or suicide.'

'What do you think?' Jake asked.

'Too many questions for a suicide, if you ask me. It feels like murder.'

'Are you looking at the husband?'

'Yep. Even though he's the one insisting that it's not a suicide, I can't say that I trust him. He's smart. He's crafty. He could just be saying that to divert suspicion from himself. He has motive – a girl-friend on the side, an impending divorce and I'd bet there's a nice life insurance policy. Still, I don't know. Maybe it was a suicide.'

'What about the girlfriend as a suspect?'

'She might have been an accessory but physically she'd be incapable of overpowering the victim,' Lucinda said, 'and intellectually she does not have sufficient imagination to do it on her own. Anything aside from the security of the nation in your day?'

'Yeah. I had a nutcase. Thought people were out to get him. Suggested that the White House was involved somehow. Amusing for a few minutes but he got tiresome real quick. Since you didn't ask, I can only assume you don't want me to come over tonight.'

'As much as I'd like to see you, Jake, it's not a good idea. You go back to sleep and I'm going to try to pull the plug on my brain so I can catch a few hours myself. Thanks for the dinner we almost had.'

'Maybe next time we can actually follow through.'

'I hope so. Good night, Jake.'

'Good night, Lucy.' Jake disconnected the call, brushed his teeth and crawled into bed. He felt as if he had just fallen asleep when the too-perky-for-the-middle-of-the-night ring tone of his cell jolted him awake.

He looked at the clock. It was 3:42 a.m. – four hours of sleep. Not enough. He shook his head and picked up the phone. 'Lovett.'

'Is this Special Agent in Charge Jake Lovett?'

'Who is this?'

'This is Sheriff Duke Cummings up in Hanover County.'

'Yes, sir. How can I help you?'

'We got a fatality hit-and-run up here and it looks intentional.'

'And you think you need the FBI's help?'

'No, sir. Not the FBI exactly. I need you.'

'One of my agents?'

'Oh, no, sir. It's just that the dead man had your card in his pocket.'

Jake's mind raced to the odd man who had visited him the day before. 'Was the victim Charles Rowland? Charles David Rowland?'

'Can't rightly say. Didn't have any identification on him.'

'What did he look like?'

'Don't know.'

'You weren't at the scene?'

'Oh, yeah, I was at the scene. In fact, I still am.'

'And you don't know what he looks like?'

'Son, have you ever seen a head after a vehicle's run over it three or four times?'

'No, I haven't had the pleasure, Sheriff, but I get your point. Tell me where you are and I'll be there as quick as I can.'

'No hurry, Lovett. The body's in an alley behind the Food Lion – as narrow as a tunnel and just as easy to block off. We'll be waiting for you.'

Jake hoped it wasn't Rowland. If it was, the fingerprints on file would make the identification a snap. But it would mean he'd made a big mistake yesterday – a mistake that no apology could rectify.

SEVEN

The default ring tone of the cell phone jarred the silence in the middle of the night. It didn't wake the sole occupant of the home. She was still up and waiting for the call. 'Yes?' she said.

'It's done,' a man's voice responded.

'Are you certain?'

'Very certain. Two down. One to go.'

'A rather trite and callous summation of your work, don't you think?' she said.

'I'm following your orders and you call me callous? I don't need to finish the original assignment if you've changed your mind.'

'Have you located the third one?'

'No. I've been very thorough. And so far, her trail ends in Trenton. Just vanished from the face of the earth. Much like Lindsey Barnaby. Makes you wonder – at least, makes *me* wonder.'

'Are you implying that I am responsible for her disappearance?' she hissed through clenched teeth.

'Wouldn't surprise me.'

She ran her tongue across her lips as she thought about how much she despised the man she'd hired. 'Then why would I want you to find her? As far as I know, she is alive and well.'

'What if she's dead?' he asked.

'I couldn't be that lucky. Find her.'

'Chances of law enforcement connecting these first two are slim, but you throw in a third death and that raises the odds exponentially.'

'Why? Not one of them has connected with any of the others in decades. The two incidents thus far have occurred in separate law enforcement jurisdictions and have been accomplished with very different methodology. Just don't get sloppy on number three and you have nothing to fear.'

'If one person stumbles on the Trenton connection, it will be the beginning of the end.'

'Highly unlikely and, besides, we have no alternative,' she insisted.

'That's not exactly true.'

'What do we have? A big pay-off? You saw how that worked with the other one. She called it a down payment. Wanted a schedule of regular payments. Do you realize how vulnerable that would make me? And the man? Intimidation, you said. He was nothing but a scared little weasel, you said. We tried that. The idiot went to the FBI. We have no idea what he told them.'

'He didn't know about the recent activities of the other one,' he reassured her. 'He couldn't have said anything about that.'

'True. But what if he gave them my name?'

'Don't you think they would have been knocking on your door by now?'

'Why should they? They couldn't have found his body yet.'

'Probably have.'

'Why?'

'There was a witness,' he admitted.

'What?'

'I don't know where he came from. There was no one around. But as I pulled off, I saw him in my rear-view mirror. He was standing there at the end of the alley, looking in my direction.'

'How could you be so careless?' she shouted, rising to her feet and pacing the room.

'There was no plate on the vehicle. The alley was unlit. The sky was overcast. He saw nothing.'

'Or so you think?'

'Yes, I do. And that's my neck on the line.'

'Find that woman. Now. She needs to be gone. She is the last person who knows. I will not be safe until you take care of her.'

'See, that's one thing that bothers me. She's not the last person who knows.'

'Yes, she is. I am certain of it. No one else had any involvement or knowledge.'

'Not quite. I wasn't there but I know.'

She stopped in the center of the room, pondering the meaning behind that statement of fact. Was he expressing fear? Or was he threatening her?

'You see,' he continued, 'I have concerns that once I take care of her, someone will take care of me.'

'Don't be ridiculous,' she said, but she thought about that truth and knew she'd follow that trail wherever it led. She knew she could not stop until she was safe or she'd lose it all.

EIGHT

Jake followed the lights past the loading dock on the side of Food Lion to the alley behind it. It was about ten feet wide with a solid wall of white-painted concrete block on one side and on the other, an eight-foot-high chain-link fence with bits of paper and other debris clinging to its base. Twenty feet beyond the fence ran a length of railroad track.

The alley stretched long before the first break – at least the length of a football field. Jake knew anyone caught in it would be at the mercy of approaching vehicles. He stared down to the other end, imagining what it looked like earlier in the evening – as dark and forbidding as a crypt at midnight. What had it been like to be hunted down in this alley? To run as fast and hard as you could and to know – even for an instant – that your best just was not good enough? No matter how hard you tried, you were going to die there among the dust and trash at the back of a strip mall. Jake shuddered. The image came too close to nightmares.

Jake slipped into a pair of Tyvec booties and pulled on a pair of gloves before ducking under the yellow tape. A middle-aged man approached him with an outstretched hand. 'Lovett? Cummings.' His small pot belly made him look like an ordinary guy and his thick, wavy head of hair gave him the look of a star – a combo of assets that had to help at re-election time.

After shaking hands, the sheriff pointed with his flashlight up near the roof line to a conical metal light shade jutting out from the building. 'We have a busted light bulb up here,' he said and swept the beam down the wall to the pavement. 'No broken glass. Musta been busted a long time ago. Now on the other end, we have another light with a busted bulb. But down there, shattered bits of glass are scattered across the street. Could have been someone did that on purpose to further his intentions tonight.'

'What else do you have to make it look like a deliberate act rather than simply a hit-and-run?' Jake asked.

'A guy who works here saw some of what happened and we have some forensics to back up his story.' The sheriff led him to about the halfway point near a cluster of suited-up techs surrounding the body. Jake saw the indentation in the chain-link fence right away. The curb beneath it streaked black with tire rubber. Possible paint scraped onto a link. And what appeared to be blood flecked here and there on the metal.

'Seems to me that poor guy over there tried to climb over the fence to get away but he got nailed by the vehicle,' the sheriff said.

'Had to be terrifying running for your life down this cattle chute, praying for a hidden exit. Makes me wonder, though, what was he doing here in the middle of the night?'

'Store closes at one a.m. so he wasn't here for shopping.'

'If the store was closed what was our employee witness doing here?'

'Restocking the shelves,' the sheriff said.

They walked over to the body and the techs parted to let them into their circle. 'Whoa, you weren't kidding about the possibility of visual identification.'

''Fraid not. Like I said: even Jesus wouldn't recognize him now. The guy you talked to have any DNA or prints on file?'

'Yes,' Jake said. 'I brought a flash drive with the digital prints as well as a hard copy of a fingerprint card.'

'Some of his fingers are squashed and flattened but there's a few that'll give us good prints. We'll do that at the morgue first thing. We'll be ready to move the body in a few minutes if you want to stick around and ride down there with me.'

'Sure. I'd like to get answers to the identity before I leave.'

'Why did he have your card?'

'If it's who I think it is, he came to me wanting protection. I thought he was a crackpot. If it is him, I made a huge mistake. A horrible misjudgment.'

'Even though it will make my job harder I hope, for your sake, it's not him. But you can't win 'em all, Bud.'

'No you can't. But you sure don't like to lose this spectacularly.'

'I hear that.'

*   *   *

Jake paced while the fingerprint expert peered through magnifying lenses, comparing the two cards. When the man pushed back from his desk, he said, 'It's a match.'

'Damn!'

'Looks like this is your case as much as it is ours, Lovett,' the sheriff said. 'The search warrant is signed and sealed. We're fixin' to deliver it to his last known address. Figured you'd want to come along.'

'But how did you get that search warrant? We just established his identity.'

'I suspected you knew what you were talking about or you wouldn't have come roaring up here in the middle of the night. I guess I sort of jumped the gun on the victim ID and called a buddy down at the Norfolk PD . . . But, hell, all's well that ends well.'

'The apartment's in Norfolk?'

'Yep. Not too far from the naval shipyard.'

'I gotta ask you, Cummings. I don't always find this much co-operation when I horn in on a local case. Are you normally this open with the FBI?'

'Hell, no. I'm usually confrontational.'

'But . . .'

'But, you see, we might have a lot of jurisdictional squabbles with the local cop shops. And I might get ticked when the Feds hire up one of my investigators just as he's hit his stride. None of that, though, stands in the way of our willingness to share gossip.'

'Gossip?'

'Yep, gossip says you play well with others. That you're not a glory hound and you don't push the locals around. I'm taking a chance that you'll prove that rumor true.'

'Appreciate that, Sheriff.'

'Make sure you consider this a probationary period. You piss me off and everything changes.'

'I'll do my best to avoid that.'

'Bear in mind, Lovett, I'm not a glad-hand politician. They might call me Sheriff Good Hair behind my back, but I earned the trust of the people of this county as a deputy for twenty years before I ran for sheriff. I'm not some tough-talking, marshmallow-middle, promise-breaking blowhard.'

Jake smiled. 'Is that your campaign slogan?'

'Should be,' Cummings chuckled. 'Let's roll.'

During the hour drive, Jake turned over the meeting with Rowland
in his mind. What had he missed? Why hadn't he taken the man
seriously? How had he reached the conclusion that Rowland was
nothing more than a paranoid conspiracy nut? Even Rowland's
pathetic routine of dropping to the floor and hugging the chair leg
hadn't moved him from his skepticism. It had only increased it. The
drama seemed more the hallmark of a scam artist than a sincere
man who needed help.

The mistake eroded his self-confidence and filled him with doubt
of his abilities. No matter how many times he'd read a situation or
a person right, it still didn't make up for one fatal error. Even in
retrospect, he didn't see any red flags warning him that he was
going down the wrong road – one that led to a literal dead end.

Maybe Lucinda could spot where he went wrong, he thought.
Maybe she could help him figure out why he thought nut or scam
artist but hardly considered the possibility of Rowland as a potential
victim. He'd hash it out with her first chance he got. Whenever that
might be.

NINE

Down a flight of trash-littered stairs they found Rowland's
basement apartment. Three white trash bags were piled on
top of one another by the door. Empty beer cans were
scattered on every surface. The place had the sickly sweet, malty
smell of overripe garbage and spilled beer.

Jake flipped on the kitchen light and watched cockroaches race
for cover. Past a sink filled with greasy water and dirty dishes stood
an old wooden table, the one nearly clean surface in sight. Surrounded
by three mismatched chairs, it had only two items on it: a pencil
and a legal pad.

He looked straight down at the yellow paper. Across the top, it
read 'Tess.' Beneath that name, a dark line dug into the paper where
the pencil went back and forth, underlining it with emphasis.
Underneath, numbered one to four, he had written: me, Candy,
Bonnie, unknown.

Beside Candy, there was a phone number with a question mark

followed by Eagleton and another question mark. 'FIND HER!!!' was written by Bonnie. Next to unknown, he'd scrawled, 'Is there anyone else?'

At the bottom of the page were several skull and crossbone doodles and the word 'danger' written multiple times. Who were these people and what did it mean? Were they all connected to the threat Rowland received? Jake pulled a small notebook out of his pocket and recreated the note there. He asked a forensic tech to bag it and mark it as evidence.

He pulled out his cell and called the number on the note. The phone rang – and rang – ten times in all before it clicked off without going to voicemail. He'd keep trying but he imagined that he'd have to match the name and the phone number to an address and pay the mysterious Candy a visit.

Jake walked into the bedroom. A single bed and a dresser barely fit in the space. The soiled socks and underwear strewn across the floor gave an added claustrophobic dimension to the tiny room.

On the top of the dresser, an old faded color photograph of a teenage couple at a prom looked oddly out of place. Jake lifted it with a gloved hand and noticed the sheen of a layer of dust underneath it. Obviously the snapshot had not been there long. Jake carried it over to a lamp and switched on the light. He could see Rowland's features in the boy's face – considering the age of the photograph, it had to be him. The girl smiling beside him looked vaguely familiar but Jake couldn't figure out why. He'd have to find out where Rowland went to high school and get his hands on a yearbook and see if he could find the girl. Could that lead to a suspect? Who knew? It was a lead and it needed to be followed until it ran off track or hit a dead end.

'Anybody find a cell phone or address book?'

A chorus of 'no' ran around the apartment. 'If you do, let me know. If you even find a stray phone number jotted down anywhere, let me know.'

Jake walked out the door where the sheriff stood keeping track of everyone going in and out of Rowland's place. 'Sad place, Sheriff.'

'Poverty looks even uglier when you know the person who lived in it is now dead.'

Jake briefed him on the two items of interest he'd found inside and said, 'I'll follow up on the legal pad note first and see if the field office from his old stomping ground in New Jersey can run down a yearbook for his high school class. I'll get back to you as soon as I have anything. Call me if you need me or if your techs find something they think I need to see.'

'We're doing a search for family but so far zilch. I kinda suspect there isn't anyone who cares if he's alive or dead.'

'Somebody must have. They killed him.'

'So all we have to do is find the one person in the whole wide world who cared enough to run him down.'

'When you put it that way, it sounds so simple,' Jake said and followed it with a rueful laugh. 'Anybody around who can give me a ride back to my car?'

'Here, take my keys. Hand them over to one of the techs at the crime scene and ask them to drive it back to the office when they finish up there.'

'Thanks. Later, Sheriff.'

By the time Jake was halfway back from Norfolk, he had an address and a name to go with the phone number written next to the name 'Candy.' He punched it into his GPS and headed straight there. Maybe he'd get lucky. Maybe Candace Eagleton at the address and Candy on the note were the same person. Maybe Candy could make sense of it all. He sighed, doubting that it would be that easy. But at least, he thought, I'll be able to scratch that lead off the list.

TEN

Lucinda made two steps past the front desk before Kristen spoke. 'Lieutenant, you have a visitor.'

Lucinda spun around and raised an eyebrow.

'Molly Smith,' Kristen said.

Kristen's habit of delivering information in bite-size morsels aggravated Lucinda and taxed her patience. She raised both hands and shrugged.

'Candace Eagleton's daughter,' Kristen said.

'And?' Lucinda said.

'And what?'

Lucinda blinked her eyes and breathed deeply. 'And where is she, Kristen?'

'Oh, interrogation room number one,' Kristen said with a smile, seemingly oblivious to Lucinda's irritation.

'Thank you, Kristen.' She paused for a moment as a number of sarcastic comments raced through her head. She swallowed every word and headed down the hall. She slipped into the observation room to observe her visitor.

Molly had long, medium-brown hair pulled back in a barrette at the nape of her neck. Her thin face was pale and drawn, making the redness of her eyes more prominent. She wore a plain maroon T-shirt, a pair of blue jeans and dark blue suede clogs on her feet. A tiny gold hoop graced each ear lobe and a simple gold cross and chain hung around her neck. Her left hand clutched a tissue. Her right hand moved around erratically from her face to the table surface to undefined locations in midair, like a little bird that did not know where to land.

Lucinda walked into the room with an outstretched hand. 'Lieutenant Lucinda Pierce.'

Molly rose, two bright pink spots of color flaming in her cheeks as she shook the detective's hand. Lucinda tried not to show her disappointment at the soft bonelessness of the other woman's grasp. 'My mother did not commit suicide,' Molly said.

'Fine,' Lucinda said. 'Let's sit down and get a little background first. Do you live nearby?'

'No. I drove most of the night. From Maine. Northern Maine. But what does that have to do with my mother?'

'It helps me to have a complete family picture, Mrs Smith. The fewer unknowns I have, the easier it is to recognize the relevant facts.'

Molly sighed. 'I haven't lived at home in ten years. Not since I graduated from high school.'

'Did you go to college?'

'Yes. For a week,' she said with a laugh. 'It didn't really suit me. But it did lead me to the man I love.'

'In one week?'

'When you're eighteen, a week seems like forever. And Matthew was so full of goodness, it radiated from his pores. He broke through my spoiled, materialistic interior and plunged into my soul the first time we met. We married seven days later and I haven't looked back since.'

Lucinda forced her face to remain placid and her tongue to stay

still. To her, Molly sounded like a groupie rather than a wife. 'Have
you been living in Maine ever since?'

'No, we travelled around to campuses delivering the Good Word
to anyone who would listen. Then, when Peter was born, we moved
north. We wanted to raise our children in the bosom of nature –
close to God, away from the materialistic trappings of the modern
world.'

Lucinda struggled to keep her eyes from rolling in her head.
'Children? You have more than one?'

'Yes.' Molly smiled. 'We have five. We planned for four. We
thought four would be perfect. But apparently God did not agree.
The fourth time I got pregnant, we had twins – Ruth and Esther.
They're six months old now. But, please, although I love talking
about my family, there are things I need to tell you about my mother.'

'OK, Molly. Why did you say that she didn't commit suicide?'

'Because she didn't. I am sure of it. I spoke to her the night before
she d-di-died.' A sob strangled off her speech. She held up a palm,
facing Lucinda as she swallowed and pulled herself back under control.
'My dad is a bully, Lieutenant. And you know how they say if you
stand up to a bully, he'll back down? Well, not my dad. Mom stood
up to him again and again but he'd always lash back. And, in the
end, he usually got his way. And you know how he did that?'

Lucinda shook her head.

'He threatened me and my brother.'

'Threatened?'

'Oh, not physically. He never hit us or my mother that I know.
He threatened to take away our favorite toys when we were little
– our cars or other prized possessions when we were older.
Sometimes, he threatened to send us off to boarding school, at
someplace far away. She always buckled. But she kept standing up
to him just the same. At least until I went away to school for that
short week. She seemed to change. She just acceded to his demands
without question. It was like she became his robot. A machine made
to do his bidding. Until recently, anyway.'

'What happened?'

'She had a plan. She was getting away from him. I was very
supportive of that plan. I warned her that even with a legal divorce,
she could not remarry. In God's eyes, she would be married to Dad
for all eternity. That did not mean she had to live with him. But to
wed again would put her soul at forfeit.'

She counseled her mother? Lucinda thought. What a self-righteous little snot.

'I think my dad killed my mother because he found out about her plan.'

'What was her plan?'

'She had a meeting with an important client. She said it was all settled. She would meet with the client at nine the next morning. After that meeting, she would be set. She'd have financial independence and could just walk out of that house and not look back. She planned to be gone before Dad got home for dinner.'

'Do you know the name of the client?'

'No,' Molly said, shaking her head and sobbing.

'Your mother wasn't expecting your father home before dinner time?'

'No. She was certain of it. She was sure she'd be gone by then. She had an overnight bag packed and in the trunk of her car. She planned to hire someone to gather up the rest of her things. She didn't want to forewarn Dad by making any obvious preparations.'

'But your father got home earlier than that – much earlier.'

'Yes. He came home early to kill her. And she promised to come visit me and the kids just as soon as she could – later this month, she said. But she never got a chance. The kids were so excited that Nana was coming. But now? What can I tell them now?' Molly collapsed on the table, her forehead resting on folded hands.

'Why are you certain that your father killed her?'

Molly's head jerked up and a cold, hard emotion took over her face, making her cheekbones stand out and her lips compress as thin as a thread. 'He always had to have his way. She was defying him, leaving him. That would not be acceptable to that man.'

'Why are you so harsh on your father?'

Molly sighed and bowed her head. When she looked back up, pain creased her forehead and the corner of her eyes. 'When I left school for Matthew, Dad hired a private detective to track us down. When he found us, he hired a couple of thugs to beat the crap out of Matthew. He nearly died in that hospital in Madison. He nearly died before he saw the birth of his son.'

Lucinda sat quietly, absorbing the dysfunctional truth of a family who should have had it all. She watched Molly, bent over the table once again, her shoulders heaving. A shudder raced through Molly's frame. Then she raised her head. 'I hadn't intended telling you all of this.'

'Mrs Smith, do you think that your father killed your mother himself – or do you think he hired someone?'

Molly thought for a moment and said, 'I've never seen my dad do anything violent. I've never seen him inflict any physical harm to anyone. And he does have a habit of hiring people to do his dirty work. But this? It seems so personal. Maybe this time . . . I don't know. I could see it happening either way.'

'Why, then, do you think your father is insisting that your mother did not commit suicide?'

'Is he? Really? That is a surprise. But my dad is very, very smart. And very crafty. It makes good cover for him, doesn't it?'

Lucinda couldn't discount the theory she and Molly shared, nor could she prove it – not yet. That left her with another problem. A wealthy man like Frank Eagleton was a flight risk. He could move money overseas and follow it at will. Right now, she knew his passport was in the top drawer of his dresser but she'd have to release the house soon. When she did, would he make a beeline for another country? Unfortunately, she couldn't think of any legal justification to confiscate his passport at this time. But what if his passport was simply misplaced? If he wasn't able to locate it where he left it? If it was somewhere he'd be unlikely to find it? Lucinda smiled. *That* could be arranged.

ELEVEN

Before Jake reached his destination, he received another call. 'She's here and she's growling,' the office secretary said.

Jake's first thought was Lucinda. Had he done something to piss her off? 'She, who?' he said.

'Sandra. Sandra Goodman. And she wants to know why you aren't here. She wants to know why she was not immediately informed that you were a person of interest in a murder investigation.'

'Person of interest?' Jake said.

'Yes. What's going on, Jake?'

'I'll be right there.' He disconnected the call and whipped on the off-ramp to cut across town. The area director never dropped by a field office unless a career was balancing on a precipice. Most people thought she was happiest when she was able to give the fatal shove over the edge. He popped a *Best of Stevie Ray Vaughn* CD into the slot and cranked up the volume.

Sandra Goodman stood near the front door as Jake walked into the office. She made a show of looking at her wristwatch and said, 'Keeping bankers' hours, are we, Agent Lovett?'

Jake clenched his jaw, biting off his words before he could speak them. He was determined not to get defensive or squabble with her in front of his staff. 'My office, please, Director Goodman?' he said as he walked past her.

'Something to hide, Agent Lovett?'

He didn't pause or turn around, refusing to respond to her baiting in any way. He went straight to his office, walked around to the other side of his desk and folded his arms on his chest.

She walked in and stopped in front of his desk, planting her palms on its surface and leaning towards him. 'Start talking.'

'Please close the door,' Jake asked.

She snorted. 'Paranoid, aren't we?'

Jake did not respond until she turned around and pushed the door shut. 'What do you want to know?'

'I think you know, Agent Lovett.'

'Please ask me specific questions, Director. I've been up most of the night and want to tell you exactly what you want to know.'

'Why didn't you inform me immediately that you were a person of interest in a murder case?'

'I am not a person of interest in a murder case.'

'Really? So why did you rush to the scene and answer the investigator's questions?'

'To help the investigation.'

'Out of the goodness of your heart? Out of camaraderie with local law enforcement? Out of an idealistic vision of your mission?'

'Because I might have information relevant to the death investigation.'

'You mean, you wanted to insinuate yourself into the case, hoping to ensure that their inquiries were directed away from you.'

'What are you getting at, Director?'

'You were possibly the last person to see this man alive, correct?'

'Possibly but unlikely. Too much time had elapsed.'

'Your business card was found in his pocket, correct?'

'Yes. He'd been to see me that afternoon.'

'Step out of your own skin for a moment, Agent Lovett. Let's say you arrived at the scene of a murder victim. The victim has no identification on him. He has no cell phone. Nothing but another person's business card in his pocket. Wouldn't that person be a person of interest?'

Jake felt a tightening in his sternum but gave an honest answer anyway. 'Yes, he would.'

'Would you not suspect this person was the possible perpetrator?'

'I might.'

'Bullshit, Agent Lovett. You definitely would. Where were you last night at the time of the crime?'

'Home. In bed.'

'Any witnesses to verify that claim?'

Jake flushed. 'No.'

'Any calls to your home landline at that time?'

'No.'

'Any calls on that line at all that evening?'

'No. Only on my cell.'

'It's clear to me, then, that you are a suspect.'

'Did you talk to the sheriff?'

She ignored him. 'You are a suspect – at least until a better lead comes along. If you are involved in this investigation in any way, it will be compromised. Can't you see yourself on the witness stand now? The defense asks: "Agent Lovett, wasn't it in your best interests to divert suspicion to my client? Wasn't that the only way to take the investigation away from your activities on the night in question?" Wouldn't that be dandy?'

Jake wanted to object but realized it was a valid point. Once the defense learned of his business card in the victim's pocket, he would be a possible vehicle for creating reasonable doubt.

'And this report you wrote about your meeting with Rowland? Doesn't it read like a plan to discredit him? To make him appear irrational, disturbed and somehow contributing to his own demise? "He appeared to be consumed by a conspiracy theory that was only in his mind." You wrote that, didn't you?'

'Yes, I did.'

'And just how do you feel about his "paranoid delusions" now, Agent Lovett?'

'I think they had a stronger basis in reality than I suspected.'

'You know what I think? It's either a stupid assessment or a crafty one. And you've never struck me as a stupid person, Agent Lovett. That makes crafty the more likely conclusion.'

'Director Goodman, it was a faulty judgment. There was no malevolence or hidden purpose behind that report.'

Goodman spun away from his desk and turned her back to him.

Jake waited, wanting to rush to his own defense but knowing he didn't dare.

She turned back. 'I wish I could believe you. I want to believe you. But at this point in time, I just don't know. For that reason, you will distance yourself from this investigation immediately. You will turn over every scrap of paper and tidbit of information you've obtained to the Hanover County Sheriff's Department. You are to tell them to feel free to ask you any questions but to take care not to provide you with any investigative information or to involve you in a law enforcement capacity.'

'But I told Sheriff Cummings—'

'I do not care what you told him. You will now tell him you are out of the investigation. Is that clear? And I do not want you in the field investigating any case until we put this all to rest.'

'Yes, ma'am.'

'If I find out you've disobeyed this order – and I don't care if it's all praise for your heroic, single-handed solving of the case – you can say goodbye to the FBI. I will see to that. You will be a dead man in our eyes – but we won't mourn your passing, we'll spit on your grave.'

Jake watched her back as she strode out of the room. He doubted she had as much power as she wanted him to believe and fear. Her over-the-top dramatic flourish at the end of her little speech told him that. Nonetheless, for now, he'd appear compliant. He'd lay low for a while, ready to make a move if it became necessary. On his personal scale of justice, a victim always outweighed the bureaucracy.

TWELVE

Lucinda lifted the yellow crime scene tape across the three steps leading to the landing at the front door. She pulled off the seal on the door and let herself back into the Eagleton home. For her, the best time at the scene of a murder was after the evidence was collected, the people all gone, the bustle at an end. Now she could absorb the environment without distraction.

If the unknown client scheduled for a meeting at 9 a.m. that morning was the person who killed her, how could it have played out? She imagined that Candace could have left the door unlocked in anticipation of her visitor. That person arrived early, snuck upstairs and surprised her as she prepared for the meeting.

Alternatively, Candace could have come downstairs at the sound of the doorbell, opened it for her visitor and been chased or retreated upstairs when she sensed danger. Or she could have gone back upstairs for another purpose? But what could that be? Or she could have been taken upstairs by force? That was unlikely. Evidence of the application of force was only seen by the small marks by and on the inside of the bedroom door frame.

Is it possible that 'client' was a code name for 'lover?' Was Candace having a surreptitious sexual encounter that went wrong? She did take great pains with her personal preparations for the meeting – well-dressed, make-up and perfume. Her outfit, though, wasn't flirtatious or seductive. Candace was dressed for success. Someone she wanted to impress was due to arrive that morning.

But what if that was the image she wanted to project to a lover? What if he came and then went upstairs? What could have gone wrong? She could have planned the meeting to dump him. To tell him it was over. That would have explained the clothing she wore. And then in a fit of rage, he . . .

No. It was not a crime of passion. It was too clinical. Too planned. Too precisely staged. Lucinda walked up the stairs and crossed half across the arched walkway. She looked down into the foyer. She imagined Candace shouting, 'Come in, the door's open,' from a position in this spot. Possible if it were a lover. Not likely if it were a client.

What if Frank Eagleton stumbled on this illicit tryst? If so, wouldn't Candace be naked or at least partially unclothed? But still, it does not appear to be a crime of passion. That would mean Frank knew about the affair. Knew and planned the killing in advance.

She pulled out her cell and called the morgue. 'Doc Sam, please?'

'Who is this and what do you want?' a gravelly voice grumbled.

'And top o' the morning to you, Doc Sam.'

'Pierce? I was getting ready to call you.'

'About what?'

'You first. Why did you call?'

'I wanted to know if you saw any indication that Candace Eagleton was dressed after her death.'

After a long pause, Doc Sam said, 'No. And thinking back, I do not recall anything to indicate that. I'll look over the photos and see if I can find anything I missed.'

'Sure would surprise me if you did,' Lucinda said.

'Yeah, well, I'm just full of surprises.'

'Why did you want to call me, Doc?'

'I found a possible injection site on the back of her hand. I dissected the area and I am certain of it.'

'Injection of what?'

'Won't know until we get the toxicology back. But I did locate her primary care physician. She hadn't visited him in the last couple of days. It could have been another doctor but he doubted it. He said she always came to him for a referral before going to any specialist.'

'That it?'

'No. There were two dislocated finger joints. Obviously happened just before death because there wasn't sufficient time for any swelling to set in.'

'Sounds like force was used to subdue her for that injection.'

'Works for me. Now stop yakking on the phone and go find this woman's killer. And don't disappoint me. I put down the husband in the office pool.'

'So it is a homicide?'

'I only bet on sure things.'

'You actually have an office pool for murder victims?'

'Maybe. Maybe I'm just jerking your chain.'

Doc Sam hung up before she could respond. She stared at her

phone. It had to be a joke – a sick morgue joke. Wasn't it? Did it even matter? Doc Sam just obliterated the slightest microscopic trace of doubt from her mind – this was homicide, not suicide.

She walked into Candace's bedroom, turned and faced the doorway. Staring at the spot marked by the victim's fingernails, Lucinda imagined her struggling, grabbing anything to escape. Did she scream? She must have – Lucinda could hear it echo in the well of her imagination.

Did anyone hear her? Colter had done the prerequisite door-to-door. Lucinda thought if she'd found anything of interest, she would have called and let her know. She'd have to check with her.

Her cell rang again. She looked at the screen – her office number. Assuming it was Colter calling, she answered with: 'Sergeant Colter?'

She was greeted with a titter. 'Oh, Lieutenant Pierce, you are so funny.'

Kristen. What now? 'Yes, Kristen, what can I do for you?'

'Not a thing for me,' she giggled. 'But there's a Mark Eagleton here and he wants to talk to you. He asked me to call and see if you'll be returning soon.'

'Frank and Candace's son?'

'I don't know,' Kristen said.

'Ask him. Please,' Lucinda said, trying and failing to hide her exasperation.

Lucinda heard mumbled voices and then Kristen said, 'Yes, he is. How did you know that?'

'Tell him I'm almost finished here. I'll be back just as soon as I can.' Kristen was still talking when Lucinda hit the end button.

She crossed the walkway over to Frank's bedroom and pulled open the top drawer of his dresser. There, under a stack of silk boxer shorts, she found the passport right where she remembered. Where to hide it – correction, misplace it? If she knew what he'd worn the last time he flew out of the country, she could slide it in a pocket. But she didn't. Where else might he leave it? She could guess but she knew it was too easy to get it wrong.

Maybe it should look intentional. Candace could have taken it. Hidden it. She snatched the passport and carried it across the walkway. Lifting Candace's mattress, she slid it in as deep as she could. If it wasn't the last place he'd look for it, Candace's bedroom certainly wouldn't be the first. She might not stop him from fleeing the country but she sure could slow him down.

Downstairs, she paused for a moment and looked up at the railing where the rope around Candace's neck had been tied. 'I'll find out why you died, Candace. And I'll find out who did it. I promise.'

She felt the pressure of a commitment made land heavily on her shoulders. She wriggled her shoulders as if balancing an unseen load and walked out of the home determined to keep her word.

THIRTEEN

Mark Eagleton looked very much like his father, Lucinda thought as she watched him through the glass. Same broad shoulders, trim, fit body, prominent lower lip and startling blue eyes. Impatience creased his brow line and put his fingers in motion, drumming the surface of the desk.

Opening the door to the Spartan room, she said, 'Mr Eagleton. Lieutenant Lucinda Pierce. You have my utmost sympathy for your loss. It doesn't get much worse than losing your mother to an act of violence.'

He responded to her extended hand with a firm handshake. 'Trying to disarm me with empathy?'

'Now, why would I want to disarm you?'

'Perhaps you think I killed my mother. Or perhaps you think I have knowledge that points to my father as the killer. You're wrong on both counts.'

'Mr Eagleton, my expression of sympathy was genuine. I do understand the magnitude of your loss.'

'Nice – an implication that you have walked in my shoes without insulting me with an actual lie. As if you really knew what it was like to learn your mother was brutally murdered.'

'Actually, I do, Mr Eagleton. My mother was murdered,' Lucinda said.

Mark gave her a hard stare. 'You're serious, aren't you?'

'Yes.'

'Were you there?'

Lucinda forced down the lump in her throat and kept her expression blank. 'Yes. Yes I was.'

'Is that when you injured your face?'

'We are not here to discuss my past trauma, Mr Eagleton, but the answer is no. I only shared that information with you in hope that you would accept my sincerity and realize that I am not here to play games with you or trick you in any way. We are here to share information together and nothing more.'

'When will you release my mother's body?'

'That is out of my hands at the moment. When all the necessary information is gathered for the autopsy report, you'll be informed and a funeral home can transport the body for the service.'

'I guess it's taking longer because Mom wanted to be cremated.'

'Actually, that's not the case. We were unaware of her wishes.'

'I'll have to take your word for that, I suppose. You're certain it's not suicide?'

'You think it might be?' Lucinda asked.

'Nothing she did would surprise me.'

'What do you mean by that, Mr Eagleton?'

'Please, call me Mark. When you say Mr Eagleton, I think my dad's in the room.'

'Why wouldn't you be surprised by a suicide, Mark?'

'My mother was unpredictable. Moody. Overly dramatic.'

'Difficult to live with?'

'Most definitely. I don't know how my dad stood it sometimes.'

'According to your father, he loved her.'

'Yes. There was that. He seemed to dote on her. For the life of me, I don't understand why. Sure, I loved her. She was my mom. But as an adult, I've stepped back and looked at her objectively. If she were my wife, I'd go nuts. I'd either kill myself or kill her. I couldn't take it.'

'Is that what you think happened here? Your father just couldn't take it any longer?'

Mark drew back. 'Absolutely not. That was a figure of speech and besides I was talking about me and not my dad. There is no way . . . '

'Are you sure?'

'Oh, I see. You've talked to my sister, haven't you?'

'Yes, I have.'

'She always took mom's side. She thought Dad was a tyrant. He wasn't.'

'Molly said that your mother had a plan. She was about to leave your father.'

'Oh, please. Where would she go? How could she possibly maintain that elevated lifestyle she enjoys so much?' Mark paused and
squinted his eyes. 'Unless she found another man. Is that what
happened?'

'At this point, we have no evidence pointing to that
conclusion.'

'Which means you're considering the possibility?'

'We're considering all the possibilities, Mark. What if she did
have a plan . . .?'

'My mother always had a plan. If it wasn't one thing, it was
another. And she never worried about the legality of any of her
whacked-out ideas.'

'Meaning . . .?'

'When I was seventeen, she found a small stash of pot in my
room. Typical teenage experimentation was all it was. But my mom
was anything but typical. She offered to bankroll me if I wanted to
be entrepreneurial with it.'

'Excuse me?' Lucinda asked.

'She said she'd give me upfront money if I wanted to deal. She
explained how I could give people good value for their dollar and
be able to have all the pot I wanted for my own use at no cost.'

Mother of the Year, Lucinda thought. 'Was she serious?'

'Seemed like it to me. She made a budget, calculated revenue
projections and did a risk assessment analysis. She figured I could
stay in business until I went to college with minimal risk of being
arrested if I were careful. Then, she thought I could re-establish my
enterprise wherever I went. She also assured me that Dad could buy
my way out of any trouble I encountered. When she said that, I
understood.'

'Understood what?'

'That she really wanted me to do it and she wanted me to get
busted. She wanted to cause problems for Dad.'

'Why, Mark?'

'I'm not sure if she was amused by it or if she felt it gave her
power over him. It was a complicated relationship.'

'Speaking of complicated, did you know your dad was having
an affair?'

'Did my sister tell you that?'

'No, your father did. He said that's why your mother moved into
the second master suite.'

'She told me separate bedrooms sparked up their marriage. She said, the yin on one side, the yang on the other with a gender gap arching between the two. She thought it was poetic. She said it would revitalize their passion. This is why I do not think she was leaving my dad.'

'But she was, Mark. She had written a farewell note to him.'

'Really? That makes no sense – unless she thought she'd have Dad on the hook for life because of his affair.'

'Actually, Mark, in her note she said that she wanted nothing from him – not his money, not his house.'

'That doesn't sound like her.'

'She had a meeting scheduled that morning with a client who she believed would provide her with the financial security she needed.'

'Client? My mother hadn't worked for that PR firm for ages. She quit to work full-time for dad before I was born.'

'Do you have any idea who that client might be?'

'No. Not a clue. Are you sure about that?'

'That's what she told your sister.'

Mark spit out a rueful laugh. 'Maybe client was a code word for lover. It had to be someone with money – lots of it. Or someone she was using to provoke Dad.'

'You don't have a very high opinion of your mother, do you?'

Mark exhaled loudly. 'She was a great mom when I was little. Always creating little adventures. Very clever at turning little things into big learning moments. She made me feel loved and safe. It wasn't until I was a teenager that I saw the other side. I didn't like the way she treated Dad.'

'What about how your father treated your mother?'

'It's not an example I'd want to follow. He was very controlling but it seemed like he had to be. She'd run off the rails without his steady hand to keep her in place. But he didn't kill her, Lieutenant, no matter what my sister thinks. You need to look elsewhere. You need to find who was responsible. Someone has to pay for taking my mom's life.'

'What if that someone was your father?'

Mark hung his head and shook it from side to side. 'I can't go there, Lieutenant. It doesn't fit with anything I know about my dad. It doesn't make any sense. There's something else going on here – please find out what it is.'

Lucinda wrapped up their conversation and watched Mark walk down the hall. His shoulders more slumped than they were earlier; his walk closer to a shuffle than the energetic stride of his father that she supposed was his typical gait. And how will he cope if he learns that his mother died at his father's hands? The old pain of her mother's death formed a hard knot in her chest. She had to set that aside and be objective. She didn't want her judgment clouded by her past and yet, her only known suspect was still Frank Eagleton.

FOURTEEN

Lucinda's cell vibrated in her pocket. She pulled it out and checked to see who called. It was her brother, Ricky. She listened to his message: 'I – I – I can't leave a message about this. Call me. Please.'

She hit redial and didn't hear a ring before she heard her brother's voice. 'Do you remember Seth O'Hara?'

'Hello to you, too, Ricky,' Lucinda said with a laugh.

'Sorry, sorry, hi, Sis. But do you?'

'Seth O'Hara? Your wife's older brother?'

'Yes. His middle son, Dylan committed suicide three nights ago.'

'Oh, that's horrible. How old was he?'

'Sixteen – only sixteen. His birthday was last week.'

'And he committed suicide? How?' Lucinda asked as she walked down the hall and entered her office.

'Gunshot to the mouth in the parking lot of the high school. The police are certain the shot was self-inflicted and I think they're right. When we dropped by the house with his gift and had a slice of birthday cake on Wednesday, Dylan seemed odd, morose, withdrawn. Wasn't even excited when Seth handed him the keys to the old pick-up truck he wanted. But no matter what I think, no matter what the police say, Seth refuses to believe it.'

'That's pretty common. Denial of a suicide happens all the time.'

'Yeah, I know. But he's refusing to allow the funeral home to embalm Dylan's body, saying he wants a full murder investigation first. Lily and I went over to the house to talk to Seth last night, to try to get him to accept what happened and stop calling the police and raising holy hell. By the time we left, though, Lily was convinced that Seth was right – some kid at school who'd been pushing him around finally pushed too far and killed him.'

'And you?' Lucinda asked.

'I still think it's a suicide. Seth showed us a snapshot of Dylan smiling and hugging his little brother around the neck that he said was taken the same day that his son died. He thinks that proves that Dylan was happy and couldn't have committed suicide. But I think I read somewhere that people who kill themselves are often euphoric once they have a plan and are ready to follow through with it. Is that true?'

'That's sometimes the case,' Lucinda agreed.

'I told Lily that but she didn't buy it. She's been pestering me ever since to call you and ask you to please come up here, look at what happened and give your opinion.'

Why don't these things ever happen when I'm not in the middle of a fresh homicide investigation? 'Ricky, I'm not sure of how quickly I can get up.'

'The sooner the better, Lucinda. Martha is crying all the time.'

'Martha?'

'Seth's wife, remember?'

Lucinda cast her mind back to the few visits she'd made to her brother's home over last couple of decades and resurrected a dim memory. 'Vaguely.'

'She wants Dylan laid to rest. She doesn't believe it's a suicide either but she wants her son buried first and worry about the rest later.'

Kristen walked into Lucinda's office and laid a piece of paper in front of her, whispering 'Urgent,' as she backed out of the room. Lucinda read: 'Ted Branson at the regional forensic center wants you to know that he has emailed screen shots of deleted emails to you.'

'Lucinda, are you still there?' Ricky asked.

'Yes, sorry, Ricky. I understand. And I get the urgency of the situation. I'm bogged down in a recent murder here. I'm not sure how open local law enforcement will be with me but I'll make a call today and see what I can find out.' She clicked the button for her email.

'Can you come up here? Lily trusts you. She'll believe you. And if you say it's suicide, too, she should be able to convince Seth.'

'As soon as I can, Ricky. I promise. As soon as I can. I've got to run now. Sorry,' Lucinda said as she disconnected from the call and opened the email. Ted, her former partner in homicide and a one-time high school boyfriend, now worked in the computer analysis division at one of the state's regional forensic labs where Lucinda had routed Candace Eagleton's computer.

His email read: 'I couldn't salvage complete messages but even with the missing pieces, the picture I'm seeing is pretty clear. Look over the screen shots and give me a call. I'd like to see if you come to the same conclusions as I did.'

Lucinda clicked on the attachment and read the choppy string of communication from the most recent email to the earliest one.

> From: ceagleton@eagletonpr.com
> To: Winordie@fastmail.com
> Glad to see you've come to your senses. I'll see you at 9 tomorrow. Make sure you bring what is required. Do not

> From: Windordie@fastmail.com
> To: ceagleton@eagletonpr.com
> Fine. I am willing to cover my debt with regular payments. We must meet face–to-face to negotiate a final settlement. I agree to the con

> From: ceagleton@eagletonpr.com
> To: Winordie@fastmail.com
> □□□□□□□□□□□□□ cooperate. □□□ I am very serious. Don't underestimate me. Or there will be no winning in your future.

Blackmail? Was Candace extorting money from someone? She grabbed the receiver of her desk phone and called Ted. 'What are you thinking?'

'You first.'

'Blackmail?'

'That's what I thought,' Ted said.

'Who is Winordie?'

'Don't know yet. I've contacted the Internet service provider but they insist: no information without a court order.'

'Can you draft the technical part of the warrant request? I'll finish it up with my side of the equation and put it in front of a judge.'

'Sure, I imagine you'll need it two hours ago.'

'As soon as, at any rate. You've just turned my whole investigation upside down. I was thinking the husband did it. This information adds another possible suspect to the list.'

'I'll get it to you as quick as I can. And don't forget.'

'Don't forget what?'

'Tomorrow is the anniversary of our first date.'

'Oh, good grief, Ted. That was twenty years ago.'

'Still a fresh memory for me, Lucinda.'

'Grow up, Ted,' she said and slammed down the phone. She regretted her little hissy fit the moment it happened. She needed his help and she chose that moment to be snippy. Lucinda sighed. As persistent as Ted is, she thought, I doubt if even that penetrated his skull.

She felt overwhelmed by the clash between the demands of the job and the needs of her family. And between the two, it seemed she never had time for herself. She'd been neglecting Chester, her cat. She'd promised a trip to the zoo for Charley and Ruby, the two little girls who became part of her life when their mother was murdered two years ago. And it had been too damned long since she'd had a relaxing evening with Jake.

'Enough of the self-pity, Lucinda old girl,' she said to the empty room. 'You have work to do.' And top of that list was another conversation with Frank Eagleton. Even with the new information from Ted, she was not ready to close the book on Candace's husband. She wanted to get Frank's reaction to what she'd learned from talking to Mark.

FIFTEEN

Lucinda called Frank Eagleton at work. As soon as he answered she said, 'Mr Eagleton, I was calling to see if you could stop by and see me this afternoon at the justice center or if you'd rather that I come there.'

He said, 'When are you going to release my house?'

'Soon.'

'When?'

'Probably after you talk to me.'

'I don't want you here. It will disrupt the office.'

'Can I expect you here soon, then?'

Frank huffed a loud exhale. 'I'd have to cancel my four o'clock meeting.'

'Shouldn't take you long to do that. I'll see you soon.'

'I didn't say—'

'You do want to get back in your house, don't you?'

'Sounds like blackmail to me.'

Lucinda suppressed a gasp. Does he know? Is he part of it? Injecting calm nonchalance into her voice, she said, 'Hardly, Mr Eagleton. I am simply trying to determine who murdered your wife. I thought that was a priority for you as well.'

'Don't play your cop word games with me, Lieutenant. I'll see you within the hour.'

'Thank you, Mr Eagleton,' she said, glad that he couldn't see her smirk of satisfaction.

SIXTEEN

Even though she was mentally exhausted when she opened her apartment door that night, her spirits lifted at the sight of her gray tabby, Chester. His happy dance to celebrate her arrival was a marvelous performance of thundering feet, chirping meows and a purr that seemed loud enough to shake the building.

She plucked a little gray mouse with pink felt ears and tail off the floor and sent it skittering down the hall. Chester raced after it, skidded as he went past it and slid into a wall. He shook off the stun from the impact, grabbed the mouse and held it between his paws, gnawing on its head.

He lost all interest in his toy when he heard Lucinda pop the top of a can of his new favorite, tuna and cheddar. He galloped back into the kitchen, meowing a loud plaint of impatience as she scooped out the contents of the tin.

Lucinda checked for messages on her landline. One was from Jake: 'I didn't want to bother you at work since I know how it is for you right now. Just wanted to let you know that I'm out from under the case that I thought would eat up my life. In fact, I won't be doing any active investigations for the time being. I'm grounded. Call me when you can.'

Grounded? That doesn't sound good. She pulled out her cell, hit her favorites list and tapped Jake's name. He answered on the first ring. 'What do you mean you're grounded?' she asked.

'The wicked witch of the north paid me a visit today and put me in quarantine. She seems to believe I'm a person of interest in a homicide investigation.'

'A person of interest? You?'

'The man who was murdered visited my office the afternoon before he died. When his body was found, there was no identification, no money, nothing but my business card.'

'And?'

'I guess good old Sandra thinks I killed him and left my calling card or something. I don't know.'

'That's absurd. What about the local investigators?'

'The sheriff himself is taking the lead on this one.'

'He thinks you might be a suspect?'

'No. He said that it was as much my investigation as it was his. He was not pleased when I turned over my file and told him I was out of it.'

'So what's the area director's problem?'

'She's old school. She might just love generating fear and loathing in her underlings. Or she might just think that being under the gun builds our character. I don't know but she seems to go out of her way to make every Special Agent in Charge under her command uncomfortable, unsettled and insecure.'

'Your job at jeopardy?' Lucinda asked.

'Nah. I don't think so. This will all blow over. She'll let me know at some point that my good name is cleared, remind me that it is, however, permanently besmirched and then expect me to express my undying gratitude for her support.'

'You're kidding me?'

'I wish. So how is your case going?'

'I'm now certain that it is a homicide.'

'That's progress.'

'Yes, but now evidence is turning me away from my chief suspect.'

'The husband?' Jake asked.

'Yes.'

'Who took his place? The mistress?'

'I still can't fathom that possibility. It's a person of mystery.'

'Totally unknown?'

'At least for the moment. Ted's analyzing the hard drive of her computer. He found some provocative email pointing to the possibility that the victim was engaged in blackmail. He's trying to identify who is at the other end of those messages and I'm going to have to talk to everyone close to the wife and find out if they knew anything about an extortion conspiracy or if they can think of anyone she might be able to blackmail.'

'Lucinda, you've got a plan. You're moving forward. It's never as fast as you want it to be but it sounds as if you're holding something back. What's really bothering you?'

'I got a call from my brother today. His wife's brother's son is dead. The local cops are saying that it's a suicide. My brother thinks they're right but his wife and brother-in-law are certain it's murder. And they think they know who did it. They want me to come up and check over the evidence and give them my opinion. But I really can't afford to walk away from my current investigation right now and I'm worried that the grieving father might decide to take matters into his own hands.'

'Why don't I go take a look?'

'You?'

'Hey, I'm at a loose end right now. My hands are tied at work and I really want to get out of the office where everyone is giving me pity looks. I could take the pressure off you and get a bit of fresh air at the same time.'

'If you're sure . . .'

'Yes. No problem. I can go up first thing in the morning.'

'OK. I'll tell my brother to expect you and I'll email directions. Thanks, Jake.'

'Thank you, Lucy. You've done me a big favor. Really.'

'Local law enforcement's not going to be pleased to have you snooping around.'

'What? They were going to throw a parade at your arrival?'

'No. They wouldn't like me sniffing around either. But you, well, you know . . .'

'Yeah. I'm a feeb. Automatically suspected of ulterior motives and a superiority complex. I'll be as humble as I can and tell anyone who'll listen that I'm not there in an official capacity.'

'They won't believe you.'

'Screw 'em.'

Lucinda laughed. 'Oh, that attitude will win you friends.'

'I don't need friends, Lucy. I have you.'

Silence thrummed through the distance that separated them. 'Lucy, you still there or did I scare you off?'

'No, Jake, you didn't scare me off. You just rendered me speechless.'

'That is a major feat.'

'Not for you, Jake.'

'I'll take that as a compliment.'

'You should,' she said. 'Now, I really need to get some rest. Tomorrow promises to be a long day.'

'Sorry – go get some sleep. I don't want to call you at a bad moment so give me a call and I'll update you on what I learned up in Albemarle County.'

'Will do. Night, Jake,' she said and hit the end button. She sighed, scooped up Chester and scratched him under the chin. 'Am I ready for a serious relationship, Chester? Or is it getting to be too much too soon? My first husband was a feeb; do I really want to run that risk again? Do I want to make myself vulnerable to any man again? Hmm, Chester?' Chester blurted out a meow. 'Yes, you're right. I am safer when it's just me and you.'

SEVENTEEN

Lucinda walked into Frank's office just after 8 a.m. The room was all glass surfaces and chrome. Even the panoramic view outside the wall of windows didn't add warmth to the sterile environment. She wouldn't give up her ratty, cramped office for this cold space for any price. 'I'm surprised to see you at work today, Mr Eagleton,' she said.

'And where else would I be, Lieutenant? I don't have a home right now, remember?'

'We released your wife's body to the funeral director early this morning. I thought you'd be out and about making arrangements for her service.'

'I wasn't in the mood.'

'Oh, not in the mood? Your wife didn't time the murder for your convenience? I am shocked.'

'Cut the crap, Lieutenant.'

'Since you didn't show up for our meeting yesterday, I thought you might be waiting for me at the justice center this morning. When you weren't, I came here.'

'I told you the office was not a good place for us to talk.'

'I recall that, Mr Eagleton but, if you remember, I gave you a choice and you didn't show up.'

'I had my secretary call. Things got complicated yesterday afternoon.'

'Well, I'm here now and I have questions.'

'Can't it wait until this afternoon? I need to prepare for lunch with a major client at noon.'

'No. I don't think so.'

'It's a federal agency, Ms Pierce.'

Lucinda took that form of address from this man as a slap in the face. She was certain it was meant to diminish her and her authority. She sat down in the chair across from Frank's desk and looked him in the eyes. 'Lieutenant Pierce, Mr Eagleton. Now are you going to answer my questions or do I need to take you with me down to the justice center? Before you answer, if I did that, I would be completely within procedure if I slapped on handcuffs and perp-walked you out the door, down the elevator and out into the street.'

'You wouldn't dare.'

'You don't want to take that gamble with me, Mr Eagleton. I am one stubborn bitch and you'd better get used to that as long as the killer of your wife is still at large.'

'Is this your way of telling me you have balls?'

'Can we stop this little skirmish in the gender war and talk about your alleged love for your wife?'

'There was nothing alleged about it.'

'Really? And was it that love that led you to commit adultery?'

'My love for Candace had nothing to do with my fling with my secretary.'

'Miss Flowers seemed to think there were wedding bells in her future.'

'If she did, then she was a fool. I never gave her any indication of any permanence in our relationship. I rewarded her in cash and expensive gifts. She was more than adequately compensated for every encounter. If you ask me, that is the working definition of whore.'

'You never told her you loved her?'

'I may have in a moment of passion but it was meaningless. In fact, I do recall one occasion when I told her "at this moment, I love you more than anything." The operative phrase being "at this moment." The moment passed – quickly.'

'You don't think you were taking advantage of a young, naïve girl's heart?'

'Oh, nothing naïve about that gold-digger. She was not in love with me. She was in love with the money and power I represented. She's shallow and insipid. And I suspect that she sent the anonymous note to Candace that ruined my marriage.'

'Oh, I see,' Lucinda said, leaning forward in her seat. 'It was the note, not your cheating, that destroyed your marriage.'

'Stop playing word games with me, Lieutenant. I loved my wife. I had no intention of leaving her. I wanted to grow old with my wife. And someone has stolen that possibility away from me and instead of looking for that killer, you are badgering me.'

'You loved your wife even though she was moody, overly dramatic and difficult to live with.'

'I never said that. Never.'

'No. Your son Mark said that.'

Frank sighed. 'I fear that boy will never grow up. He's so much like his mother and he rebels against it constantly. He's said some asinine things in his life, but that's probably the worst. I'm sure he only said that in a misguided attempt to protect me.'

'Actually, it had the opposite effect.'

'Figures. You have any children, Lieutenant?'

'No.'

'Don't. They're lots of fun when they're little but they grow up too fast. Once they hit twelve, you have years of heartache and worry. You think once they get past their teens, it's a major accomplishment. But then, they always disappoint you again.'

'You sound awfully bitter, Mr Eagleton.'

'Listen, I love my kids. But they can be really aggravating. My daughter always thinks the worst of me; my son has nothing good to say about his mother. Where are the rewards of parenthood in that?'

'You have a point there, Mr Eagleton. But perhaps your attitude towards child-rearing is not a universal truth. Maybe it just means you aren't parent material.'

Eagleton snorted. 'I told that to Candace a long time ago but she told me I was crazy. And she wanted children so much . . .'

'And you just went along?'

Frank nodded.

'Was that your usual reaction to her plans – even if you didn't think they were right?'

'No. I wouldn't say that.'

'Did you help her plan her extortion attempt?'

'Extortion attempt? You mean blackmail?'

'Yes.'

'Candace wouldn't blackmail anybody.'

'We think she may have done just that. Who would she be able to blackmail?'

'No one. She didn't know anyone's deep, dark secrets – that I know of.'

'If not that, perhaps she was involved in the commission of a crime or in an unethical act.'

'Candace? Please! She was always hounding me if she thought I stepped a little too close to the ethics line. When she didn't approve of a business deal I made, she told me so – particularly if she thought I was taking advantage of someone in an untenable situation. She was merciless in her judgment – she didn't let me slide on anything.'

'Interesting. So she could have been blackmailing you?'

'OK,' Frank said, throwing his hands in the air and rising to his feet. 'That's one stupid comment over my quota for the day. Enough. I have work to do. Get back to me when you have something sensible to say.'

Lucinda sat for a moment, looking up at his scowling face, the hands on his hips, the impatient way he shifted his weight from one foot to the other. She made deliberate movements as she left the chair and took two steps toward the door. She turned and looked back at him. 'You are not exhibiting the attitude I would expect from a grieving husband. If you played any role in the death of Candace Eagleton, I will find out. Maybe not today or tomorrow. But I will not rest until I know every detail of your involvement.'

'Next time you want to talk to me, Lieutenant, I suggest you contact my attorney. April can provide you with his details.'

EIGHTEEN

'I wanted you to know that I am a little closer to locating Bonnie Upchurch,' he said.

'Where are you?' she asked.

'I'm in Texas – Dallas, to be exact.'

'Did you find her?'

'No.'

'Then why are you calling? We need to keep our contact to a minimum.'

'But this is important. I was certain you'd want to know.'

'What's so important?'

'In the Dallas County Courthouse, I found a record of a woman by the name of Bonnie Louise Upchurch who legally changed her name to Olivia Louise Cartwright.'

'When did that happen?'

'Nineteen years ago. No wonder her trail was cold.'

'Is she still there?'

'No. The apartment building she lived in at that time is no longer standing.'

'Then it's a dead end.'

'No. Not at all. I've got leads sprinkled throughout the Southwest. I'm driving west to follow up on them as soon as I get off of this call.'

'When you find her?'

'I will try to find out what she knows. It's possible that she will not have a suspicious memory. If not, there's no reason to take action.'

'How will you know she's not lying?'

'You don't need to know my methods – in fact, it's better if you don't. If you recall, Candace confirmed everything before I was finished with her. She was honest even when she knew she was going to die.'

'How many times have I told you to be careful with your choice of words?'

'Get off your high horse. This is your operation. I am just your humble servant. Don't get all high and mighty with me. I know your secrets. And I know what to do if trouble gets too close. No matter what happens, I will not go down alone. That is my promise and my threat. Get used to it.' He slammed down the receiver in the phone booth and got back in his car. He headed west on Route 20 planning to rendezvous with Interstate 10 just north of Alpine.

NINETEEN

J ake slid into the spacious interior of his 1966 Impala Super Sport, pleased that he had an opportunity to make the two-hour drive that took him through the rolling hills of the Albemarle County countryside. The silvery-blue convertible was more than just a car – it was his legacy from his dad. He never turned the key in the ignition without a flash of memories about his father galloping through his head with a power equal to the 325 horses under the hood of his beautiful, gas-guzzling glide ride.

He avoided the major interstate and took the back roads, cutting over to Route 29 when he reached Lynchburg. He had a favorite section of that highway between Lynchburg and Charlottesville – a place where the trees formed a crowded canopy wrapping the road in green light as the hills created an undulating ribbon of asphalt.

He followed Lucinda's directions as he turned off the highway onto a secondary road. He drove past alternating patches of verdant woodland, rocky fields where cattle grazed and green patches of row after row of field corn or soybeans. One family farm after another – many 200 acres or more – created a bucolic atmosphere that made Jake feel drowsy.

The sight of the name 'Pierce' on the side of a large silver mailbox waving its red flag brought him back to alertness. He turned in, crossed the cattle guard and headed up the lightly graveled dirt driveway. On his left, in the front of the house, rough, whitewashed horizontal boards defined a paddock where the horses pranced in the sun.

On the other side of the drive stood a faded red barn and a field filled with grazing polled Herefords. Beyond them both, nestled in the hillside stood a traditional, two-story white farmhouse surrounded by a white picket fence. Around the outside perimeter of the fence, a host of fowl – Plymouth Rocks, Rhode Island Reds, guinea hens and generic white chickens – scratched the dirt looking for bugs.

A tractor sat idling by the bare patch of dirt in front of the barn door. Jake pulled up next to it and parked. A rangy man with tousled hair walked out of the barn, wiping his hands on the rump of his denim overalls. 'That's some car,' he said. 'What a beauty!' He ran a hand across one fender, a look of love or lust in his eyes. 'Where are my manners?' he said as he wiped his right hand on the denim once again and stretched it out toward Jake. 'Ricky Pierce. And you're Lucinda's FBI friend?'

Jake shook Ricky's hand. 'Jake. Jake Lovett. And I'm here as your sister's friend. This is not an official FBI investigation. I'm technically off-duty.'

'Understood. Glad you could make it. Seems like my sister works too hard sometimes but she's never been one to do things halfway. Follow me up to the house. We'll sit down with some coffee and talk this thing over.' Ricky swung in the tractor seat and made a broad turn back out to the drive.

Inside, Jake sat down at the plain wooden table in a farm kitchen that looked like an old set from *The Waltons*. There were new, shiny stainless steel appliances but there was also a green enamel wood cook stove with a stainless steel pipe rising up from behind it and venting out of the wall.

The cabinets were wood painted white – the ones on top had glass-paned doors, the lower set was covered with floral chintz curtains. The countertops were a mottled brown marble. The upgrades to the kitchen made it appear streamlined and efficient. The remaining traditional farmhouse features gave it a cozy, homey feel. Jake wondered what it looked like when Lucinda lived here as a teenager.

When both were seated with a steaming mug of coffee, Ricky said, 'I imagine Lucinda's filled you in on the problem here?'

'Yes. As I understand it, law enforcement and the medical examiner have ruled your nephew's death as a suicide but your brother-in-law and your wife are convinced he was murdered by someone who was bullying him at school.'

'To tell you the truth, I think they're grasping at straws. My sister-in-law Martha wants to bury her boy but Seth won't let anyone embalm Dylan because he's certain his son's body has evidence of foul play. I was hoping if Lucinda looked at the evidence and agreed with law enforcement that would help Seth accept the reality of his son's suicide.'

'You know, if I do reach the same conclusion, it still might not help. Not only am I not Lucinda, but Seth could be too entrenched in his denial to accept logic or reason.'

'The authorities are giving him a little time to come around but the sheriff told me they'll seek a court order if he doesn't accept the reality of a suicide soon.'

'I guess my first stop is at the sheriff's office and then I'll call on the doctor who performed the autopsy. It might go smoother if you were with me. Can you get away?'

'Yep, sure can. Made sure I took care of everything that had to be done before you got here. You gonna talk to Todd Childress, the kid that was pushing around Dylan?'

'Yeah, but it's probably better if you weren't along for that.'

'Makes sense,' Ricky said, and upended the contents of the mug into his mouth as he pushed away from the table.

'We'll take my car if that's all right,' Jake said.

'More than all right – looking forward to the ride.'

Initially, the sheriff balked and peered at them through suspicious, slitted eyes. He was not the stereotypical sheriff with a pot belly and swaying jowls. He carried his six-foot-three height on a thin frame. His chin jutted out firm and solid without a trace of middle-aged slackness. The two men assured him that Jake was not on the scene in any official capacity. Eventually, a wary but more relaxed sheriff opened up about Dylan's death.

'I do want a resolution here. If Seth doesn't let go of this, the county will be forced to bury him with the unclaimed bodies. I don't want to do that to the family. It just doesn't seem right. But I can't make Seth budge.'

'What makes you certain it's a suicide?' Jake asked.

'Let's start with the gun. It's a pearl-handled ladies' pistol – the same one Martha's father gave her for her sixteenth birthday.'

Jake looked at both their faces. 'He gave his daughter a pistol for her sweet sixteen?'

The sheriff chuckled. 'Oh yeah, ol' hanging Fred Clooney. He was a judge in criminal court. No defense attorney ever wanted to be in front of his bench. He was as tough as beef jerky left out in the sun.

Why, he even wore a gunslinger's holster with a pair of six-shooters under his robe. Don't make 'em like that anymore.'

'What about fingerprints on the weapon?'

'Nobody'd wiped off that gun like they were trying to hide anything. Most the fingerprints belonged to Dylan. The other couple of prints we found matched Seth and Martha. It seems to me like they're the only folks that coulda killed the boy if he didn't kill himself.'

'What about the truck he died in? What did you find there?' Jake asked.

'Nothing you wouldn't expect. It was messy. Blood spatter, pools of blood. But it was only one person's blood and it all belonged to Dylan. No signs of a struggle. Lots of full and partial fingerprints on the dash and the door panels – some identifiable, some not. And before you ask, we did check that boy Todd's prints – not one matched.'

'Did he have an arrest record?'

'Nah. His parents gave us permission to print him.'

'Really?'

'Yep. His father's one of my deputies – not like he could say no.'

'I'd like to talk to the boy.'

The sheriff cocked his head sideways. 'I don't know. I told Deputy Childress that there wouldn't be any problems.'

'Sheriff, the boy knew Dylan. He can give me some perspective on the boy – help me deal with the family.'

'Let me think on it.'

Jake nodded. 'Did you do any interviews after his death?'

'Quite a few. Talked to a lot of kids at the school – but it didn't seem like he had any real friends. He was a loner. Lately, they said, he'd withdrawn even more. One kid told me that Dylan fretted a lot about the end of the world. He seemed to think the death of Osama bin Laden would herald the commencement of the final jihad that would annihilate the world. Pretty dark musings for a kid.'

'So you think, psychologically, it all fits a suicide scenario?'

'Not just my opinion – I talked to Dylan's guidance counselor. She was very concerned that he might be clinically depressed. She recommended that the O'Haras take him to see a psychiatrist six months ago. She said that Martha seemed willing to try anything but Seth simply said it was against their religion.'

'What religion is that?'

The sheriff shrugged.

'Ricky, do you know?' Jake asked.

'Can't say that I do. I know he doesn't come to my church – but Martha does sometimes. When Dylan was younger, she used to bring him to Sunday School. But I can't recall Seth ever going to any church.'

'Folks out in these parts tend to see visiting a shrink as a sign of weakness. Old prejudices die hard out here in the country.'

'I think people cling to their biases everywhere, Sheriff. They're just probably a bit more honest about them out here.'

'That's a kind way of putting it. Anyway, physical evidence, psychological evidence and interviews with everyone but Seth O'Hara point to suicide. I've looked but I can't find a thing to tell me otherwise.'

'Thank you, Sheriff. I'll be talking to the medical examiner next but I'd like to speak to Dylan's counselor, too, if you'll give me a name. And I really want to talk to Deputy Childress's boy.'

'His counselor's name is Jane Salvadore. And I'll talk to Childress and set up a meeting for you.'

'Thanks again, Sheriff.'

'I really want this resolved. I really want the boy to be put to rest. I know how upset his mother is – I don't want it to drag out any longer. But – but – if you find anything I missed, anything that indicates a possibility of foul play, I want to know about it. If you find evidence that someone took Dylan's life, I will not ignore it, even if it's my deputy's son. I'm more interested in protecting this county than I am in protecting any individual. If we missed something, I truly hope you find it.

'Oh, and you might want to sit down with little Becky Carpenter. She seemed more upset about his death than anyone outside of the family. She was the only person I could find who considered Dylan a friend. She indicated that she wasn't surprised that he committed suicide but I had a feeling she was holding something back. Maybe you could find out what it is – if you can get her to stop crying long enough to talk.'

TWENTY

After leaving Frank Eagleton's office, Lucinda checked for messages on her cell. Ted Branson had more information about the computer analysis. She hit the call back button. As soon as she heard the ringing stop, she started talking. 'What have you got, Ted?'

'The Internet Service Provider got back to me with the origin of the email. It came from a computer at Scott Technologies.'

'As in Scott computers?' Lucinda asked.

'Yes, and Scott phones, Scott printers, Scott modems, you name it.'

'Whose computer?'

'There's the tricky part. The ISP claimed that they can't go any deeper into the origin. It seems Scott has a built-in security system that randomly switches IP addresses on all their computers. Because of that, they can't pin down the specific device.'

'You're kidding?'

'Wish I were. And it gets worse. Scott employs more than sixteen hundred people. Everyone has access to a computer – most have their own personal computer. Not counting what's on the assembly line, that easily means more than a thousand PCs on the premises.'

'So now I have sixteen hundred persons of interest?'

'You got it. But, while I've been waiting for your call back, I used the original search warrant request to draft a new one for you to serve on the security department at Scott. They should have data that can lead you to the exact computer at the time the messages were sent. I'm emailing it right now.'

Lucinda added a few details to Ted's draft, printed it out and headed down to courtroom level to find a judge to sign it. It was a busy day on everyone's docket but finally the detective found a jurist on break to handle the warrant and she was on her way to the campus of Scott Technologies. As she drove she wondered who was the first technology company to call their compound of offices and factories a campus and why. Odd use of the word, she thought. Was it to make freshly graduated computer engineers feel comfortable? Or did they think it somehow enhanced their corporate image?

The center front of the main building was a wall of glass. She pulled open the door and heard the sound of a camera activating. A bodiless voice said, 'State your name, corporation and your business, please.'

'Lieutenant Lucinda Pierce, police. I have a warrant.' She held the document and her shield towards the camera. She heard a click and pulled open the interior door. The ceiling of the lobby soared up three or four stories. To her right was the reception desk. Straight ahead was a solid wall broken only by a steel door with an identity card scanner standing beside it. To the right of that was a one-station security checkpoint that looked just like the ones at the airport.

Lucinda walked over to the front desk. The young woman behind the counter had a set of headphones with a mouthpiece wrapped around her head. Her right eyebrow was pierced and a partial tattoo was visible on her neck – it looked like the top of a dragon head. She raised one eyebrow at Lucinda but didn't say a word.

'I have a warrant.' Lucinda held up the signed papers.

'So you said.'

'I have a court order from a judge granting me permission to search the databases in the security division.'

'As if,' the girl snorted.

'Excuse me?'

'Hold on. I'll call up to security.' She turned away from Lucinda and put her hand over the mouthpiece. Lucinda could hear the sound of her talking but could only recognize a word here and there.

She disconnected and turned back to Lucinda. 'Someone will be with you shortly. Have a seat.'

Lucinda thought about demanding immediate access but then thought better of it and sat in the waiting area. She checked the email on her iPhone but found nothing of interest. She went to the Internet and pulled up the day's headlines, read a story or two and grew bored. Twenty minutes after she'd sat down, she was still waiting. She walked over to the receptionist and said, 'This is unacceptable. I demand admittance now.'

'I was told to tell you to wait.'

'I'm sorry, waiting time is over.'

With sarcasm dripping off every word, the receptionist said, 'No, ma'am, I'm the sorry one 'cause I just can't do that.'

'Oh, really. Then I guess you leave me no choice. I'll have to cuff you, stuff you in my back seat and take you to the justice center.'

'On what grounds?'

'Obstruction of justice.'

'You can't do that.'

'You don't want to dare me.'

The receptionist pushed a button and turned away from Lucinda again. Although her words were still unintelligible, her voice rose an octave, making her state of mind obvious. She spun back around. 'OK. You're going to have to go through security first.' She removed her headset and stepped out from behind the desk. She pointed to the security set-up and said, 'Over there. Empty your pockets into the bin and walk through the metal detector.'

'I can't do that.'

'No outsider goes into the facility without going through there. You have to.'

'I am a police officer.'

'That doesn't matter. Do you have a pacemaker or a plate in your head?'

'No.'

'Then you have to go through here.'

'I'm carrying a weapon.'

'Weapon? You can't take a gun in there. What's wrong with you?'

'I am a police officer.'

'You'll have to give the weapon to me.'

'Not hardly.' Lucinda chuckled.

'Then put it in the bin.'

'I don't think so.'

'Then there's nothing I can do.'

'Play it your way, then,' Lucinda said as she pulled handcuffs out of the waist of her skirt.

The receptionist squealed. 'No. Get away from me!' she shouted as she took shelter behind the front desk.

Lucinda walked towards her as a man in a suit walked through the outer doors. The girl slammed a hand down on the release button and he stepped into the lobby. 'Lieutenant Pierce?' he said, his hand outstretched, a plastic smile plastered on his face.

'Yes,' she said, without reaching for his hand with hers.

'I am the attorney of record for this corporation. At this moment, my colleague is presenting a motion to the judge requesting a stay on that warrant. I expect to receive a call any moment informing me of his success.'

'You think you can squash a warrant?'

The attorney pushed the corners of his mouth a bit broader. 'Yes, Lieutenant. I do believe we can. As a high technology corporation with multiple government and commercial research and development projects in progress at any given time, we have a vast amount of proprietary information on our servers. It would create a breach in security to allow anyone to have access to our data. We have successfully fought these attempts before in a number of instances.'

'You have a number of employees engaged in criminal enterprises?'

'Of course not.'

'Then why would you fight a court order?'

'We have successfully proven that there are other ways to obtain information without putting our company at risk of corporate espionage. Even an innocent leak from a police officer could endanger my client's viability as a profitable business.'

'Mr – you didn't introduce yourself.'

'Fischer. William Fischer.'

'Could I have your card, Mr Fischer?'

He hesitated for a moment, then pulled one out and handed it to her.

'Mr Fischer, I am involved in a homicide investigation. Someone in this building has information I need. I'm sure Scott Technologies doesn't want to be known as a corporation who shelters killers.'

'We also included a motion for a gag order to prevent you from going to the media and smearing the reputation of my client.' His cell phone trilled a tidbit of classical music. Lucinda was annoyed by the pretentiousness of his ring tone and downright angry when she saw a genuine smile sneak across his face.

He disconnected the call and turned to face her. 'We have a stay, Lieutenant. My secretary is scanning it now and will email it to my phone. You can wait to see it if you like. Otherwise, I believe our business here is concluded.'

Lucinda clenched her teeth and rose to her feet. Anger sent vicious comments flying to her tongue but she kept her mouth shut. She walked away without saying a word. That a corporation could trump law enforcement and impede the pursuit of justice seemed wrong to her on many levels. But she wasn't going to roll over and die – this was only the first volley. She could not let them win. At that thought, the email address, Winordie@fastmail.com, ran through her thoughts and she knew that person would not be an easy adversary.

TWENTY-ONE

J ake was disappointed after his visit to the medical examiner. The doctor was cooperative and forthcoming but unfortunately could not point to any additional indicators of suicide.

He headed to the sheriff's office where Deputy Childress was waiting for him with his son, Todd. He went straight to the booth on the other side of the glass from the interview room and sized up the pair. Todd, his T-shirt and jeans full of holes, slouched in the metal chair, legs outstretched, hands in his pockets and a scowl on his face. His father, in his neat, pressed brown uniform looked to be the polar opposite of his son as he paced back and forth in the room. Jake suspected harsh words had been spoken judging from the boy's expression and the red flush that had risen in the deputy's neck.

Jake eased the door open and stepped into the room, both pairs of eyes pivoted in his direction. He introduced himself, explaining that he was not here on official FBI business; he was just a friend hoping to find answers for a family. 'What can you tell me about Dylan O'Hara, Todd?'

Todd shrugged. The deputy tapped his foot against the chair leg. 'Answer him, with words.'

'I don't know him.'

Jake sighed. 'We know you know him. We have many witnesses to that fact.'

'I don't *know* him know him.'

'Well, what do you know, Todd?'

'Nothin'. I don't like him.'

'Why don't you like him?'

Todd shrugged again.

'You've been seen talking with him, Todd.'

'Talking *at* him,' Todd objected. 'I talk *with* my friends. He's not one of them.'

'What did you talk *at* him about?'

'Well, I tell him to get out of my way. To stop hoggin' my oxygen. To get lost.'

'I understand you harassed him a lot. Why was that?'

'He was taking up space. He was a useless consumer of oxygen. Why else?'

'When is the last time you saw Dylan?'

'How am I supposed to know? I try to ignore him.'

The deputy slapped an open palm on the desk in front of his son. He let the concussive sound reverberate a moment before he spoke. 'Todd, we are not playing games here. This is serious business. Some people have pointed the finger at you saying you killed the O'Hara boy.'

'I want a lawyer,' Todd said.

'Don't be stupid, Todd,' the deputy said.

'I may be your son but I still have my rights. I want a lawyer.'

'Don't be ridiculous. You haven't been charged with anything. But if you don't straighten up and start answering this man's questions, I'm apt to get arrested for assault. You understand me, boy? Now sit up in that chair.'

Todd slouched down a little further. He was now at an extreme angle, his head on the back of the chair, his heels propped up. Jake wondered how long he could hold that position without sliding down on the tile floor.

'Dad, do you really think that somebody from the FBI comes down to this rat-trap town out of the goodness of his heart?'

'Yes, I do. Now answer the man's questions.'

'I don't believe you, Dad. You've always told me that the FBI is a lying bunch of shits. You always said you can't trust them past the tips of their noses. You told me you'd never willingly help one of those s.o.b's if you could help it. And now that they've got their sights on your own kid, you're acting like this jerk is your best friend. You're such a hypocrite.' Todd straightened up with a smug smile on his face.

The deputy raised his arm in the air as if to strike his son then lowered it and shoved his hand deep into his pocket. 'I'm sorry, Agent Lovett, my son has turned into a real shit.'

Jake nodded and turned to Todd. 'Listen, if I walk out of here with my questions unanswered, you will remain a person of interest in this investigation.'

Todd shot to his feet and faced his father. 'I told you I didn't kill that dweeb. I wouldn't waste my fucking energy. I want to go back to school. I'm going to miss my civics test.'

'Sorry again, Lovett. I'm sure he's telling the truth about not killing the boy but I can't say I can vouch for anything else including his sudden concern about academics.'

Jake nodded and watched father and son walk out of the interview room. Before the door closed behind them, Jake saw the deputy cuff his son on the back of the head. Todd squealed as if he'd been stabbed.

The agent wasn't sure if that meeting had been productive or not. If it had been murder, the boy's lack of cooperation made him look as guilty as sin. But that was the problem. Was it murder or suicide?

He called Becky Carpenter's mother, who agreed to bring her daughter into the sheriff's office after school. He hoped that interview would be more obviously helpful but he doubted it. He had higher hopes for the appointment he had with Jane Salvadore, Dylan's guidance counselor.

TWENTY-TWO

Lucinda bent under the yellow tape on the front porch of the Eagleton home, unlocked the door, removed the seal and stepped into the foyer. The home had a hollow feeling, as if she could feel the presence of the woman of the house fading away as if she never existed.

She'd been through a family photo album and knew there had been happy times here – adult parties, birthday parties for the kids, Christmas gatherings around the tree. She'd seen unexpected snapshots of Candace and Frank showing expressions of delightful surprise. Where did it all go? Is happiness that fleeting? Is love always doomed to die? A vision of Jake flashed across her mind and she tucked it away.

She sighed, turned and left the house. She ripped off the yellow tape and dialed Eagleton's office number on her cell. 'I have a message for Frank Eagleton.'

'Would you like me to put you through?'

'No. Just tell him law enforcement has released his home. He can go back any time he wants.'

Back at her office, Lucinda asked for background information on Scott Technologies from the research department. Lara said, 'You're going to get an avalanche. That place has been in the news a lot lately.'

'Why?'

'Their CEO is running in the Senate primary.'

'The woman in the race?'

'That's the one. Tess Middleton. Do you want me to weed out anything connected to the election?'

'Yes. No. Abstract the essence and send it all on.'

'You got it, Lieutenant.'

Next, Lucinda rang Audrey Ringo to check on the toxicology results. She knew it was too early to expect anything but miracles did happen.

Audrey's irritation was evident the moment she asked: 'Do you think I'm a magician?'

Lucinda sighed. 'What's the latest from your oncologist, Audrey?'

'Doctor Ringo, if you don't mind, Lieutenant. Who told you I have an oncologist?'

'Everybody knows, Audrey. Your bout of breast cancer is not a secret.'

'It is, too. If I hear anyone else speak of it, I'll know they got it from you. And you will regret that,' the lab director shouted into the phone, then slammed down the receiver.

Lucinda sighed again. No good deed goes unpunished. Last time I show concern for the health of that red-headed witch. She looked at her watch. Time for her appointment with the district attorney.

When she walked into Michael Reed's office, he looked up and said, 'You just can't pass up an opportunity to make my job difficult, can you?'

'I imagine that means you've heard about the stay.'

'Why didn't you come to this office first?'

'It seemed so routine, Reed. I didn't think I needed the big legal guns.'

'Well, obviously you thought wrong. They are so connected. I got a call from the mayor, three councilmen and even an underling at the governor's mansion. Scott Technologies is a sacred cow. Do you know how much money they bring into this state?'

'I never considered money more important than a person's life.'

'There you go again – acting all self-righteous on me. Any time a little political maneuvering is in order, you get on your high horse and act like you're too good to sully your hands with diplomacy. What am I going to do with you, Pierce?'

'I've never shied away from diplomacy, Reed, but I will not compromise my principles nor curtail my investigation of a homicide simply because it's not politically convenient for your office. Is Tess Middleton among your campaign contributors?'

'That is irrelevant.'

'Is it? And is she?'

Reed pursed his lips. 'Yes. If you must know, she has given to my campaign in the past. Not this year, though. She's funneling her money into her own campaign.'

'Are you supporting her?'

'Does that really matter?'

'I think so. Full disclosure and all that.'

'They've asked but I haven't endorsed anyone yet. I need to back the winner, whoever that will be. Right now it's too close to call.'

'If the odds look better, you might want to think about it a bit. I got the impression from the corporate attorney that there has been quite a bit of law enforcement interest in her company. Might not look good if you endorse her one day and the next someone serves her with an indictment.'

'Do you know something I don't?'

'I've told you all I know.'

'Can you check with that FBI friend of yours?'

'I don't think that would be appropriate.'

'Oh, c'mon, professional courtesy. A little pillow talk and nobody is the wiser.'

Lucinda stalked out of his office without another word. She stormed down the three flights of stairs and into her office. She wished she had a door on her cubicle so she could slam it. *How dare he bring my personal life into an investigation? How dare he be so presumptuous to assume I am sleeping with Jake?* She folded her arms across her chest and stewed for a moment.

She badly wanted to snap at someone to release her pent-up anger. Unfortunately, Kristen took that moment to step into the doorway of her office. 'Lieutenant, someone called for you while you were upstairs. He sounded very angry.'

'Who was it?'

'He didn't leave his name.'

'Then why are you even telling me? What purpose does it serve? Someone else is pissed at me. So what? Can I figure out the reason why without knowing who it is? No. Next time, get the name.'

'I'm sorry, Lieutenant, I—'

'Sorry doesn't solve the problem, does it, Kristen?'

The moment Kristen stepped back into the hall Lucinda regretted venting on the poor, underpaid, overworked staffer. She picked up the phone and called the Giant Cookie Company. For a fee, they would take rush orders. She asked them to write Kristen's name on the cookie and attach a note that read, 'I'm sorry, Kristen. Lieutenant Pierce.' They promised to deliver within the hour. Lucinda hid in her office until they did.

Busy with paperwork, she almost paid no attention to the squeal of delight from the front desk. She stood up and stepped into the hall just in time to collide with an excited Kristen. 'You're forgiven, Lieutenant. Nobody has ever done anything so sweet for me before.' She wrapped her arms around the detective and gave her a hug. Lucinda felt even worse now. No one has ever been that nice to her? And I had to chew her ass out without cause before I was?

Awkwardly, Lucinda patted the receptionist on the back. Kristen skipped back up the hall, pausing at the corner to wave her fingers back at her and shout, 'Thank you!'

Lucinda returned to her paperwork and was just about caught up when her cell phone rang. 'Pierce.'

'I've had it with you, Lieutenant.'

'Excuse me?'

'You know what I'm talking about. I called you at your office number earlier and you refused to take my call. It took me a while to find your damned card with your cell phone number on it.'

Am I supposed to apologize because Frank Eagleton can't keep his collection of business cards straight? Lucinda wondered. 'I wasn't in the office earlier.'

'Then why didn't you return my call?'

'Because you didn't leave your name, Mr Eagleton. All I knew was that an angry person called.'

'I guess that means I'm not the only person you're harassing this week. Gee, and I thought I was special.'

'Mr Eagleton, all I did was call and leave a message with your secretary to inform you that your house had been released and you were free to occupy it again.'

'Oh, yeah, the timing of that was a dead giveaway.'

'Mr Eagleton, you are not making any sense to me.'

'Right. Play dumb. You lured me to my home so you could sic your goon on me. And he can act all innocent while he asks to speak to my wife. My dead wife. That's sick, Lieutenant.'

'What are you talking about?'

'I know you sent him over here. You are so transparent.'

'Mr Eagleton, I sent no one to your home. Did a police officer come there?'

'As if you don't know. No, Lieutenant. He was wearing a sheriff's department uniform. But that didn't fool me. I know you sent him. I know you guys all stick together. And I'm warning you. When I said if you wanted to talk to me you needed to go through my attorney, I was serious – dead serious. And if you or one of your goons bothers me again, we're going to file a lawsuit against you and your department.'

'Mr Eagleton, please,' she said before she heard the dial tone. She stood for a moment, lost in thought. What did it mean? Did someone from one of the sheriff's departments stop by his house? If so, why? Or did someone connected with Candace's death visit posing as a deputy? If so, what did they want to know? Is Frank's life in danger? Or is Frank just full of crap? She brought up the area law enforcement directory on her computer.

TWENTY-THREE

Jane Salvadore's office was a refuge of neat located through a door behind the counter in the chaotic main office of the high school. Neat enough, Jake thought, to be obsessive. The woman herself was just as tidy and picture perfect. Her nails cut close and freshly manicured. Her hair coifed just so with every strand in place, and an understanding smile spread across her face.

When Jake mentioned Dylan, her expression fell into a frown. 'That poor boy,' she said. 'He was so troubled.'

'What was bothering him?'

'I never could figure that out. I opened doors for him to talk to me but never touched any deeper than the surface. But I know he was struggling. It was in some ways typical adolescent angst but beyond that there was something deeper. I suspected it was something for which he had a great deal of shame or anxiety.'

'What about Todd Childress? Do you know what was going on between Todd and Dylan?'

'I do know that Todd tormented him. Todd is a bully. He pushes around a lot of kids but seems to lose interest in them quickly. On the other hand, Dylan was his constant target in the last few months. Why? I don't know. But Dylan seemed a bit more sensitive than the average boy – at least more demonstrative about it – maybe it was that. It was as if he held a painful secret inside that he was afraid to share but somehow Todd knew what it was.'

'Did something happen to set Todd off?'

'There was a fight in the shower of the boys' locker room after gym class. They were both naked and wet. The PE teacher broke it up and neither boy would tell us what it was all about. But Todd has been on Dylan's back ever since.'

'How was Dylan doing in class?'

She flipped open a file folder on her desk and scanned the contents. She pulled out three report cards, opened them and spun them to face Jake. 'As you can see, he had excellent grades until the last two reporting periods. A lot of A's and a few B's in his sophomore year. More A's and fewer B's in his junior year. Not a C in sight. His senior year started out fairly well – more B's than A's, but still . . . Now D's and F's are more common. He stopped turning in homework even though it seemed as if he completed his assignments.'

'What do you mean?' Jake asked.

'Two of his teachers saw him drop papers into the trash can as he walked out of the room. Each one pulled it out when he left and realized that it was the completed homework assignment that he claimed he hadn't done. It really made no sense. But then teenagers often don't.'

'Have you talked to his teachers?'

'Oh, have I. Dylan was well liked by the faculty. He seemed to have better social skills with adults than he did with his peers. He was polite to his teachers. He did his work. He studied. When it all fell apart they were perplexed. I was asked if his parents had divorced, if he'd lost someone close to him, all the usual torments. Or if he'd started using drugs or drinking alcohol. We had some sessions with his parents trying to get to the bottom of what was going on in Dylan's life but they were as clueless as we were. That's when I began to suspect he was depressed or had some other serious mental health issue. I told Seth and Martha that they needed to get help for Dylan.'

'It sounds as if you have no doubts about the conclusion that Dylan committed suicide?'

She shook her head. 'If you try to be suspicious that it's something more, you come up with Todd Childress. Have you met him?' she asked.

Jake nodded.

'He's been a rather obnoxious boy of late. He acts all tough but, believe me, he's one of the biggest babies in the school and he's a coward. Are you going to be talking to any of Dylan's friends?'

'Does he have any close relationships besides Becky Carpenter?'

'Other than her I can't think of anyone he's close to. In fact, he seemed to have pushed everyone away this year except for her. But there were other friends before that. I called them into my office to see if they were having grief issues after Dylan's death. A couple of them were angry that he took his life. The rest appeared indifferent. But I think that was an act. The whole student body was rocked by his suicide – even kids who didn't know him. Most of them want to attend his memorial service but no one seems to know when that will be. Do you?'

Jake shook his head, unwilling to share that Dylan's father was the reason for the delay.

'Ready for the nickel tour? Get an idea of the lay of the land?' she asked.

'Lead the way.'

Walking out into the hallway, she said, 'If I see any students that knew Dylan well at any time, I'll point them out.'

'I don't want to question any of the kids without their parents present.'

'Of course not. But who knows what one of them might volunteer,' she said and flashed him a smile.

She pointed out the library and named the teachers behind each closed door and whether or not Dylan had been in one of their classes. Jake wondered if she knew all of her students that well.

At the door to the boys' locker room, Jane stopped. 'I don't like going in there unless it's a genuine emergency. Tends to make everyone uneasy – including me. But I thought you might want to go in and see where the fight took place.'

Jake pushed open the swinging door and the smell hit him – the odor of mildew, percolating hormones, stinky feet and sweaty adolescent bodies. Memories of his high school days rushed back. This place was one of the cruelest on earth. Ridicule for any perceived defect – the boy with big feet, the one with a prominent birth mark on his back, the one with the pimply butt. And God help any boy with a smaller than average penis. Jake never instigated any of the harassment over that deficiency but he was always willing to join in the laughter at the other boy's expense. At the time, it seemed the right thing to do. Now, it left him with a sense of shame. How would he have reacted if one of the boys he'd ridiculed had committed suicide? Was that Dylan's problem – a small penis?

He knew that if he had any problem with an emotional component when he was in high school he wouldn't dare talk to his friends; he would talk to his mom or one of the girls. But would he even have considered that if the problem was penis size? That afternoon's interview with Becky Carpenter took on a new importance. Does she know his secret?

Back in the hall, he asked, 'Do you know if there was anything unusual about Dylan's body? A scar, a mark, or—'

'Or a small penis? You guys are so obsessed with that. I wouldn't know. Neither he nor his parents ever said anything about that. One of his PE teachers might have known – but maybe not. They're so careful in the locker room – they don't want to be accused of staring at the boys' bodies. I don't think they really see them.'

The possibility of more conversation temporarily came to an end with the ringing of the class bell. Students erupted from classrooms with their thundering feet and babbling voices.

Jane nodded and smiled as one student after another acknowledged her presence with a simpering sing-song, 'Hello, Mrs Salvadore.' Then her expression changed without warning and Jake followed her gaze. 'Eli! Eli!'

A small young man turned towards her and walked in her direction. Unlike most of the teenagers, he didn't slouch. He stood as rigidly upright as he could as if he believed it made him look taller. 'Hello, Mrs Salvadore.'

'Eli, this is Agent Lovett from the FBI.'

Eli's eyes widened. 'FBI? Is somebody getting busted?'

'No,' Jane said with a laugh. 'Agent Lovett is not here on an investigation. He's just trying to help Dylan's parents come to grips with what happened.'

Eli's head dropped and he stared at the floor. 'Oh.'

'You and Dylan were pretty good friends, weren't you?'

'We were. I mean, like last year – even the beginning of school this year. But then, like, he freaked out. He didn't want anybody near him. You got too close and he'd back away.'

'Do you know what was bothering Dylan?'

Eli shrugged. 'I really need to get to class, Mrs Salvadore.'

'Go ahead, Eli,' she said. 'Well, that wasn't much help. Let's swing by the cafeteria. It's time for the third and final lunch period of the day.'

The noise level in the cafeteria was even higher than it had been in the hallways during class change. In there, hundreds of simultaneous conversations mingled with the ring of dropped silverware, the slam of trays slapped on tables, the clatter of serving spoons against stainless steel bins as workers scooped food onto students' plates.

'Not an environment conducive to good digestion, is it?' Jane said with a laugh.

'I won't be bringing a date here.'

'Oh, look,' she said, pointing across the room. 'There's Becky Carpenter.'

'The blonde?'

'Yes. The one in the black T-shirt and black jeans.'

She was a petite girl with a pretty face but her expression was so solemn and sad, Jake had a hard time imagining it with a smile.

'She's so quiet, it's painful,' Jane said. 'She's not one of my students but her counselor told me that it takes a major effort to get her to say anything but "yes," "no" or "I don't know."'

'Great. Her mother's supposed to bring her in to talk to me this afternoon. That'll be a fun conversation.'

'Good luck with that.'

They made their way back to the front of the school. As they stood in front of the doors to the outside, Jane said, 'I am nearly certain that Dylan committed suicide but if I'm wrong, I want you to find whoever hurt that boy and hold him accountable.'

'Any idea who that might be?'

'I know I mentioned the Childress boy but I'm sure he couldn't have done it. He doesn't have it in him. I guess if I were theorizing about possible culprits, I'd look closer to home. I'd look at Seth O'Hara.'

TWENTY-FOUR

Lucinda called the sheriffs of Powatan and Goochland Counties without any luck. Her fortunes changed when she placed a called to Hanover County. 'Yes, I paid a visit to 2210 Churchill Lane. I called your chief and gave him a heads-up first. Is there a problem?'

Lucinda rolled her eyes at the knowledge that the chief was aware of his visit. It boggled her mind to think that he didn't recognize the address where a leading citizen was recently murdered. 'No problem with your call on the house but I got a blistering phone call from Frank Eagleton. He thought I put you up to it.'

'He's an ass. He went nuts before I even talked. What's his problem? I mean, I know his wife just died but there was no need to talk to me like that.'

'Sheriff, do you know how his wife died?'

'Nah. Eagleton didn't say.'

'She was murdered.'

'You're kidding me? In that house?'

'Yes. I just released it today.'

'You think the husband did it?'

'Maybe, but right now I'm following a slightly more promising lead. Could you tell me why you went looking for Candace Eagleton?'

'Well, I got a murder up here and I found her nickname and a phone number written on a piece of paper in the victim's apartment. It was the best lead we had but since we can't talk to her, we're back to square one.'

'Who was killed?'

'Some fella named Charles David Rowland. Not a big-time criminal. Pretty much just a sad sack plodding along in life looking for his rightful place in the world long after he should've found it.'

'How was he killed?'

'Trapped in an alley behind a grocery store and run down like a dog. The last few minutes of his life musta been hell.'

'It wasn't just a hit-and-run?'

'Nope. Whoever drove that vehicle left enough marks back there to make re-creation a breeze – he did it on purpose, all right. On top of that, the dead guy had no wallet, no money, no cell phone. Not a thing in his pockets except one small item.'

'What was that?' Lucinda asked.

'A business card. Now here's the really weird part – it was an FBI business card.'

'You're kidding me.'

'Nah. Wouldn't do that. Pretty strange, though, isn't it?'

'Stranger than you know,' Lucinda said. 'It was Jake Lovett's card, wasn't it?'

'How did you know that?'

'We work together from time to time. And it looks like fate has just brought us together again. Do you have any idea of the connection between Candace Eagleton and Charles David Rowland?'

'Not a clue. In fact, I was right surprised when that phone number led me to an affluent community. Seemed a little out of Rowland's class.'

'Still, looks like we'll be working this case together, Sheriff. I'll put the research department to work finding the connection between those two victims. Maybe if we do the wicked witch will allow Agent Lovett to join us in the investigation.'

'I called that woman to set her straight but she never returned my calls. I never thought Lovett was a suspect. I wouldn't have called him to the crime scene if I thought he was.'

'When we find the link, I'll get the chief to call her. She'll have to return his call. Anything else I should know about?'

'There were two more names on that scrap of paper we found: Tess and Bonnie. Next to Bonnie's name he wrote "Find her" in all caps. He also wrote "unknown" and a question mark,' the sheriff said.

'Not particularly useful unless the connection between Candace and Rowland somehow brings us closer to knowing their identities. I'll get back to you as soon as I find anything or learn something new.'

'And I'll do the same. Nice talking to you, Pierce.'

Lucinda disconnected the call and pushed in the extension of Lara Quivey in research. 'Hi, this is Lieutenant Pierce.'

'Did the report have everything you needed?'

'The report?' Lucinda said, looking across the desk surface for an overlooked document.

'Yes. I emailed it. Everything you wanted to know about Scott Technologies and a few things you could probably live without.'

'I'll check for that as soon as I get off this call. I have another request now.' Lucinda ran down the two names and everything she knew about them.

'Do you need that today?' Lara asked.

Lucinda was tempted to say 'yes' but if she did, she'd feel guilty making her work late when it wasn't a genuine emergency. 'No. But can it be a priority in the morning?'

'Sure can, Lieutenant. I'll be here for about another half hour if you think of something else you need.'

Pulling up her email, Lucinda spotted the one she wanted right away. She opened the attachment and scrolled down, scanning through the document. She didn't see anything of interest until she passed the narrative section of the report and hit the timeline. She read it and passed by it at first before it hit her. She scrolled back, looking for the name that she thought should have popped out right away. She smiled when she found the entry. October 29: Bartholomew Scott hands over the reins of the corporation to his daughter Tess Middleton. Tess. Not a very common name. And the email came from Scott Technologies. What if the unknown person using the Winordie@fastmail.com address was the CEO herself? She grabbed the receiver and called down to Lara again. She was pleased when the call was answered. 'When you find something that puts Candace Eagleton and Charles Rowland together, see if it also pulls in Tess Middleton, the CEO of Scott Technologies.'

'Wow. Really?'

'You know her?

'My choice for senate.'

'You might want to hold off on that decision for a little while and get me a detailed bio on Middleton, too.'

'Maybe I should work late tonight?'

'I'm not asking you to do that.'

'No. You never do. But once you threw in Middleton's name, it all got very interesting. My curiosity is craving gratification. I'll put in a couple of hours at least and, hopefully, everything you need will be ready for you by lunchtime tomorrow.'

'I couldn't do it without you guys. Are you alone in the office?'

'Nope. Vicki's here, too.'

'I'll order a pizza for you – mushrooms, Canadian bacon and green pepper, right?'

'Yes, ma'am. Thank you very much.'

After ordering dinner for the two in research, Lucinda printed out the Scott Technologies report so that she could write on it as she read along. She pulled her cell out and placed it on the desk. She was antsy about Jake's call. She knew he'd phone as soon as he finished up for the day but she was anxious to know what he was thinking about Dylan's death. And even more apprehensive about Jake and Ricky's compatibility.

TWENTY-FIVE

Jake looked through the glass of the door leading to the lobby. Becky Carpenter stared down at her feet. Her mother Dolly fussed with her hair, trying to push it back from her eyes. Becky shrugged her away and voiced her annoyance in one word that she stretched to three syllables, 'Mo-o-om.'

Pushing open the door, Jake stretched out his hand to the mother, who took it loosely. Her short pixie cut framed a youthful face. Jake wondered if the pain he saw in her eyes was because of the situation of the moment or a permanent state. He reached out to shake Becky's hand but she wouldn't acknowledge it at all – she kept her hands wedged into the front pockets of her black jeans.

'I have a room where we can talk in private. Follow me.' The door buzzed and Jake ushered them through and down the hall to an open interrogation room. Inside he asked if he could get them anything to drink. 'I would love a bottle of water if that isn't too much trouble,' Dolly said.

'Becky? How about you?'

Becky shrugged and shook her head.

'Becky?' Dolly said and then turned to Jake. 'She was just asking for a Dr Pepper while we were waiting. I'm sure she'd like one.'

'Coming right up.'

When Jake returned with two waters and a Dr Pepper for Becky, Dolly was whispering urgently to her daughter. She looked up and said, 'Thank you. I've told her how important it is to tell you everything she knows.'

'Thank you, Mrs Carpenter,' Jake said. 'Now, Becky, what is it that you know?'

'Nothing,' she muttered, without looking up.

'You did know Dylan O'Hara, didn't you?'

Becky's shoulders heaved as she choked off a sob.

'Becky, please, look at me,' Jake asked.

The blonde head rose, revealing tear-filled eyes and flushed cheeks. Jake's heart went out to her. He didn't want to press her but knew he must. 'You knew Dylan, right?'

'Yes.'

'Do you know anything about his death?'

'Yes.'

'What do you know, Becky?'

She pulled her cell phone out of her back pocket, pressed buttons, scrolled down and handed it to Jake. 'Here.'

Jake read a text message from Dylan: 'Now is the time. Goodbye, Becky.' He looked at the time. It was sent at the approximate moment of Dylan's death.

'It's my fault,' Becky blurted out.

'Why is it your fault, Becky?'

'I didn't think he'd really do it.'

'Do what Becky?'

'Commit suicide.'

'Do you know why he committed suicide?'

'I told him it didn't really matter,' she sobbed, the tears flowing freely down her cheeks.

'What didn't matter, Becky?'

'That no one that counted cared about that any longer.'

'Cared about what, Becky?'

'It was late but I should have snuck out of the house.'

'Becky, what was bothering Dylan?'

'I should have been with him.'

'Why, Becky?'

'I shouldn't have cared if I got caught and grounded.'

'Becky, why was Dylan so distressed?'

'I was selfish and now he's g-g-g-gone.' She threw her head toward the table, cradling it on her folded arms as her wrenching sobs filled the room.

Jake exhaled and leaned back in his chair. Dolly threw an arm around Becky's shoulders and whispered words of love and comfort. Both of the adults waited for Becky's bout of grieving to run its course. After a long two minutes, Becky raised her head, sniffled and wiped her eyes with the back of a hand.

'That's all I can tell you,' Becky said.

'Becky, do you know why Dylan committed suicide?' Jake asked.

'Yes,' she said with a nod.

'Will you tell me why?'

Becky shook her head side to side.

'Why not, Becky?'

'I promised.'

'I respect your honor in keeping a promise, Becky. But Dylan is gone now. Nothing can hurt him. Telling me can only help. If I understand why Dylan took his life it will enable me to help his parents accept the reality of the situation and move on.'

'Dylan did not want his parents to know.'

'What did Dylan do that was so awful, Becky?' Jake pushed.

Becky compressed her lips and shook her head as fresh tears began to fall.

'Becky,' Dolly said, 'you need to tell him what you know. This is not a game.'

The teenager squeezed her mouth together even more tightly, making her lips nearly disappear. She blinked her eyes and gave a sharp negative jerk of her head.

'You are not a child any longer, Rebecca. Stop acting like one,' Dolly said.

Becky turned her head to stare at the wall on the opposite side of the room, her chin outthrust and her arms folded across her chest.

'Rebecca Ann Carpenter, how do you think I would feel if you committed suicide and someone knew why but refused to tell me? That is how you are being selfish. That is how you are not being a good friend. Don't you care about Dylan at all?'

Becky jerked to her feet, glared at her mother and walked to the side of the room where she rested her forehead on the concrete block wall, her back to both of them.

Jake stood and walked next to her with a business card in his hand. 'Here, this is my card. Take it. Give me a call when you're ready to talk.'

'That will be never.'

'I'm willing to wait. My office number and my cell are on here. Please take it and think about it.'

Becky wouldn't touch it. She walked to the door and faced it. She said, 'Can I go now?' without turning around.

Jake sighed. 'Yeah, it's unlocked, go ahead.'

Becky left the room. Jake and Dolly listened to the shuffle of her feet as she went back down the hall. 'I am sorry,' Dolly said.

'Don't be, Mrs Carpenter. You tried. Now, we just need to give her time.'

'I don't know, Agent Lovett. I've never seen her acting this stubborn since she was a toddler.'

'You have any idea of what Dylan's secret might be?'

'I wish I did,' Dolly said. 'Let me have your card. I'll try to work on her.'

Jake slid the card into her hand. 'Don't push too hard. She'll be ready when she's ready. It shouldn't take too long – the burden of carrying that secret will soon get too heavy for her to bear alone.'

Dolly walked to the door and then turned back. 'I am very frightened, Agent Lovett.'

'About what, Mrs Carpenter?'

'I am afraid that she'll try to follow Dylan's example.'

Jake wasn't going to mumble any phony platitudes. He knew the mother's concerns were real. He knew the suicide risk was higher for every student in that school right now. He'd seen the epidemics happen elsewhere.

Dolly held Jake's gaze for a moment, unshed tears welling beneath her eyes. And then, she was gone. Jake stood in that same spot, feeling impotent, frustrated and powerless over what would happen next.

TWENTY-SIX

J ake checked his watch – 5:30 p.m. He had more than enough time to get back for the supper Lily had offered before he left that morning. After the meal, he'd call and see if Seth O'Hara was home and willing to talk. He had to follow up the lead pointing to Seth as a murder suspect but, most of all, he wanted to begin the work of Seth accepting the verdict of suicide. He really doubted it was anything else.

With a little bit of time on his hands, he called Lucinda.

'Pierce,' she answered.

'The perfect way for you to answer my call.'

'What? All I said was "Pierce."'

'But the sound of your voice pierces my heart every time.'

'Stow it, Lovett.'

'Not the effect I intended at all. What do I need to do to get back to "Jake?"'

'Tell me something good about your progress investigating Dylan's death.'

'I am almost completely convinced it was a suicide. But in order to convince Seth, I think I'm going to have to find the reason why. From my conversation with your brother Ricky and his wife, I don't think he'll accept it otherwise.'

'You're probably right but with time such an issue now, maybe you could try talking to him,' Lucinda urged.

'I planned on it. I'm going to go talk to him after supper if he's home.'

'Oh, supper? It didn't take you long out in the country to start picking up the lingo.'

Jake chuckled. 'Lily invited me to supper and I accepted. She didn't offer dinner. How's your investigation going?'

'Funny that you should ask. I could put on my detective hat and ask you why you felt such an urgent need to leave town.'

'You know why, Lucinda,' Jake said, knowing that she was jerking his chain and wondering where it would lead.

'I know what you told me. But right now, I need to ask if you took Candace Eagleton's life?'

'What? How did I get involved in that case?'

'Very simple. You remember that piece of paper with names and a phone number on it that you found at Rowland's apartment?'

'Sure. What about it?'

'Do you recall that the name with the phone number beside it was Candy?'

'Yes. Oh, no. You've got to be kidding. Are you saying "Candy" is Candace Eagleton?'

'Yes, indeed. And if Sheriff Cummings has the timing right, if you'd made it to the house when he thinks you tried to the other day, you would have found me there on the other side of the yellow tape.'

'Bizarre,' Jake said. 'Are you and Cummings working together on this now?'

'For the time being, yes. We're trying to figure out how there could be a connection between an upper-class supporter of the arts like Candace and a lowlife like Rowland. It seems unlikely but there has to be something or her name and number would not have been in his apartment.'

'I'll call the field office in the morning and see if I can't get someone to run some reports for you. You can't have too many details. I imagine that any relationship between the two would have had to have been rooted in the past before either of them settled into their current positions in society.'

'Good point. I've got people working on it, too. I've been trying to run down Candace's family but no one seems to recall her ever mentioning where she lived before moving to Virginia. We know she went to Sweet Briar College in Amherst but we can't seem to find anything prior to that. The college is clutching its confidentiality tight to its chest and Frank Eagleton is no longer speaking to me.'

'Listen, Lucy, I've got to run or I'll be late for supper. You want me to call later?'

'Yes, I'd very much like to know how it goes with Seth.'

'Will do. Love you,' Jake said.

Lucinda inhaled deeply. 'Goodnight, Jake.' As she hung up, she wondered why he did that. The 'love you' thing was happening with greater frequency. She told him she wasn't ready for commitment yet, particularly not with an FBI agent. Her first husband was FBI and he once said 'Love you' a lot, too. It didn't last long. One day, he just packed up his things while she was at work and left – no forwarding address. Bastard. She'd had to go through his mother to get the divorce finalized. That was a humiliating moment in her life – not the worst, but close.

A ding signaled incoming email. The message from Lara in the research department was marked urgent. A note read: See attached. Your link is in New Jersey. She scanned the detailed bios of Charles David Rowland and Candace Monroe, now Eagleton. Both went to Livingston High School in the middle of New Jersey. Both graduated in the class of '78.

Unbelievable. It seemed very unlikely that the two former classmates had maintained a connection throughout the intervening years. They must have recently renewed contact. But why would they be reuniting now? What happened to stir it up? Does it have anything to do with Ted's suspicions that Candace was blackmailing someone? It sure didn't make sense that she was trying to extort Rowland – he had no money to give and no reputation to save. Was he Candace's partner in crime? And does this high school make the connection with the other names on Rowland's note?

She hit reply. 'Please see if you can obtain a copy of the 1978 Livingston High School yearbook as soon as possible or sooner. Thanks!'

She hardly hit send before a reply came back: 'I'm already on it – if they get it to the Fed-Ex box in time, we'll have it tomorrow.'

Lucinda pulled down a victory fist and hissed, 'Yes!' Once again, she owed the whizzes in Research big time. Would she find the Bonnie person and unknown individual on Rowland's list?

She printed out the reports, packed them and the rest of the documents connected with the investigation into an empty file folder box, closed the lid, tucked it under her arm and headed home to review it all once again.

TWENTY-SEVEN

'I stopped in Reno and now I am in San Diego. Air flights and hotel bills are running my expenses high. I wanted to make sure you're good with that. I don't want to be cheated because I went through more money than you expected.'

'Of course I'm good for it. Don't be an ass.'

'I know you have the money. But having it and giving it to me are two different things.'

'I can't believe you're pulling this shit on me now. What do you want?'

'I need more cash. I'm using currency when I book these flights and I'm running out.'

'Doesn't a cash transaction get you flagged with security? Might you be remembered?'

'Do I strike you as stupid?'

'No. I'm not saying . . .'

'In case you find yourself on the lam before this is all over, Ms Diva, book your flights at a travel agency. They want your business and they're not going to cause problems.'

'That's a smart idea.'

'Yeah, yeah, yeah. The cash?'

'Where should I send it?'

'There's a Wells Fargo on San Ysidro Boulevard. Send it there. I'll be there first thing in the morning to make sure everything is set up to receive the funds and give me the cash.'

'How much do you need?' she asked.

'Twenty.'

'Twenty thousand?'

'Hey. This woman's a nomad. If she keeps going west, where will I find her next – Hawaii? New Zealand? Thailand? You don't want me to find her, you just say so, I'll head on home – but the cost of that flight will be on you, too.'

'Of course I want you to find her. Don't be so damned prickly. Every day the risk gets a little greater. I need her found and I need her gone.'

'Send the cash and your wish is my command, Ms Diva.'

'Stop calling me that.'

'But it suits you so well.'

'Go to hell,' she said and disconnected the phone. She grabbed the dog's leash and called his name. A golden lab came galloping. She shouted up the stairs. 'Back soon. I'm taking Dufus for a walk.'

She listened for the mumble of acknowledgment and walked out the door. Stupid name for a dog. That man was getting tiresome in many ways. But at least his stupid dog with its stupid name has served its purpose well. She walked a mile before dropping the disposable cell phone in a storm sewer. In another half mile, she was at Walmart. After tying Dufus to the bike rack, she went inside and bought another phone. Before walking outside, she sent a text message with the new number to another disposable in San Diego.

On the other end, he would get the number, memorize it and ditch his cell, and use yet another one the next time he needed to call.

TWENTY-EIGHT

Martha O'Hara answered the phone when Jake called. After a muffled exchange in the background, she invited him to come over to the house. Martha opened the door the moment Jake stepped into the deep, enclosed porch, where muddy work shoes and boots lined up against the wall.

He thought he saw a pretty face lurking behind a mouth drawn downward in grief, a reddened nose and the sagging bags beneath her eyes. The emotional toll of losing a child always ravaged a parent, leaving them damaged inside and out. Jake wanted to give her a hug but her husband Seth hovered in the background with a scowl on his face.

Dylan's father appeared to have transformed all of his grief into seething anger and resentment. His pursed lips, furrowed brow and a pair of hands that kept clenching unbidden into fists were a clear reflection of his state of mind. Jake knew a lot of pain was buried behind that anger and wanted to hug him, too, but suspected the response might be a punch or a shove.

They gathered around an old, large round oak kitchen table, darkened by the passage of time. The chairs were plain, sensible oak without any real style. On each seat, plump cushions covered with yellow gingham made them look more inviting and comfortable.

Adjacent to the porch, a U-shaped kitchen with the same depth had counters of worn tile and knotty pine cabinets with black, wrought-iron handles and drawer pulls. A window above the sink had a bright yellow valance and matching café curtains. Jake imagined that during the daytime, the sunshine streaming through the curtains would cheer the space a lot. Right now the outside darkness seemed to creep into the room, making it look tired and dreary.

Martha set out two pots of coffee – one regular, one decaf. Jake sipped with delight after dumping a dollop of the farm-fresh cream into his mug. Martha and Seth sat silent, waiting for him to begin.

Jake cleared his throat, unexpectedly nervous about this encounter. He'd been doing this so long; those occasional moments of unease always took him by surprise. He kept his eyes on his mug, hoping not to telegraph his feelings. 'Good coffee, ma'am. Thank you very much.'

Martha smiled. 'I see you like that cream.'

'Oh, yes. Don't get it this fresh very often. How do I begin? First of all, I want to express my sympathy to you for your loss. I can't pretend to know the depth of your feelings. I've lost my parents but I know that losing a child is much worse. And I know you want to understand why. I know that the reality is difficult to comprehend – it's unnatural and is an affront to the natural order. I know these things,' he said, tapping one temple, 'but I don't know them,' he said, poking his chest above his heart. 'I need to ask for your forgiveness and understanding in advance in case I say anything insensitive or inappropriate.' He scanned both their faces, watching them as they nodded before he continued. 'Everything I've found and everyone I've interviewed have pointed to the likelihood that Dylan did commit suicide.'

'I bet they have,' Seth said. 'I imagine at the top of that list are the cops who are trying to cover up for the deputy's boy.'

Jake closed his eyes, inhaled deeply and looked at the O'Haras, ready to be as empathetic and understanding as possible. 'I'm talking about my conversations with others, Mr O'Hara – Dylan's teachers, counselor, friends. I am looking into the decisions made by the sheriff's office and the medical examiner. I've set aside their conclusions for the time being.'

'Yeah, right.' Seth's sarcasm was apparent as he folded his arms across his chest and glowered at Jake.

'One person who believed that Dylan took his own life suggested that if wrong, then the most likely suspect was you, Mr O'Hara. Why would you think anyone would say that?'

'Because they are covering up for the deputy.'

'But that person could have pointed the finger at anyone. Why you?'

'Who was it?'

'I'm sorry, I can't reveal that name,' Jake apologized.

'Why not? I thought this was America. I thought we had a right to confront our accuser.'

'This is simply an investigation,' Jake said, instantly regretting that choice of word. 'It's not even an official investigation. I'm just trying to shed some light on the circumstances surrounding Dylan's death. I am making an inquiry as a friend of the family. Your right to confront your accuser exists in a trial situation.'

'A friend of the family,' Seth sneered. 'You're no friend of my family. We don't want you nosing around here. We want justice for our son. If you were here to arrest Todd Childress, I'd call you a friend of the family. As it is, you're just a troublemaker, stirring things up. *My* family just wants you to go away.'

Jake stared at him, attempting to size him up. He couldn't help but wonder if there was something Seth wanted to hide.

Martha broke the silence. 'That's not true. I am glad Agent Lovett is here. Thank you, sir. Thank you very much. All I want to do is put my poor son to rest. Ask me any question you want.'

Seth's face reddened and he glared at his wife. She ignored him and held her head high, for the moment replacing her sorrow with steely resolve.

Jake jumped in to take advantage of the moment. 'Mrs O'Hara, do you have any idea why someone would point the finger at your husband?'

'Yes, I do . . .'

Seth bolted to his feet, his chair scraped across the floor, filling the room with an irritating, abrasive sound. 'Martha!'

She kept her eyes on Jake, not sparing a single glance for her husband. 'We need to tell him everything, Seth. We need to be totally honest to get the answers we need about our boy.'

Seth spun around, went to the opposite side of the room and leaned his back against the wall. His muscles tingled with tension, causing tics around his eyes and on one upper arm. His face reddened except for the areas around his mouth and eyes – they turned stark fish-belly white.

'You were saying, Mrs O'Hara?'

'Dylan and Seth were going through a very rocky time in their relationship. There were lots of arguments.'

'About what?'

'About Dylan's declining grades. About all the time he spent in his room. About how he always had ear buds in his ears playing so loudly, the sound of the music seeped out around him. About borrowing the car. About going to college. About life, politics, religion – everything. Seth and Dylan saw eye-to-eye on nothing. Sometimes I got the feeling that if one of them expressed a viewpoint, the other one would automatically take the other point of view.'

'That's a lie, Martha,' Seth interjected. 'That might have been true of Dylan but it was not true of me.'

Martha turned and looked straight at her husband. 'It didn't seem that way, Seth. I know our boy could be very frustrating. I know he could be very negative. I hoped it was just a phase,' Martha said and a sob tore from her throat. 'If only I'd listened to that lady at the high school and accepted that it was much more serious. If I'd only suspected he would take his own life. If I—'

'Dylan did not take his own life,' Seth yelled.

'OK, OK. Let's calm down here,' Jake urged. 'We're all in this together. We all want to find the truth. Right?'

Martha nodded as tears flowed down both cheeks.

'All I want is the person who killed my son behind bars. I think we all know who that is,' Seth insisted.

'Mr O'Hara, we are not there yet. We first need to determine how your son died – homicide or suicide.'

'Are you sure you're not on the Todd Childress defense team?' Seth taunted.

Jake ignored that remark and turned back to Martha. 'Ma'am, were there ever any public displays of this alienation between your husband and your son?'

Martha sighed. 'Probably more than I know. I was present a couple of weeks ago when they butted heads in the feed store. They were shouting at each other over the choice of dog food, of all things. Dylan wanted the brand with the highest protein content because he believed that our working dogs herding the cattle and the sheep deserved it. Seth wanted to save money with a cheaper brand. Dylan said, "I'd be better off dead. You'll wish you listened to me then," and stormed out of the store.'

'The boy acted like the farm was a cash cow,' Seth complained. 'No expense was unjustified. I knew one day the farm would be his. I had to talk sense into him.'

'And you thought the best place to do that was in a crowded feed store? And the best way to do it was screaming at him and calling him a naïve idiot in front of all those people?' Martha retorted.

'I did not call him a naïve idiot.'

'Yes you did, Seth. I heard you. Sometimes you get so wound up you don't know what you're saying.'

Seth slumped against the wall. 'It's not my fault. I did not cause him to commit suicide. He did not commit suicide. He was murdered.'

'Not your fault?' Martha shouted. 'Then why did you scoff at the counselor when she suggested that we get professional help for Dylan?'

'That has nothing to do with this.'

'Maybe if he'd had help, he wouldn't have committed suicide.'

'He didn't commit suicide!' Seth screamed.

Martha rose to her feet, her face mottled and twisted. 'If he didn't then I guess that leaves you as a suspect. Did you kill our son?'

'I can't believe you said that. Married twenty-five years and you can say that to me? You can doubt me that much? I thought you knew me, Martha.'

'So did I, Seth. So did I,' Martha said as she sank back down into the chair and buried her face in her hands.

'This is on you, FBI man,' Seth said, jabbing a finger in Jake's direction. 'This is all on you. You owe it to me to tell me who made that accusation. Who put that thought in my wife's head?'

'I'm sorry, Mr O'Hara. I can't say that.'

'Why not? It has to be someone I know. Probably someone close. Maybe that loud-mouthed, self-righteous prick of a brother-in-law. Yeah, that's it,' Seth said, shoving himself away from the wall. He stomped over to the rack by the door, grabbed a ball cap and shoved it on his head. 'I'll take care of this, right now.'

Jake stood, reached out an arm in a conciliatory gesture, and said, 'Mr O'Hara, let's talk this over a little more.'

'I've done all the talking I want to do here. I did more listening than I wanted to in the first five minutes of your visit.' Seth jerked open the door, stepped over the threshold and slammed it so hard that the panes of glass rattled in their frames.

'Mr O'Hara,' Jake called out again.

Martha's lower lip quivered. 'I'm living in hell,' she whispered.

The sound of a starting engine reverberated in the kitchen. The pings of flying gravel rattled against the side of the house. Jake headed for the door, pulling it open; he turned and asked, 'Ma'am, will you be all right? I really should follow him over there.'

Martha nodded mutely.

Jake jumped in his car, started it up and the race began.

TWENTY-NINE

Lucinda entered her apartment in a high rise on the banks of the James River to an energetic and noisy greeting from Chester. The gray tabby circled her legs without causing her any distress. She was grateful for her ability to cope, remembering the time in the immediate aftermath of the loss of her eye years before on a domestic violence call. Chester's figure eights churned up dizziness and nausea then.

She fed Chester, grabbed a glass of Beaujolais and spread her files out on the dining table. After an hour of intense perusal, her working eye burned and watered. She stood, stretched and stared out her window at the river flowing below. A kingfisher soared down the middle of the water, seeking prey lurking beneath the surface.

A lone kayaker slipped down the river, a sleek silver arrow of fluid motion. On the opposite bank, a leggy blue heron stalked through the tall grasses at the water's edge, its golden eye peering in the river for any sign of shad or catfish. She felt a lot like that bird, hunting through the files, hoping to snag a tidbit of information that would nurture her investigation.

She exhaled deeply, decided against another glass of wine and returned to the table. Her eyelids were growing heavy when she picked up the document on the history of Scott Technologies. She read past the important clue and flipped the page when it suddenly hit her. She turned back. Did she read what she thought she read? Yes.

'Bartholomew Scott started the business in a carriage house next to his home in Trenton, New Jersey, in 1972. A series of progressively larger manufacturing facilities housed the company in New Jersey for the next several years. Dissatisfied with the economic situation in his home town, Mr Scott searched for a more fertile location for the continued growth of the company. He opened his first manufacturing facility in Virginia. Three decades later, Scott Technologies sits on a fifty-acre campus in a manufacturing facility producing more than seventy products to improve the technological environment for businesses, homes and government entities.'

New Jersey! Trenton, New Jersey. Tess Middleton, the current CEO of Scott Technologies, is the daughter of Bartholomew Scott. The email came from Scott Technologies. That definitely strengthens the connection. How could it not be the same Tess as on Charles Rowland's note? Did she go to Livingston High? Getting that year-book now seemed even more urgent.

She got up and paced the room. Chester interpreted that move as a signal to play. She noticed him and absent-mindedly threw a little purple mouse down the hall. He chased it with galloping feet and returned with the head and tail hanging out of his mouth. Lucinda was oblivious to his muted meows. He dropped it and let out a lusty yell. She startled out of her reverie and tossed the toy back down the hall. Chester ran up to it, flopped on the floor and chewed on its tail.

Lucinda pulled out her cell phone and looked for any missed calls or voicemail messages. Nothing. Why hadn't Jake called? Maybe she should call Ricky and find out if he knew what was keeping Jake busy. Ricky's cell rang four times and went to voice-mail. A little more anxiety and apprehension disturbed her peace.

She called Ricky's landline, thinking that Lily would answer. But that phone rang ten times without an answer. She hadn't tried Jake's number yet because she didn't want to disturb him if he was in the middle of an interview. That no longer mattered. She called Jake's cell. It, too, rang four times then went to voicemail.

She grabbed her keys, thinking she had to drive up there but stopped herself before she reached the door. If something was wrong, she wouldn't get there in time to make any difference. Should she call the sheriff? She feared she would sound like an unprofessional, hysterical woman.

She started pacing again. Did she have Seth O'Hara's phone number? She pulled out her cell and checked her contacts. No. He wasn't there. She opened up her laptop and searched there. In a couple of minutes, she found it. Placing the call, she realized she was holding her breath. She exhaled forcefully and Martha answered the phone. 'Hello, Martha. This is Ricky's sister, Lucinda. I couldn't reach him on the phone so I thought I'd call your place and see if that FBI agent was still there.'

'No, he's not,' she said with a sob.

'Martha? Is everything all right?'

'No. It's not.'

'What's going on?'

'Seth thinks that Ricky is telling people that he killed Dylan. He went over there to straighten him out.'

'Omigod!' Lucinda exclaimed, her face blanching at the prospect.

'That FBI guy chased after him. That was almost half an hour ago. I haven't heard a word since.'

'Did you call Ricky and warn him?'

'No.'

'Why not?' she shrieked.

'Seth is my husband, Lucinda. He's the one that matters to me the most. He's all I have left with Dylan gone.'

'But . . .' Lucinda sputtered out and stopped. She couldn't expect anything more of a woman devastated with grief by the death of her son. 'Thank you, Martha,' she said and disconnected. She called the sheriff's office and asked them to send a deputy to respond to a bad situation developing on Ricky's farm.

Then she knew she simply had to wait. She couldn't drive up there and get caught up in that investigation. Not now. Things were heating up here in her own case. She had to be here first thing in the morning.

It was getting late but she knew she couldn't sleep. She placed her landline and cell phone beside her recliner, scooped up Chester and leaned back to stroke him and gather up as much comfort as she could from his purr.

THIRTY

Jake raced down the gravel drive, wincing at the sound of the little rocks bouncing off the body of his vintage car. He had little hope of catching up with Seth before he arrived at Ricky's house. He called the landline there first but it was busy. He tried Ricky's cell and got an answer.

'Ricky, this is Jake. Seth is on his way to your house and he's very angry. Don't let him in.'

'Angry at me? Why?'

'He thinks you alleged that he killed Dylan.'

'I never—'

'I know. I know. I couldn't tell him who it was but he jumped to the conclusion that it was you.'

'Damn!' Ricky said. 'Uh, hold on a second.' Off the phone, he shouted, 'Lily, don't answer the door.'

Jake strained to listen to the conversation.

'It's OK, honey, it's my brother.'

'Don't let him in.' Ricky put the phone back up to his face. 'Hey, I gotta run . . .'

'Ricky, leave the phone on. Hit the speaker button.'

Jake heard a click and the voices became more distinct.

'Seth, why are you bringing your rifle into my house?' Lily asked, sounding more curious than concerned. 'Oh, Seth, put that gun down.'

'Out of my way, Lily. I'm not here for you.'

'Stop pointing that rifle at my husband. You stop it right now, Seth.'

'I wanted to know why he said it,' Seth said. 'You want to explain that to me, Ricky the Righteous?'

'Said what, Seth?' Ricky said, talking slowly and calmly.

'Don't move, Ricky. Lift up your hands or I'll shoot you right now.'

'OK. My hands are up, Seth. Can you explain the problem?' Ricky said.

'This is ridiculous, Seth,' Lily shouted. 'Mama would be ashamed of you. Bringing a weapon into your sister's house and pointing the barrel at her husband.'

'You leave Mama out of this and get out of my way!'

Jake heard an 'oof,' followed by a clatter and a thump. He could only imagine that someone had just fallen.

Ricky continued in a slow and soothing voice. 'Now, Seth, we both know you don't want to hurt your sister. Keep your hands off of her. You don't have a problem with her – you have a problem with me.'

'If you have a problem with my husband, you have a problem with me, too!' Lily shrieked.

'Lily, please,' Ricky said. 'Now, Seth, if you'd just lower that barrel, we can talk this out.'

'I'm not going do that, Ricky. Not until you tell me why you told that FBI prick that I killed my son. And if I don't like your answer, I'm pulling the trigger.'

Jake heard a wordless scream, then more sounds of falling objects and tumbling bodies. A shot rang out. Jake pushed the accelerator to the floor, then had to brake hard as he reached the driveway, sending his car into a fishtail. He righted the vehicle and roared up the gravel drive. This time, the sound of the rocks hitting the car body didn't register in his thoughts.

Jake screeched to a halt in front of the house and grabbed his cell, even though he hadn't heard a sound since the weapon fired. He pulled out his gun and cautiously climbed up the two steps. Easing open the porch door, he approached the interior door.

He turned the knob and pushed, stepping to the side behind the wall. He leveled his weapon and spun around the corner. Lily was on the floor, her arms wrapped around Seth's ankles. Seth was flat on his back. Ricky stood near them, his mouth agape.

'Is anyone hurt?' Jake asked.

Ricky pointed up to the ceiling where a bullet had poked a hole in the plaster. Jake breathed a sigh of relief. 'Is the rifle the only weapon in the room?'

Ricky nodded. 'I think so.'

'Everyone stay where you are. Seth, take your hand off the rifle and put both of them on top of your head,' Jake said as he eased his way over to Seth. Jake kicked the weapon out of Seth's reach. Jake grabbed the rifle then holstered his gun.

'Ricky, Lily, go sit on the sofa. Lily, let go of Seth's legs. He's not going anywhere until I tell him.'

Lily looked up at Jake with doubt.

'Lily, please,' Jake said.

She released her grip with obvious reluctance, crawling backwards to get some distance from her brother before standing upright. She circled around and joined her husband on the sofa.

'Seth, you can get up now,' Jake said. 'But make your movements slow and deliberate. I want you to sit down in the chair to the right of the sofa. Don't speak until I ask you a question.'

Sitting up, Seth glowered at Jake, then turned his scowl to his sister and her husband. He placed his hands on the floor and pushed up. After he'd taken a seat, Jake said, 'Ricky did not tell me that you killed Dylan.'

'You're a liar,' Seth hissed.

'No, I am not, Seth. Ricky did not accuse you because Ricky is certain that Dylan committed suicide.'

'Well, righteous Ricky always has an answer for everything. And besides, he's always right. If you don't believe me, ask my damn wife and sister. Why, they don't see a need to use their own brains any longer. They just listen to Ricky and say "that's what I think." I don't give a damn what Ricky or either of those women think, 'cause anyone who says my son committed suicide is wrong.' He pointed a finger at Ricky. 'You think that son of a bitch knows my son better than I do?'

Ricky opened his mouth to speak but Jake held his hand up, cautioning him to remain silent. 'I'm not finished looking into Dylan's death, Mr O'Hara. But I will tell you, I'm leaning in the direction of suicide.'

'Of course you are. Everyone sides with Ricky and you cops stick together – you'd never dare contradict the sheriff.'

'Yes, I can dare and I dare often but this time he may be right. I can't prove that your accusation isn't true, Seth. All I can do is to keep searching until I find the reason why Dylan would take his own life.'

'You mean concoct a reason why,' Seth said with a sneer.

'You have no idea of how much I hate telling a parent that his child has committed suicide. I do not want that to be true. But everything is pointing in that direction. The only thing I can conclusively say is that Ricky is not part of your problem, Seth. He never said a negative word about you. He was only concerned about your state of mind. He only wanted to help your wife put your son to rest.'

'What about the boy who killed my son? You're protecting him because he's a cop's kid, aren't you?'

'Seth, I promise you that I will continue looking at Todd Childress until I know with absolute certainty that homicide is not even a remote possibility. Can you accept that and stop going off half-cocked, threatening family members?'

Seth grunted but did not say a word.

'Seth,' Jake continued, 'can you ask your sister's forgiveness for coming into her home brandishing a weapon?'

Seth nodded. 'I'm sorry, Lily. I should have waited till I found him in the barn or out in a field.'

Jake grabbed Seth's collar and jerked him up. 'Quit screwing around, Seth. I call that a threat. Do I need to come to your home and confiscate all of your weapons?'

Seth sneered and laughed. 'I thought this wasn't an official investigation, Mr Agent.'

Jake released Seth's collar and pushed him back into his seat. He rested a palm on each chair arm and leaned into Seth's face. 'It is now, buddy. It was the moment you walked into this house with lethal intent. Right now, I want you to stand up and walk outside with me. I'm going to take any other weapons out of your vehicle and then you're going home to your wife, who is understandably upset.'

Jake let Seth lead the way until they were twenty feet from Seth's pick-up truck. 'Put your hands on your head and kneel on the ground, Mr O'Hara.'

'I've got a shotgun in there on the rack but that's it,' Seth protested.

'On your knees, O'Hara.'

Seth sunk down, gravel digging into his knee caps.

'Lace your hands on top of your head.'

'Aw, c'mon. I'm not going to try anything.'

'Do it. Now.'

Seth grumbled but complied. Jake seized the shotgun and then checked under and behind the seats and in the glove box for any handguns. He straightened up and was looking down the drive when a siren pierced the peace of the country night.

The vehicle came to a halt with a hail of gravel. A deputy stepped out of a marked car, a shotgun resting in the cradle of his arm. 'What the hell's going on here?'

'FBI, Deputy.'

The deputy lifted a flashlight and shone a bright beam on Jake's face. 'Martha told me one of your kind was around these parts. Pull your shield out slowly and hold it up in the light.'

Squinting, Jake slipped his identification out of his pocket and held it aloft.

'All right, then. Now what the hell did Seth do?'

Jake explained the situation and the deputy asked, 'Ricky and them pressing charges?'

'I don't think so,' Jake said. 'But you'd have to ask them.'

'Is it OK to let Seth up?'

Jake nodded.

'C'mon, Seth,' the deputy said, offering him a hand. 'You go sit in your truck. We're going to go in and have a word with your sister and her husband. You sit right here. When I come out I'll follow you home and make sure everything's OK on the home front. Can't have you running home and taking out your frustration on Martha.'

'Yes, sir,' Seth said as he climbed into the cab, sliding behind the wheel.

The deputy pointed a finger at the man's chest. 'And you listen good, Seth. You take off without me and so help me God, I'll run your sorry ass down, slap on a pair of cuffs and carry you down to lock-up. You understand me?'

'Perfectly, sir,' Seth said.

Seth seemed passive at the moment, Jake thought. But with his hair-trigger temper, he believed the odds were fifty-fifty that he'd bolt before they came back outside.

THIRTY-ONE

Back inside Ricky's home, Jake stayed in the background while the deputy got details of the incident for his report and discussed the possibility of charges against Seth. Ricky and Lily sat side by side on the worn, comfy sofa, oblivious to any comfort it had to offer. Ricky, though a bit rattled, was recovering from the shock of the incident.

Lily's brow furrowed, her shoulders slumped and her hands were in constant motion, wringing against each other, until Ricky secured one of them in his hand. Her mouth smiled in response but the other signs of distress reflected on her face and in her posture did not relent for a moment.

The deputy sat on the edge of the matching easy chair, leaning towards them with his elbows resting on his knees. Jake could tell he wanted to file charges and suspected, like him, the deputy was worried about Seth repeating the night's performance, but with a more lethal conclusion.

To no one's surprise, Lily adamantly rejected the idea, tears forming as she pleaded on behalf of her brother. Ricky indicated that he would not oppose charges being brought against Seth except for the trauma and anxiety it might cause Lily. He was willing to go along with whatever she wanted.

Jake heard the unmistakable sound of a pick-up truck starting up and the subsequent revving of the engine. 'Deputy?'

'I heard it,' he said. 'Seth's gonna have to decide how this thing's gonna end. I'm not making a move until he drives off.'

Jake would rather step out to the truck and give Seth another warning but he deferred to the deputy's decision and held his peace. His body tensed on high alert, listening for any change in the sound from the truck as he wondered how it all would end. He doubted Lucinda would be pleased if tonight's events turned ugly. He imagined a dead Seth in a wrecked truck after a hot chase down the narrow winding roads. He thought of Seth arriving home first, taking his wife hostage, getting into a gunfight, being shot by the deputy – or worse, by him. He did not relax at all until he heard the engine shut off three minutes later. And then, only partially – his body remained coiled for instant response in case he heard the motor come to life again.

After the deputy left with his complete report and no charges filed, Jake pulled out his cell and pressed Lucinda's number. 'Hey, Lucy, it's Jake. I'm not going to be able to talk long. I'm expecting a call from the deputy about Seth's arrival back home. I wanted to update you on what's been happening. Let me start with the fact that no one has been hurt but things were a bit out of control there for a while.'

'Ricky's OK?' Lucinda asked.

'Yes.'

'And Lily?'

'Yes. You knew there was a problem?'

'Yes, I talked to Martha and then I called the sheriff.'

'OK. Basically you don't know what happened at Ricky's house. Seth pulled a rifle on Ricky, knocked his sister to the floor and scared the crap out of me. Do you want to speak to your brother for a moment?'

'Yes. But then I need to tell you about something that's developed here.'

'You got it,' Jake said and handed the phone to Ricky.

Ricky said, 'Hey, Sis. All's well here. Lily will probably have a few bruises from tonight and we have a bullet lodged in the ceiling of the living room – but that's the total extent of the damages.'

'Do you feel safe, Ricky?'

'Yeah, Seth's not going to come back here any time soon. We're not pressing charges – Seth might be an ass but he's part of the family and Martha will give him plenty of grief for shoving Lily. I'm not at all worried about him coming back here.'

'Lock the doors anyway, OK?'

'Yes, big sister, I'll lock the doors.'

'Throw the dead bolt, too.'

'Yes, ma'am, will do. Now, you stop worrying. Your FBI guy has everything under control. And he is staying here at the house. But tell me, is there something serious going on between the two of you?'

'Not now, Ricky. I really need to speak to Jake again. Could you hand the phone back to him, please?'

'That sounds like a "yes" to me.'

'Ricky! Give the phone to Jake.'

Lucinda listened to her brother chuckle as he passed the phone.

'Yeah, so what was your answer?' Jake asked.

'To what?' Lucinda said, playing dumb.

'Is there something serious going on between us?'

'You know the answer to that as well as I do, Jake.'

'I know it's serious for me, but what about you?'

'This is not a good time for this discussion, Jake.' Lucinda bristled.

Jake sighed. 'When, Lucy? When will it be a good time?'

'I don't know, Jake. I just know it's not now. Can we change the subject, please?' Lucinda felt like damaged goods. People make commitments every day. People take risks on relationships all the time. Why couldn't she? Why did the thought of it make her stomach churn and cause a dull, aching throb at the base of her neck?

'Sorry, Lucy. I won't bring it up again until we're face-to-face. Promise. Now, what's going on with your case? Am I still a suspect?'

'Of course you are, Agent Lovett. You are on the top of my list,' Lucinda teased.

'OK, I'll work on my alibi,' Jake said with a laugh. 'But seriously, what have you learned?'

'Rowland and my victim were in the same high school graduating class in Trenton, New Jersey. And it seems that we have a possible ID for the mystery Tess on that piece of paper – Tess Middleton, CEO of Scott Technologies.'

'Big name means big trouble. Are you sure about that?'

'No. But I'm hoping to get a class yearbook in the morning. I'll see if she was in the same class and I'll try to locate a Bonnie as well.'

'Good work. I guess I should call off my researchers.'

'If you don't mind, I'd rather keep them on it. It's possible your guys will find something mine couldn't access.'

'No problem. Hey, I've got another call coming up. Catch up with you tomorrow.'

And he was gone. Lucinda reached a hand down to stroke Chester's head. He jumped and chirped at her touch as it roused him from a deep nap. 'Sorry I startled you, Chester.'

The cat relaxed back down in her lap, purring like a well-oiled motor. Lucinda laughed. 'It's so simple for you, itty bitty kitty boy. I wish I could fall to sleep with half your ease.'

She wondered how she would sleep tonight. Her mind galloped through imaginary yearbook pages, searching for Tess and Bonnie. Would they be there? Or would it be another dead end? And if they were members of the same class, what brought them together then? And what connects them now?

If she did find a connection to Tess Middleton, would the DA block her efforts to confront the high-powered woman with the financial ability to make or break any political campaign? Or would he do the right thing? That open question created the greatest anxiety about the investigation now but she didn't even know if it would go that far.

Would she find the answers she wanted tomorrow, or only more questions?

THIRTY-TWO

Lucinda arrived in her office just after 6 a.m. the next morning – far too early for a Federal Express delivery but she couldn't help herself. The day was too young for almost everyone else.

She called Ted to ask about the computer search but his cell went straight to voicemail. The laboratory was empty and no one was present in research.

She fretted at her desk, trying to review her notes but failing to maintain her concentration. A little after seven, Ted called. 'I drove down last night. I'm going before a judge this morning. With a little luck, we'll have a subpoena for the computer records at Scott Technologies this morning.'

'Do you need me there?'

'I sure wouldn't mind having you if you have free time. But someone from your district attorney's office is meeting me at the court so I should be OK. And I'll personally deliver the subpoena to you if you're going to be in the office.'

'I should be. If something comes up, I'll give you a call. Thanks, Ted.'

'At your service, as promised.'

'How are the kids doing?'

'They settled into life here as if they've never known any place else. Both are doing well in school and growing out of clothes faster than we can buy them. They seem very happy that we're all under the same roof, even though they know Ellen and I have separate bedrooms.'

'How's your dad?'

Ted sighed. 'A little worse every month. But, at least, up to now, he's remaining cheerful.'

'The downward spiral is inevitable, Ted. Terribly sad but inevitable. It's the worse way to lose someone you love. I've got to run. I'll see you after court and we can talk some more.' Lucinda disconnected the call, a little uncomfortable about her lie – at the moment, there was nothing urgent to do. She just wanted to get off the phone.

She caught up on some long-avoided paperwork and then pulled out her reports on the death of Candace Eagleton. She started a to-do list: 1. Review yearbook – confirm Candace, Rowland, Middleton and look for people named Bonnie: 2. Check on lab results – most important contents under the victim's fingernails: 3. Serve subpoena on Scott Technologies (if we get one): 4. Check up on Jake's progress. She scratched the last off and started a second list. She wanted to keep the original one strictly for items connected to the Eagleton murder investigation.

When the phone on her desk interrupted her concentration, she snatched it up before it finished one ring. 'Pierce.'

'Hello, Lieutenant. This is Beth Ann Coynes. I wanted you to know that we have isolated the DNA of one male from the scrapings under Candace Eagleton's fingernails.'

'Whose is it?'

'We don't know that yet. It would be helpful if we had a DNA sample from her husband for comparison.'

'OK. I'll call his attorney.'

'Ouch. It's come to that already?'

'Afraid so. Can you run the profile through AFIS in the meantime?'

'Right now, it's going through our local database. When that finishes, if there's no hit, I'll run it through the national database.'

'Good. Keep me posted each step of the way, please. I want to know even if you come up empty-handed.'

'Will do, Lieutenant. Good luck getting your guy.'

'Thanks, Beth Ann. Anything else of significance?'

'Not here. I'm hoping we'll find something you can use in the toxicology but none of those results are in yet. I hate husbands who kill their wives.'

'We don't know that's what happened here. It's possible but we have other leads to follow first.'

'The techs on the scene got a creepy vibe from him. I'd wager a week's salary that in the end you'll end up at the husband – either he did it or he hired someone to do it.'

Lucinda recalled the nastiness of leaks to the media in other cases and worried. She'd always trust Beth Ann but what if she was wrong? 'I trust you will not mention your opinion to anyone outside of this investigation.'

'Of course not. We've already had calls looking for results. Doctor Ringo chewed them up and spat 'em out. Then we had to sit through a long lecture about the need for everyone in the lab to keep their mouths shut about any and every case. She promised suffering if we did anything to compromise any investigation.'

'Good old Audrey. Fear and intimidation – what a way to manage.'

Beth Ann chuckled. 'No other method would work for her. She's not the most likeable person on the planet.'

'And she sure doesn't like me,' Lucinda said with a laugh and looked up to see research guru Lara Quivey step across her threshold. 'Lara just walked into my office bearing a package. Gotta run.' She dropped the receiver and said, 'Is that it?'

'I think so but I haven't opened the package.'

'Do it. Do it. Do it,' Lucinda urged.

Lara pulled the tab on the FedEx package and slid out the 1978 yearbook. 'Ta da!' she said, handing the book to Lucinda. 'If that's all you need from me now, I'll get back to work.'

'Thank you, Lara. Thank you a lot. I'm sure I'll be back to you when I get through digging in this.' Lucinda opened the book to the Class of '78 senior pictures. She quickly located Candace Eagleton, nee Monroe, Charles Rowland and Theresa Scott, now Tess Middleton. She searched through all the photos of the class and did not find a single person named 'Bonnie.' But what if it was a nickname? A nickname for what? First, she thought, she'd search for 'Bonnie' in the juniors and sophomores – then she'd worry about possible other names.

She'd just begun looking at the photos of the Class of '79 when her cell phone rang. 'Pierce.'

'Oh, Lucy. I need you. I need you real bad.'

'What's wrong, Charley?'

'Oh, please, come right away. It can't be right. You need to help me. And Ruby's just sucking her thumb.'

'Are you at school?'

'No. I'm at home. It's a teacher work day. Please come. Please hurry.'

THIRTY-THREE

Jake thought he was rising early that morning. He believed that Ricky and Lily would still be sleeping after last night's drama. He was sorely mistaken. When he walked into the kitchen, both were at the table reading sections of the newspaper. Plates covered with crumbs and smears of egg yolk were pushed to its middle.

'Well, look who's up,' Lily said.

'You've already had breakfast?' Jake asked.

'Oh, sure,' Lily said. 'But I planned on fixing some for you soon as you got up.'

'I guess we should have waited for you,' Ricky said, 'but after doing our morning chores we were pretty hungry.'

'How you like your eggs, Jake?' Lily asked. 'Scrambled, poached, sunny side-up . . .'

'How about once over light?'

'You got it. Toast or English muffin?'

'Muffin, please.'

Jake sat down at the table with Ricky. 'You've done chores already? What time do you get up?'

'You never lived on a farm?'

'No, city and suburbs – no bucolic bliss for me.'

'I heard the sarcasm around that bucolic phase. You gotta be a morning person to make it as a farmer. We get up at five, slug down some coffee and get busy. If we don't get out to the dairy cows before six, the cows start lowing so loudly you can hear 'em in the next county. And the hens start picking on the weakest one something fierce if we don't let them out in the yard by then.'

'Hens fight?' Jake asked, amazed at the prospect.

'More like they bully. You can look at them and see who's at the bottom of the totem pole. Always got a bare spot or two where the others plucked out her feathers.'

'Why do you lock them up at night?'

'Coons, foxes, skunks, weasels – they'll all snatch up hens that wander too close to the fence after dark. Bite their heads off and leave the bodies there since they can't drag that part through the wiring.'

'Yuck. That's disgusting.'

Lily slid a plate in front of Jake. 'Hope Ricky's big mouth doesn't put you off your feed. And don't forget, there's more where that came from.'

'Did you know that Lucinda was a champion milker? She got a blue ribbon at the competition at the county fair one year,' Ricky said.

'Really? Amazing the things she's never told me.'

'I wish I still had her here,' Ricky said. 'She was the hardest-working farmhand I've ever seen. And she was fearless. She'd walk out into the field and bring the meanest bull up to the barn to service one of the cows without blinking an eye. She'd put on the chain and lead him up as easy as a trained dog.'

'You're kidding?'

'Nope. C'mon, you know her. Have you ever seen her back off from doing anything out of fear?'

'You're right about that. But she just doesn't act like a farm girl.'

'Well, she's got a layer of smooth polish overlaying her roots – our grandmother up north saw to that. But if you dropped her out here and told her she had to earn her keep on the farm she'd do it and probably earn the keep of three or four others while she was at it.'

Jake scratched the back of his head. 'It's going to take me a bit to incorporate those images into my picture of Lucinda. But I can already see how they all fit together.'

'Speaking of together, just what are your intentions regarding my sister?' Ricky asked.

'Ricky, how rude!' Lily objected.

'Ah, c'mon, Lily. You wanted to know, too. You're just too much of a scaredy cat to ask.'

'Scaredy cat? No, Ricky, I'm just polite.'

'So, who looks after my sister, then? She has no dad to do that for her.'

'I think your sister can take care of herself,' Lily said. 'She's proven that time and time again.'

'Still . . .'

'Still, Ricky? Oh, you go on ahead and do your protective brother routine. If I try to stop you, you'll just corner Jake out of my earshot and I'll never get to know the answer.'

Ricky laughed and pointed his finger at his wife. 'You see, I got your number, Lily. You want the question asked; you just want to act superior by not being the one who does the asking.'

'I don't need to ask, husband dearest. I am superior – I am the woman,' she said with a grin.

'See, Jake, if you get serious about my sister, you'll have to try to never be alone with her and Lily. Either one of them alone is debilitating to our fragile male egos – but together, you'd best be wearing a cup.' Ricky jumped up, put a hand on each side of Lily's back, spun her around and planted a kiss on her lips.

'Oh, cut it out, Ricky. You're really going to spoil Jake's appetite now,' she said as her face flushed and her dimples danced.

He still held Lily tight when he asked again. 'Enough fooling around, Jake. What are your intentions toward my sister?'

'I think maybe you oughta talk to Lucinda about that.'

'Jake, you know she won't talk to me about it. Give it up.'

'Man, she's your sister, Ricky. If I start talking about her to you, she'll never trust me again.'

'Hey, I won't tell her.'

'Still, Ricky . . .' Jake began, interrupted by the sharp ring of the telephone.

Lily pulled away from her husband, walked across the kitchen and picked up the receiver. After a moment, she said, 'Martha, calm down. I can't understand a word you're saying.' She paused for a moment and said, 'Martha, you are not making any sense.'

Lily sighed and dropped her shoulders. 'OK, Martha, don't cry. Jake is right here. I'll let you talk to him.'

Jake stepped over and took the receiver from Lily's outstretched hand. 'Yes, Martha. What can I . . .?' Jake listened, his brow furrowing and his jaw tightening. 'All right, Martha. I'll be there as quick as I can.'

Jake hung up and turned to Ricky and Lily. 'Seth's acting crazy enough to scare Martha. I'm not sure what's going on but I'm going to run over and check it out.'

'You want me to go with you?' Ricky asked.

'No. Because of his attitude towards you, you may make matters worse. I'll be fine. I think Martha's probably overreacting.'

'He's my brother. I can go,' Lily said.

'That might be a good idea, Lily. But let me go over there alone. If it seems like you're needed, I'll give you a call.' Jake shoveled a fork full of egg and bacon into his mouth, pulled open the outside door and, still chewing, said, 'Wish me luck.' A moment later the gravel was pounding the sides of Jake's vintage Super Sport once again.

THIRTY-FOUR

'I've found her,' he said.

'Where?' she asked.

'She's back in New Jersey.'

'See, I told you she'd be trouble. I told you she was going to try to destroy me. Her return to New Jersey proves that.'

'Maybe she just wanted to get back to her roots,' he argued.

'Are you backing out on me?'

'No. I'll do what you want me to do but I doubt if she's planning anything. If she wanted to cause trouble, wouldn't she come down to Virginia?'

'Ha. That just says she's still afraid of me. That's why she ran. That's why she changed her name. But coming back east means that she is determined to make me pay as she promised all those years ago.'

'I guess that means we're still a go.'

'Yes. Make it look like some sort of accident – but not an automobile accident. That worked once. It won't work again. Are you sure she's in New Jersey? Are you sure she hasn't moved on again?'

'I called the phone number at her address. She gave her name on the voicemail message. She has to be there.'

'In Trenton?'

'Yes.'

'Make sure this doesn't come back to me.'

'Don't worry. There's enough violence in northern New Jersey to cover up anything you want.'

'Just eliminate her. And don't let them suspect murder. That's all I want. Where are you now?'

'Seattle.'

'When will you be in Jersey?'

'Not until this evening. I couldn't get a direct flight but I'm on the first plane out of here.'

'How long will it take you to set it up?'

'It depends on where she lives and if she's living alone or with someone else, where she works and how much of a creature of habit she is. It'll take some reconnaissance time.'

'Don't make it take too long. If she speaks out before you get to her, I'm ruined and I'll give you up in a heartbeat to make a deal. I will not go to prison.'

'Thanks for that vote of confidence. You really do make me sick. I can't wait to get this job finished, get the rest of my money and scrub you out of my life.'

'The feeling is mutual.'

'And just in case that feeling takes you to the next step of hiring someone to eliminate me, let me warn you. I put what I call my insurance policy in the hands of my attorney. Don't worry, I sealed it. He will only open it if something happens to me. If he does, he'll read every detail implicating you.'

'Aren't you charming? I'll call you with a number as soon as I get a new cell. When this is over, you can just go to hell – I'll even provide the hand-basket.'

'Boarding call, I have to run. It'll all be over in a matter of days. Make sure you have the final payment ready. I want this wrapped up immediately. I need some R&R in the tropics where I can wipe out the memory of you over a bottle of rum.'

'Yo ho ho,' she said and disconnected the call.

THIRTY-FIVE

Eleven-year-old Charley Spencer slid out of bed early that morning. Her little sister Ruby didn't stir when Charley looked into her bedroom. Her father was far away on a Doctors without Borders mission in Africa–Libya, she thought, but wasn't sure she remembered correctly. Kara, the woman caring for them in her father's absence, had been a constant in her life since her mother's murder three years ago.

The sight of her mother's body on the floor had begun to fade from her mind – the edges were no longer sharp but she could still envision the image like a blurred charcoal sketch. The one thing that continued to burn hot in her mind was the sound of Ruby sucking her thumb. That's where she found her that day – pressed tight against their mother's body, making that noise that still sent Charley close to panic.

Ruby was six years old now but when she was stressed she still reverted to her thumb. When Charley heard the sucking sound her heart raced, her mouth went dry and she had to force her breathing to stay smooth and regular.

Ruby was more prone to suck on her thumb when her father was away, making Charley feel guilty for her negative reaction to it. With Dad gone, Ruby needed her more but all Charley wanted to do was get as far away from her as she could when she heard that distinctive slurping.

This morning, however, Charley was the only person in their apartment making any sound and she tried to be as quiet as possible so as not to wake the others. She turned on the coffee pot and went to the bathroom to brush her teeth and hair. When she emerged, she poured half a cup, added enough sugar to bake a cake and then filled the cup with half-and-half.

She went out onto the balcony overlooking the James River and sat down sipping her highly adulterated coffee. She was lost in the beauty below when Ruby stumbled out to join her.

'I want coffee, too,' Ruby said.

'No you don't. You're too little for coffee. I'll make you a mug of cocoa.'

'No. I want coffee!' Ruby pouted.

'Ssshh. Don't wake Kara.'

'But I want coffee,' Ruby said even louder.

Charley sighed. 'OK. I'll put a little coffee in your cocoa.'

The two girls went into the kitchen. Charley dropped a small dollop of coffee into Ruby's hot chocolate and added a shot of half-and-half, then fixed a second cup of coffee for herself. She carried both out to the balcony and the sisters sat side by side watching the river flow. 'I don't like this, Charley,' Ruby said, placing her mug on the table and pushing it away.

'See. I told you that you're too little for coffee.'

'I want some cocoa,' Ruby whined.

'All right. I'll go make you another cup. I'll just be a minute. You sit in your chair and don't go near the railing.' In the kitchen, Charley fixed a fresh hot chocolate while keeping her eye on her sister to make sure she stayed firmly seated. She carried the steaming mug and set it down in front of her. 'Careful now. It's hot. Blow on it before you sip.'

Ruby took a noisy taste of her cocoa, set down her mug and smiled at her big sister. 'Thank you, Charley. This is good.'

'You're welcome, Ruby. Now let's sit and listen to the birds and the river for a bit.' Charley was amazed that Ruby actually did as she asked. Baby sisters could really be aggravating and contrary and big babies. Charley suspected that Ruby was a bigger baby than most – and she knew why. They were both branded by their mother's brutal murder.

Sirens disrupted their serenity. Charley leaned over the railing but could see nothing even though she was sure the sound was nearby. 'C'mon, Ruby, let's go see what's happening.'

Charley led her sister out the door into the hallway and stopped. Across the hallway, policemen walked in and out of Mr Bryson's apartment. Holding Ruby's hand she walked up to the open door. 'Is Mr Bryson hurt?' she asked the first uniform she saw.

'Go back into your apartment. We're taking care of everything.'

'But Mr Bryson? Is he OK?'

'Do you live in this apartment?'

'No.'

'Then it's none of your business. Go back to your apartment.'

'But Mr Bryson is my friend.'

'Your friend?'

'He meets me in the lobby and gives me M&Ms and talks to me almost every day after school.'

'Well, Mr Bryson can't talk to you right now, little girl; go back to your place. OK?'

Charley just stared at him as he went into Mr Bryson's apartment and shut the door. She hated it when someone called her a little girl. Ruby was a little girl. She wasn't. 'C'mon, Ruby, we're going downstairs to see if they know at the desk.'

The two sisters rode down ten floors in the elevator and entered a lobby full of milling people and uniformed officers. She tugged Ruby toward the front entrance. Looking through the double glass doors, she saw paramedics busy over a body lying flat on the sidewalk in a pool of blood. She gasped. Ruby wailed and stuck her thumb in her mouth, sucking as if her life depended on it. Too late, Charley thought of her sister and how traumatic it would be for her to see the scene outside the building.

Charley dragged Ruby back into the lobby, 'You don't want to look at that, Ruby. Please take your thumb out of your mouth, please.'

Ruby looked up at her with big eyes and an ashen face and sucked her thumb even harder. Charley held tight to Ruby's hand and went up to a uniformed officer. 'Is that Mr Bryson lying on the ground?' she asked.

'You shouldn't be down here. Where is your mother?'

'My mother is dead – somebody killed her. Is Mr Bryson dead, too? Is that him on the sidewalk?'

'Your mother is dead?'

'Yes.'

'Is she in your apartment?'

'No.' Charley thought that a preposterous question. Did he really think she'd be down here if her mother was dead upstairs? 'Of course not. She died before we moved here.'

'Where's your father?'

'He's in Libya but that has nothing to do with anything. Is Mr Bryson dead?'

'Who's taking care of you?' he said, crouching down to her level.

'Kara.'

'Where is she?'

'She's still asleep,' Charley said, wiping the tears from her eyes.

'Did somebody kill Mr Bryson?'

The officer paused for a moment. 'Listen, let's go upstairs and I'll talk to Kara and she'll know how to explain this to you.'

'I'm not a baby. I know about people dying. My best friend is a police lieutenant. I'm not a stupid baby.'

'I know you're not a baby. But please, I don't know how to explain this to you, and I don't want to say the wrong thing, particularly in front of the little girl – is she your sister?'

Well, at least he knows the difference between me and a little girl, Charley thought. 'Yes, sir. Her name is Ruby.'

'She seems very upset. Why don't we go up to your place and talk to Kara?'

Charley was irritated that she couldn't get an answer to her simple question about Mr Bryson but gave in to the policeman's request, thinking it might be the only way she'd learn what happened. She turned away from him and headed to the elevator.

The officer followed her in and asked, 'Which floor?'

Charley didn't answer – she just hit the button and stared at the closed doors. When they reached the apartment door, she noticed that Mr Bryson's door was open again and the dreaded yellow tape blocked off that section of the hallway. Bile rose into her throat at the sight of it. She'd hated yellow ever since that day.

Charley slid the key into the lock but before she could turn the knob, the door jerked open. Kara, with disheveled hair, wearing a terrycloth robe, stood just inside. 'Where have you been, Charley? Don't you know better than to go traipsing off with Ruby without saying a word?'

'Somebody killed Mr Bryson!' Charley shouted at her.

Kara turned toward the policeman. 'Officer?'

'Can we step out into the hallway?' he asked.

Kara put a hand behind each of the girl's backs, gently shoved them inside and pulled the door shut behind her as she joined the officer in the hall. Neither noticed when the door creaked open a crack. They had no idea that Charley was listening to every word.

'Your neighbor, Jim Bryson, jumped from his window this morning. I don't know where she got the idea that someone killed him. He left a suicide note – he'd lost his job, his father died and his girlfriend dumped him – all in the last month.'

'Ohmigod!'

'The older girl told me he was her friend and I just didn't know how to explain a suicide to her . . .'

'Yeah. How do you do that? Thank you, Officer. I'll handle it now – not quite sure how. Wish me luck. I sure don't want to traumatize those girls anymore.'

'Was their mother really murdered?'

'Yeah. Three years ago. They're still dealing with it. It hasn't been easy – they found the body.'

'Oh, man,' he said. 'Well, best of luck. Sorry to have to put you in this situation.'

Kara took in a deep inhalation, exhaled loudly and turned the knob, surprised to see that the door was not shut tight. The moment she stepped in, though, she knew why.

'It's a lie!' Charley yelled. 'Mr Bryson was a nice man. He was my friend. He wouldn't kill himself – it's a lie. He wouldn't leave me like that.'

'Charley, I am so sorry—' Kara began.

'Tell me the policeman is a liar and I'll believe you're sorry,' Charley interrupted.

'Oh, Charley, the truth often hurts more than any lie. But you need to accept it no matter how much it hurts.'

'I hate you,' Charley said and rushed out of the living room and into her bedroom. She grabbed her phone and called the other woman who was a constant in her life, Lieutenant Lucinda Pierce – Lucy. The investigator who solved her mother's murder and became a friend, confidant and the woman she most wished could take her mother's place.

'Oh, Lucy. I need you. I need you real bad.'

THIRTY-SIX

Only two miles separated the justice center from the Spencer's luxury apartment building but the traffic was beastly that morning – stopping, starting and seeming to go nowhere. Lucinda tapped her fingers on the steering wheel, suppressing the desire to turn on a siren and peel out around them all. Abuse of privilege, she kept telling herself. She knew others did it all the time but it was a personal matter and she was loath to take advantage of the fact that she was law enforcement.

She had no idea what caused Ruby's distress but she knew that it always boiled up anxiety in Charley. The traffic was so maddening. Finally, she pulled into the parking garage, wondering what the cause of the commotion in the front of the building was and if it was connected to Charley's need to see her. Waiting for the elevator was torturous but she knew it would get her up there faster than pounding up all those flights of stairs from the lower parking level to the tenth floor.

Lucinda was startled to see the yellow crime scene tape blocking off the hallway just past the Spencer apartment. She instinctively knew that it had something to do with Charley's problem. Should she cross the line and check out what was happening? Or check on Charley first? Making a quick decision, she hit the doorbell and Kara whipped open the door and stepped into the hall.

'Our neighbor across the hall committed suicide this morning – jumped from his window onto the pavement. I was still asleep when Charley took Ruby down to the lobby to see what was happening – and they did. Ruby isn't speaking and Charley is refusing to believe he killed himself. Their father is going to kill me when he gets back,' Kara said, speaking as quickly as possible.

Lucinda started to respond when the door pulled open again. 'Lucy!' Charley cried out. 'The police are lying.'

'Let's talk inside,' Lucinda said, pushing gently on the young girl as she walked across the threshold. 'OK, Charley, why do you think they are lying?'

Charley pointed at Kara. 'She believes them. I don't want to talk around her.'

'All right, Charley. Let's go up to your room.' Lucinda shrugged apologetically at Kara.

The babysitter smiled softly and mouthed, *Don't worry about it.*

Walking into Charley's bedroom that morning, she noticed how much it had changed in the last couple of years. It was no longer the refuge of a child. The stuffed animals still lined the shelves above her tousled bed but not one of them lay on the sheets or pillows – she used to sleep with two or three of them for comfort. On the walls, where pictures of cartoon characters once hung, were photos of Johnny Depp as a pirate, Justin Bieber, Miley Cyrus, Lady Gaga and others Lucinda didn't recognize decorating the wall along with a poster covered with photographs of protein crystals and another one with a collage of Janis Joplin photos. She's growing up, Lucinda thought as she was hit with a wave of emotion that was a blend of pride and anxiety.

'OK, Charley, why do you think the police are lying?'

'Because Mr Bryson liked me. He told Daddy that seeing my smile made every day worthwhile. So he couldn't have killed himself.'

'Well, sometimes the things adults do don't make sense to kids – or even to other grown-ups.'

'But he didn't. Someone killed him. Just like Mommy. Someone killed him. You've got to find out who did it. You've got to put them in jail,' Charley wailed.

Lucinda wrapped her arms around her and held her tight. She felt the trembles of Charley's small body, heard the hiccups mixed with her sobs and felt a damp spot forming on her shirt where Charley's little head rested. 'Please, Lucy, please. You have to help Mr Bryson.'

Lucinda let Charley cry herself out. Then she held her out at arm's length and said, 'Charley, I'm going across the hall. I'll talk to them. I'll look at what's in his apartment. And then I will give you an honest answer. I'll give you my professional opinion, OK?'

Charley sniffled and rubbed the back of her hand across her nose. 'OK, Lucy.'

'You trust me?'

'Yes.'

'Will you believe me, no matter what I say?'

'But, Lucy . . .'

'Charley . . .'

'I'll try. No matter what. Even if I don't like it.'

'OK, sweetie,' Lucinda said and kissed her on the forehead. 'I'll be back as soon as I can.'

Across the hall, Lucinda read the suicide note detailing all the bad news that had befallen Jim Bryson. She looked at the balcony for any indication that someone else had forced him over the railing. Instead she saw a table with an overflowing ashtray, a bottle of Glenlivet, three-quarters gone, and a crystal tumbler with less than half an inch of whiskey.

She looked down at the sidewalk below where one foot stuck out from beneath the blanket thrown over his body. 'He was barefoot when he jumped?'

'Yeah,' a detective told her. 'His shoes with socks stuffed inside are sitting beside the sliding glass door.'

'No doubts that it's a suicide, then?'

'None at all. I've run into a fake suicide once before and I'm always suspicious. Nailed the husband on that one. But here? Nothing even closely resembling anything else. I sent someone to see his mother who said he's been very distraught for the last few weeks. He called her yesterday evening and told her he loved her. She thought the outpouring was just a by-product of his sorrow – now she's beating herself up for not dropping everything and driving into town to see him. She said her son had a long history with depression and suicidal ideation and she should have known it was serious. Is there something you know that I don't, Lieutenant?'

'No, Sergeant. I just have a sad little girl who doesn't want to believe that Bryson took his own life. I'm not sure if she feels his death was a personal affront or if she's just feeling guilty that she did nothing to stop him.'

'Not much a little girl could have done in a case like this.'

'No,' Lucinda said. 'But that is something she is too young to understand.' And every time anyone dies suddenly, Charley will probably instantly suspect murder – the pain of her mother's death will never completely go away. Just as her own hadn't, Lucinda thought. She closed her eyes and sighed.

'Lieutenant? Are you OK?'

'Not really. I've got to explain suicide to an eleven-year-old. Not a pleasant or easy task.'

'Wish you luck,' he said.

'Thanks,' Lucinda said as she exited the apartment and walked slightly down and across the hall. She went straight to Charley's bedroom.

Charley, startled, looked up at her. 'Well, who did it?'

Lucinda exhaled with force. She sat down on the girl's bed and patted a spot beside her. 'Come sit with me, sweetie.'

'No!' she said, shaking her head from side to side. 'You believe their lies. You're part of the cover-up.'

'Oh, Charley, there's no cover-up. Please come and sit here,' she said, patting the mattress again. 'C'mon. Let me tell you what I learned.'

Charley stood for a moment with her arms folded, looking out the window. Then she slouched over to the bed and sat down. Her body was rigid and she would not look at Lucinda.

'I read his suicide note, Charley.'

'I saw a show on TV. Somebody faked a suicide note when they killed someone and fooled the police.'

'That was a typed note, wasn't it?'

Charley finally looked at her with a furrowed brow. 'I think so.'

'This one was handwritten. It looked like all the other writing in the apartment.'

'Well, it was a really smart killer. He learned to forge his handwriting before he murdered Mr Bryson.'

Lucinda sighed. 'No, Charley. There are certain distinctive quirks about a person's handwriting and they were all there in the note. No one could get it that perfectly.'

'But I never saw him cry.'

'You brightened every day for him, Charley. You gave him a little bit of happiness each time he saw you. But so much had gone wrong in his life recently. He just did not see any other way out. He's been battling depression all his life. Do you know what depression is?'

Charley shook her head. 'Sort of.' Then she bent over double and sobbed. 'I should have been better. I should have been nicer. I should have spent more time with him.'

'Charley. Charley,' Lucinda said and put an index finger under her chin and turned her face up to hers. 'Listen to me, Charley. There was nothing you could do. You couldn't get his job back. You couldn't fix his relationship with his girlfriend. You couldn't bring his father back to life. It was out of your hands. But you should be proud of yourself. You brought a little bit of sunshine into his life. The time he spent with you was a break from his sorrow. His mother said he'd been battling depression all his life. This isn't on you – not in the least little bit.'

Charley shook her head. 'It is my fault. It's everybody's fault.'

'In a way, yes. But in another way, it's no one's fault. Suicide is a sad thing. It always devastates the people left behind. Those who loved that person never forgive themselves. But they should. I'm sure Mr Bryson was trapped in a circle of darkness where he could find no way out.'

Charley's face squeezed tight. 'If he only asked, I would have given him my flashlight.'

Lucinda wrapped her arms around the little girl she loved so much and wished as hard as she could to protect her from every pain that waited along the arc of her life.

THIRTY-SEVEN

Jake's stomach dropped when he turned into the O'Hara's driveway and saw dust hanging in the air over the dirt road. Someone had recently been in or out of the farm. He feared Seth had left in a fit of anger and hoped Martha would know where he went.

Before he cut off the engine, Martha ran outside. 'You're too late!' she shrieked. 'He's gone. He's gone. Ohmigod! I don't know what he'll do.'

Jake stepped out of the car and placed his hands on her forearms. 'Martha. Start from the beginning.'

'Someone called.'

'Who?'

'I don't know.'

'Do you know what that person said to Seth?'

'I only know what Seth said after he hung up. He said that Todd Childress was bragging about killing Dylan.'

'What?' Jake said. Murder did not fit into the picture he had formed thus far.

'I asked him how? But Seth said it didn't matter. It was time for him to pay.'

'Did he go to Todd's home?'

'I think so. But maybe he went to the school. But he grabbed ammunition and got another rifle and shotgun to replace the ones you took from his truck last night.'

'Any handguns?'

'No. I checked. It's still in the drawer by his night stand.'

Jake found it difficult to believe the deputy hadn't secured all the firearms in the O'Hara house after that incident. 'OK. I'm going to go to Todd's and if he's not there, I'm going to the school. Stick close to the phone. If we end up in a hostage situation, I might need you.'

Jake tore off back down the driveway, wincing at the sound of gravel against his beloved car. The dust would wash off but he was certain if he made many more trips down ratty drives he'd have to get a new paint job.

When Jake arrived at the Childress home he saw no sign of Seth's truck but he did see a big hole in the front door. Mrs Childress answered his knock. He flipped open his ID and asked if her husband or son were at home.

'No,' she sobbed. 'I'm waiting for my husband. That crazy Seth O'Hara blasted a hole in our front door. I thought he was going to kill me.'

'OK. Tell your husband I'm heading to the school to make sure he's not there. And please ask him to call my cell if he finds Seth.' Jake fidgeted as Mrs Childress wrote down his number, then he was off again.

At the high school, Jake spotted Seth's truck in the circular drive in front of the building. The door to the cab hung open and neither a rifle nor a shotgun were in the gun rack on the back window.

He raced toward the entrance to the school. When he pulled open the door, he heard excessive commotion in the main office and screams coming from down the hall. He followed the screams, pulling his gun as he ran. He just hoped to God he didn't have to use it.

He turned a corner and heard a multitude of shouting voices and sobbing hysteria. He followed the sound and stopped beside the open doorway to a class. He peered around the corner. A female teacher stood in front of the class with her back pressed against the blackboard. More than twenty frightened faces stared back at him as they sat with scrunched shoulders in the one-piece chairs, an attached writing surface curving around in front of their bodies.

Todd Childress stood up against the far wall, hands up, blubbering that he didn't do anything.

In front of him stood Seth O'Hara, pointing the end of a rifle into the teenager's face. The shotgun was attached to a strap looping over his shoulder and resting across his back. Jake swung through the doorway and into a shooter's stance. 'Drop the rifle right now, Seth.'

'Leave me alone. Y'all won't take care of business so I'm going to do it for you and for my boy.'

'Seth,' Jake said as he crept forward, 'you don't want to shoot him in front of all these kids.'

'Get out of here, FBI man.'

'Seth, let's get everyone else out of the classroom.' Jake waved his hands and pointed toward the door. As Jake passed a cluster of students, they darted behind his back out into the hall.

Seth did not turn around. He kept his eyes on Todd, who cried and pleaded, 'I did not kill Dylan. I swear to God. I didn't. Please don't kill me.' A wet stain spread across the front of the boy's jeans.

Jake took one cautious step after another, ready to freeze if Seth looked in his direction. When the last student left the room, followed by their teacher, Jake moved faster until he was behind Seth with the muzzle of his gun pressing against the base of his skull. 'Drop the rifle, Seth.'

'Not unless you promise to arrest this bastard.'

'I promise you, I'll take him into the sheriff's office and ask him a lot of questions.'

'Slap his wrist and send him home, too,' Seth accused.

'Seth, you're going to have to trust me. I want to get to the bottom of what happened to your son – no matter where it leads, I want the truth.'

Seth stood still without turning around. Sounds of running footsteps and shouted orders came down the hall. Jake glanced back to the door where a cluster of deputies stood with weapons drawn. If Jake couldn't talk Seth into standing down, blood would be shed soon.

'There's no way out, Seth.'

'I don't care if I die. I'll pull the trigger, get justice for Dylan and then I don't care what happens to me.'

Todd whimpered. Seth stabbed at him with the rifle barrel and said, 'Shut up, sissy boy.'

'Martha cares,' Jake whispered. 'She's heartbroken over Dylan's death. Don't make her grieve yours at the same time. Don't leave Martha all alone. She's a good woman. She deserves more. She's the one who carried Dylan inside of her body for nine long months. She's the one who labored for hours to bring him into the world. She's the one who held him to her breast and gave him sustenance. Don't destroy her, Seth, with rash, impulsive behavior. And how will Martha explain your death to your mother? I know your mom's not doing well; your death could kill her.'

After an eternity of silence, the barrel of the rifle slowly tilted down. At the moment it aimed toward the floor, Jake jerked Todd away, flinging him across the room, slammed Seth's body up against the wall and snatched the rifle out of his hand. He tossed it into a far corner, removed the shotgun from Seth's back and cuffed his wrists behind him.

Jake turned Seth over to the waiting deputies and said that he wanted Todd Childress taken to the station, too.

'Agent, that's Deputy Childress' boy. There's no call to run him in.'

'Yes, there is. I wouldn't care if he were the FBI Director's son. He has information. And I want answers. Stick him in an interrogation room. I'll be right behind you. And see if Becky Carpenter is in class – if she's not, go to her home. I want her in an interrogation room, too.' Jake headed down the hall to the school office to inform the administration that everything was now under control.

At least here. At least now. Jake sighed. So much more was out of control and he feared it may get worse.

THIRTY-EIGHT

After calming Charley, Lucinda rushed back to her office to continue her review of the yearbook. In the class of '79, she found one Bonnie – Bonnie Upchurch. She found a Bonnie Alder in the class of '80. She flipped through page by page, looking for connections between the four players.

Tess and Charles Rowland both worked for the high school newspaper, *Gator News*. Tess and Bonnie Upchurch were on the debate team. Bonnie Upchurch and Candace were in the Senior Chorus together. Rowland and Candace were members of the photography club. Bonnie Alder had no photographs indicating a connection to any of the other three. Lucinda sent an email to Lara Quivey asking for background on both Bonnies just the same, indicating the top priority was Bonnie Upchurch.

She then placed a call to Frank Eagleton's attorney, William Quillian, requesting that his client voluntarily submit to DNA testing. When Quillian balked, Lucinda snapped, 'Don't you think you should confer with your client on this matter, counselor?'

'We know that our client's DNA is all over that house. It would not be surprising for his DNA to be under her fingernails. If you got a match to my client, you'd arrest him and charge him with her murder on the flimsiest of causes. I will not put my client through that.'

'If it's not your client's DNA suspiciously jammed beneath the victim's fingernails, your client is cleared. If it is his DNA, he merely remains on our suspect list.'

'You're telling me that a positive result will not cause his arrest?'

'The DA would put my butt in a sling if I used that as cause for charging your client.'

'I want it in writing.'

'I don't think so, sir. My captain would have my scalp.'

'Seems like everyone is trying to get their hands on your body parts, Lieutenant.'

'Hazard of the job, counselor.'

'I'll talk to my client but I won't make any promises. In fact, I will advise him against it.'

'You succeed and I'll get a warrant to compel him to provide samples.'

'I have an excellent track record in fighting those warrants, Lieutenant. I would not count on your success prematurely.'

'I do nothing prematurely, Mr Quillian. How about you?'

Quillian made no response.

'Call me after you confer with your client, please.'

'I'll think about it,' Quillian responded.

'You do that,' Lucinda said and disconnected the call. She wondered how Jake was doing and if he was anywhere near finding the answer to why Dylan took his life – or if it might be one of those questions destined to go unanswered.

Ted Branson's arrival with a Scott Technologies search warrant broke off her reverie. 'Good. One thing's gone right this morning,' Lucinda said. 'You're coming with me to serve it?'

'I was hoping you'd ask,' Ted answered.

On the drive to Scott Technologies, Ted explained the decision of the judge. 'We've been given a very limited warrant. We can only access the company's data to identify the sender of the email. Nothing more. Once we do that, unless the company gives us voluntary clearance, we need to have a hearing before the judge as to whether that individual might communicate proprietary business information before we can access that person's email account.'

'You're kidding me?'

'Wish I were. Apparently there was an incident with another high-tech company and an investigator leaked company secrets that reached the ears of the competition. He doesn't want a repeat performance of that screw-up. He said that with both parties present, an agreement can be reached about how we can maintain confidential information for the company, and at the same time allow law enforcement to obtain any other communication that would be relevant to the investigation.'

'That's right – the almighty corporate dollar needs to be protected from the blowback of a murder investigation. Money is always more important than people. How could I have forgotten?'

'You might want to stow your sarcasm while we're out at Scott Technologies. It could make things more difficult,' Ted said.

'Do I look like an idiot to you, Branson?'

'Lucinda, you know you can be too—'

'Don't start, Branson. Don't start.'

They rode the remainder of the trip in silence. Upon arrival, they went to the front desk with the warrant in hand. The receptionist said, 'One moment, please,' and made a phone call.

The moment stretched into five minutes. Lucinda approached the desk. 'Excuse me. Is the data center that far from this desk? Can it really be taking them that long to get here? Call them again, please.'

'We are waiting for our attorney. I cannot contact the data center until he arrives.'

'Excuse me, miss. This is a search warrant, issued by a judge. It means we get immediate access to the data center.'

'I am following procedure, Lieutenant.'

'How about I follow procedure and slap a pair of cuffs on your wrists?'

'I cannot do anything but what I was instructed to do.'

'Fine. I am instructing you to press the button that gives us access beyond this welcome area.'

'I cannot do that.'

'Really? Well, I can arrest you for obstructing justice and I can bring in a uniformed officer to relieve you of your post and allow me to serve my warrant. Is that what you want?'

'No. I would like you to please sit and wait patiently. Our attorney will be here as soon as he can.'

'And this time gives the data center the ability to erase data, wipe out the information we need. This is unacceptable. I'm giving you thirty seconds to make up your mind.'

The receptionist grew more agitated with each passing second. When only eight remained until the deadline set by Lucinda, the door opened to reveal a man of medium height, dressed in a suit, shooting his cuffs as he walked. 'Lieutenant,' he said with a nod of his head. 'Could I review the document, please?' He slid a pair of half-glasses on his face and focused on the paper she handed him.

'If anything has been destroyed while we've been kept waiting out here, I will hold you responsible. The bar will not be pleased with a tampering with justice charge.'

He looked over the top of his glasses and said, 'Please, Lieutenant. This is not a game of cops and robbers; we consider it a serious business matter. We can't just have anyone claiming to possess a warrant to come in and run roughshod over our data. Now, if you will stop interrupting, I will complete my review and we can proceed.'

Lucinda wanted to snap back at him but she held her tongue and looked over to Ted, rolling her eyes. Ted covered his mouth with his hand to hide his smirk.

Finally, the attorney looked up, stowed his glasses in his suit jacket pocket and said, 'Everything appears to be in order. If you will follow me, we will get the information authorized in this document. After that, if you want to take this matter any further, have the court clerk contact me so I can check on my availability for a hearing on any further information you may want to obtain.'

Lucinda, eternally impatient, walked behind the attorney, bristling at his slow progress up the hallways. She wanted to give him a shove to hurry him forward but suppressed that primitive urge.

A computer tech in the lab brought up the email in question and jotted a code down on a piece of paper. 'We do not keep the designated codes and the name of the person on the main frame computer. We have that data on a separate laptop kept in our safe.'

'Get the laptop,' Lucinda said.

The tech turned to the attorney, who nodded.

'One moment, please,' he said and left the lab.

Lucinda sighed and turned to Ted. He appeared to be paying no attention to the course of events. He seemed more fascinated with observing the size of the main frame and the intricacy of the technology present in the room. Lucinda jabbed him with her elbow.

Ted looked at Lucinda and shrugged. 'Professional curiosity,' he whispered.

Lucinda gave him a withering stare.

When the tech returned, he placed the computer on his desktop and fired it up.

'Can you turn it this way so I can see the screen?' Lucinda asked.

'No. Do not turn it. No, Lieutenant. When he locates the record in question, you may then look at the screen but not before.' The attorney stepped behind the tech and watched as he pulled up the correct file.

The tech turned to the attorney again. This time his eyes widened and a spot of white appeared beside each nostril. The lawyer's jaw clenched tight.

'Well?' Lucinda said.

'May I see the search warrant again, please?'

Lucinda handed it to him, wondering at his sudden politeness. What has he found that is making him so nervous?

The attorney laid down the document and exhaled loudly. To the tech, he said, 'We have no choice.'

The tech turned the laptop around with slow, deliberate moves, making Lucinda want to jerk it out of his hands. As the screen came into view, she looked down and saw the file of Tess Middleton, CEO. 'Ah ha!' leapt to her tongue but she bit down and refused to let the words escape her mouth. She cleared her throat. 'May we please look over her email messages?'

'Absolutely not,' the attorney said, swiveling the screen away from her. 'As I am certain you've noticed, that is the account of our

CEO. Nearly all of her communications are proprietary. We cannot allow a fishing expedition through them.'

'I can get another warrant,' Lucinda said.

'Yes, but we have the right to a hearing before you do so.'

Lucinda was fuming but she swallowed it down to keep her voice level and calm. 'You certainly do. I suppose that means you believe your CEO has something to hide.'

'I did not say that. I did not intimate that,' the lawyer snapped. 'We are a business with extreme security issues, including some government projects that are subject to classification on different levels.'

'Mm, hmm,' Lucinda said. 'And amidst all that, there may be messages that lead to the identity of a killer and you simply do not care.'

'I believe you have everything you are entitled to according to the court document. It is time for you to leave the premises, Lieutenant.' He pushed at her shoulder.

Lucinda spun towards him with her fists clenched at her sides. Ted pushed himself between Lucinda and the attorney. 'Do not ever again put your hands on the lieutenant or on any member of law enforcement.'

'Excuse me for my familiarity,' the lawyer said after a pause. 'If you'll follow me, I'll escort you outside.'

Lucinda fumed as she walked to the car. She was now convinced that Tess Middleton was the Tess on Rowland's note. And she was hiding something. But what?

THIRTY-NINE

Jake considered his options. He had three rooms filled – one with Seth O'Hara, another with Todd Childress and a third with Becky Carpenter. Who should go first? He decided that he should save Seth for last. He could play Todd and Becky off one another – they both knew something. Todd was eighteen years old, he could interview him without any concern about his parents. While he did, he'd send a deputy for Becky's mother.

Todd had a sneer on his face when Jake stepped through the door.

The fear he felt for his life earlier had now been replaced by a surly cockiness backed by the strong, fit body of a football linesman. Placed on an NFL team, Todd would look small and puny in comparison – as he did when he begged for his life a short time ago. But isolated in that small room, his shoulders appeared broad, his upper arms massive. Jake knew he had to knock down the boy's false front if he was ever going to get to the truth.

'I understand that you and Dylan had a fight.'

Todd shrugged.

'You lost, right?'

'No,' Todd snapped back.

'It makes a sick sort of sense. You have a fight. He humiliates you with a loss. You kill him to get revenge and prevent him from telling others about the way you sniveled on your knees, begging him to stop.'

Todd leaned back in his chair, folding his arms across his chest. An ugly, arrogant smile crossed his face. 'Yeah, right.'

Jake instantly realized that he needed a different twist. 'OK, I admit it. I was just jerking you around. I like to toy about cold-blooded killers like you.'

'I didn't kill anybody.'

'That's not what I hear.'

Todd turned his head and stared at the wall.

'A murder charge will blow your football scholarship out of the water, Todd.'

'You'll never prove it.'

'You think not?'

'It didn't happen.'

'Don't you know? I don't need to prove it. All I need to do is charge you. The moment I do, the Crimson Tide will roll up on the shore and spit you out.' Jake watched as that statement crept into Todd's thoughts.

The young man jerked his attention back to Jake. He blinked and the corners of his mouth quivered. 'My dad won't let you do that.'

'Hey, Todd, wake up. I'm FBI. I'm a Fed. You think your father, the deputy – a county official – can stand in my way?'

Nothing remained of Todd's smile. The spastic blinking of his eyes betrayed his apprehension. 'You can't bring charges without proof.'

'Is that what your father told you?'

Todd pursed his lips and shook his head.

'Does your father know you killed Dylan? Is your father helping you cover up this crime? Do I need to arrest him, too?'

'There was no murder.'

'Then why were you bragging about killing him?'

'I wasn't. Dylan committed suicide.'

'Really? And why would Dylan do that? He had excellent grades, great prospects for the future. Why would he take his own life? Doesn't make sense to me. No, I think it was murder. And I think you did it. What happened? Did he humiliate you? Did the nerd steal the football star's girlfriend?'

'That's stupid.'

'Why is it stupid, Todd? Jealousy is often a motive in murder.'

'It wasn't murder.'

'So who's the girl?'

'There is no girl.'

'What about Shawna, then? I heard you two were a pretty hot item. Until recently, that is. Did you catch her under the bleachers with Dylan?'

Todd turned away again without a word.

'Was it worse? Did you walk in on them doing it?'

Todd's head jerked back. 'She wouldn't do it with him.'

'Why? 'Cause he's a wimpy nerd and you're a big football player? Don't you ever go to movies? It happens all the time, Todd. You might as well admit it. Your girlfriend, your Shawna, cheated on you with Dylan.'

Todd shot to his feet and kicked the leg of the table. 'She wouldn't let that faggot touch her!'

'What was that, Todd? What did you call Dylan?'

Todd slumped back into the chair. 'Faggot. I called him a faggot.'

'Is that just a casual insult, Todd? The response of a homegrown bigot and homophobe? You know what they say about homophobes, don't you, Todd? They say that homophobes are homosexuals in denial. Is that what you are, Todd? Are you homosexual?'

'No!' he shouted, slamming a fist into the table.

'Some homophobes' distress about their own sexual identity makes them hate anyone who is gay. They hunt for them. Beat them up. Kill them. Sometimes, they didn't mean to kill them, they just got carried away. Is that what happened, Todd? Did you put a bullet in Dylan's head because he was gay? Or was it because he found out you were gay?'

On his feet once more, Todd shouted, 'No! I did not shoot him. I did not do anything but threaten to tell. I didn't think he'd kill himself.'

Jake allowed that statement to hang in the air, filling the room, seeping into the walls for a long minute. While he did, Todd heaved with an intense emotion that caused him to sway in place.

'Have a seat, Todd,' Jake said. He waited until Todd sat down, bending over in the chair, shoving both of his hands between his thighs. 'What did you threaten to tell?'

'You know,' Todd squirmed. 'I told him that when I got to the microphone at the pep rally the next day, I'd tell everybody. He begged me not to. That's when I said that just before the rally I'd call his dad and let him know first.'

Leaning forward in his chair, his voice barely above a whisper, Jake said, 'Know what, Todd?'

'He begged me not to tell his dad.'

'What did you say you'd tell Mr O'Hara?'

'I said – I said I'd tell him that his son was a faggot.'

'How did you know that, Todd? Did you catch him with another boy?'

Todd hung his head and shook it hard.

'Did the two of you—?'

'No, no! It wasn't like that.'

'What was it like, Todd?'

'We were in the locker room. In the shower. Dylan was looking at me. He was all excited, you know. He turned away and covered himself with a towel but it was too late – I'd seen it. But he should have known I wouldn't tell anyone.'

'Why should he have known that, Todd?'

'Because if I told anybody I got him all worked up, what would they think about me?' Todd turned his face up to look at Jake. Tears formed in his eyes. 'If they thought I turned on gay boys, what would they think was wrong with me?'

Jake closed his eyes and rose to his feet. 'I'm going to leave you here for a little while, Todd. You think about what you've just said. See if you can think of a reason why that wouldn't give you a motive for murder.'

Jake left the room, hoping some time to think might bring Todd to a point of epiphany – make him understand what great harm bigotry can inflict. He wasn't sure that Todd had the maturity or insight about himself to understand. He was fairly certain, though, that Todd did not kill Dylan and felt he now knew why Dylan committed suicide.

He stepped down the hall to the room where Becky Carpenter waited with her mother. If she was clinging to a promise to keep Dylan's secret, he needed to scare it out of her.

FORTY

Lucinda dropped Ted off at his car and returned to Scott Technologies. She parked outside of the gated, guarded parking lot, watching for Tess Middleton's car. She knew it was a new red Lexus ISC and she had the license plate number. She also knew Tess's home address. She wanted to catch her off guard away from the security of her corporation. She thought about sitting outside the woman's home but that could prove to be a long wait without any awareness of when it might end. Instead, she decided to follow her and know exactly where she was at all times.

The red Lexus pulled out of the lot at 4:37 p.m. Lucinda wondered if Tess always left at that time or, she hoped, the warrant and its results had sent her fleeing from the office earlier than usual. Lucinda was certain that the attorney had informed his boss what the search had uncovered.

Lucinda followed her prey downtown where she stopped in front of her campaign office and went inside. The plate-glass windows of the former storefront were plastered with posters, allowing Lucinda to hide behind them and peer in through the clear glass in between. She watched as Tess patted some workers on the back, looked over paperwork and engaged in an earnest conversation with a young man in a suit. When Tess turned from him, he was beaming.

Back in her car, Tess led Lucinda out to the suburbs and up to a gated community. Lucinda pulled to the side of the road outside the gates and waited. Once the Lexus was out of sight she pulled up to the gate with her badge in her hand.

'The name of the guest you're visiting?' the guard asked.

'Sorry. That's police business. Open the gate.'

'I can't admit you without knowing where you are going.'

'Yes, you can and you will,' Lucinda insisted.

'I am sorry, Officer . . .'

'Lieutenant. Look closely. Lieutenant.'

'Sorry, Lieutenant. But it is against policy to admit anyone without knowing a destination.'

'So, you're telling me that if I had reason to believe that one of your residents was being stalked by a dangerous man – a man who possibly scaled the stone wall in the far corner of your community – that you would not allow me in to hunt him down.'

The guard grabbed the phone.

'What are you doing?' she asked.

'Calling the security office.'

'Hang it up, now.'

'I have to report this.'

'You dial that number and I'll have you in cuffs before the call connects.'

He looked at her, really seeing her for the first time. Lucinda saw that combined look of fascination and repulsion as he absorbed the damage on one side of her face.

'You call anyone – you tell anyone that I am here or the purpose of my visit and I will arrest you for obstruction of justice.'

He slowly lowered the receiver.

'Is that clear?' she asked.

The guard nodded.

'While I'm on this property, not a word. When I leave, you can tell anyone you like. Do you understand?'

'Yes, Lieutenant,' he said as he pressed the button to release the gate.

Did you really have to lie? Lucinda asked herself. You didn't lie, you just gave a possible example, she responded to her conscience. She followed the directions from the GPS on her iPhone, taking one turn after another until she pulled into a position that blocked the driveway in front of a white columned home with black plantation shutters.

Lucinda walked up the sidewalk and onto the porch. Above her head hung a large, crystal-festooned chandelier that she estimated would cost at least six months of her salary. She pressed the doorbell and heard a few notes that sounded vaguely like *Hail to the Chief.*

The door opened before the sound faded. A young woman wearing a tan uniform and a white apron stood on the threshold, one hand on the edge of the door. 'May I help you?'

Lucinda flipped open her badge. 'Tess Middleton, please.'

'I'll see if she is at home.'

'I know she's at home. Get her.'

The maid flushed. 'I'll see if she is available,' she said and started to shut the door.

Lucinda shoved out her hand, blocking the closure and stepped inside.

The woman winced. 'One moment, please.'

Lucinda watched her ascend the stairs. When she was out of sight, Lucinda shut the front door behind her.

A moment later the woman reappeared at the top of the stairs and walked down saying, 'It is not convenient at this time. Ms Middleton is preparing to go out this evening. She said she would be delighted to speak with you tomorrow if you would just call her appointment secretary and set a time that is mutually convenient.'

'I certainly wouldn't want to disturb her preparations. I'll be glad to talk to her upstairs,' Lucinda said as she walked up and met the young woman midway.

The maid threw her arms across the stairway from wall to banister. 'No. That is not possible.'

Lucinda grabbed the woman's wrist and wrenched it from the banister. 'Now, are you going to step aside or am I going to arrest you?'

'I'll lose my job,' she pleaded.

Lucinda genuinely regretted that possibility but could not allow that to stand in her way. She stared at the woman, silently counting to ten before making a move.

The woman stared back at her and then relented, backing against the wall. Lucinda ascended and followed the sound of running water. She entered the master bedroom suite and approached the door of the en suite bath. Standing in the threshold she studied Tess wrapped in a robe, staring closely at her face in a swing-away mirror.

Tess's eyes drifted to the large wall mirror and startled when she saw the person behind her. 'Lieutenant,' she said without turning around. 'I'm certain you've been informed that it is not a convenient time.'

'Yes. I was informed.'

'As you can see, I am in the middle of my toilette. I don't have much time. I have a fundraising event to attend.'

'I doubt they'll start the program without you, Ms Middleton.'

'Call my secretary in the morning and set an appointment. And on your way out, please inform Juliet that I need to see her immediately.'

'I think she's busy packing.'

'What?'

'She knows you're going to fire her for allowing me up here. But let me assure you she did try to keep me out. I'm a bit taller than her and I'm armed. I don't think it was a fair fight.'

'Leave my home immediately or I will call . . .'

'The police? I'm here, Ms Middleton.'

'My attorney,' she spat.

'I could arrest you now and let you call your lawyer from the jail.'

'On what grounds? All you know is that my computer and my email account sent a message to a woman who committed suicide. If you arrest me, I will sue.'

'Those kinds of threats have never stood in my way, Ms. Middleton. All I want to do is ask you a few questions about Candace Eagleton.'

'I barely knew the woman.'

'And Charles Rowland.'

'Who?'

'And Bonnie Upchurch.'

At that name, Tess blanched. She thought she'd burned that bridge with the deaths of Candace and Rowland. Interesting.

'If you want to ask me any questions, contact my attorney. You met him today, I believe. I have nothing to say to you.'

'Not now, Ms Middleton. But let me warn you, I don't mind slipping information to the media. Even if you are not involved in the murders of your two former high school chums, it will ring a bell that cannot be unrung. Your campaign will be dead in the water.'

'That, Lieutenant, is a threat. I will inform my attorney. Now leave my premises and don't come back without a search warrant.'

Lucinda smiled and waited to make sure Tess caught sight of it in the wall mirror. Then she turned and walked away. On the way out, she turned to Juliet and said, 'I told her it wasn't your fault.'

'I doubt that will do a bit of good,' Juliet said and slammed the door behind Lucinda as she stepped out on the porch.

Lucinda walked to her car and turned to stare back at the house. There was a secret buried there and she was determined to unearth it.

FORTY-ONE

Jake paused at the door to the room holding Becky and Dolly Carpenter. He hoped to dig the truth out of Becky but knew it wouldn't be easy. The teenager's expectant face turned toward the sound of the opening door and, just as quickly, looked away as she folded her arms across her chest.

Jake sat down across from them, nodding at Dolly as he took a chair. 'Becky, were you romantically involved with Dylan O'Hara?'

'What?' she asked.

'Were you sexually intimate with Dylan O'Hara?'

'With Dylan? No.' Becky gave her mother an anxious sideways glance.

'I heard some secrets from another student today. It made me wonder if you are pregnant with Dylan O'Hara's child.'

Becky's mouth flew open and she shot to her feet. 'No. No. Who told you that?'

'It made me wonder if Dylan committed suicide because of your pregnancy.'

Becky planted her hands on her hips. 'No. If you say I'm pregnant one more time . . .'

'If he didn't commit suicide because you are carrying his child, then why did he do it, Becky?'

'He did it because . . .' She paused, looked over at her mother, then gazed down at the floor, shaking her head.

'Because, Becky?'

The girl kept staring at the floor, shaking her head.

'I know you made a promise, Becky. But things have gotten out of control. Dylan's dad threatened to kill someone today because he thought that young man murdered Dylan. People are being hurt because you won't tell the truth.'

Becky looked up at Jake, her eyes vibrant with pain. She looked at her mother and again at the floor. Her head swung slowly back and forth.

Jake stepped over to Dolly and whispered, 'I don't know if it will help but it might – would you let me speak to Becky alone?'

Dolly stared into his eyes for a moment, then nodded her head. 'Becky, I'm stepping out for a moment. But I'll be close by. You need me, you call me. OK?'

Becky nodded without looking up.

'Have a seat, Becky,' Jake urged.

The teenager slid back into the chair and refocused her gaze on the table's surface.

'Becky, maybe I'm wrong, but it seemed like you were more concerned about speaking in front of your mother than you are about talking to me.'

'Because I know she'll tell Mr O'Hara. Actually, Mom is a big gossip. Everyone would know before we got back in the car.'

'You sound very critical of your mother.'

Becky sighed. 'I won't lie. I like listening to her dish it out most of the time. This is just different. I couldn't bear to have her talking bad about Dylan.'

'You've got to tell me, Becky.'

'I bet you'll tell Mr O'Hara, too.'

'So what if I do? Mr O'Hara has a right to know why his son died. His heart is broken, Becky. He needs answers.'

A long moment of silence stretched between them. At last, Becky looked up. 'More than anything, he didn't want his father to know.'

'What horrible thing could Dylan have done?'

'He didn't think his dad would ever speak to him again.'

'What did he do, Becky?'

'It wasn't what he did. It was who he was.'

Jake knew where the conversation was leading but acted as if he didn't. 'What do you mean by that?'

'Dylan wanted it to be different. He wanted to be like everyone else. I tried to help him. One night, I completely undressed, hoping it would turn him on. But, nothing . . .'

'Becky, are you saying that Dylan committed suicide because he was gay?'

'It was more like he did it because he didn't want anyone to know he was gay.' Becky shuddered. 'I can't believe I broke my word. I hope he doesn't know it. I know you have to tell Mr O'Hara but please try to make him understand. Please don't let him hate Dylan.'

'I'll do the best I can, Becky. And I think you need to explain everything to your mother. She's very worried. Put her mind at ease. And give her some credit – she does know some things are not meant to be the subject of gossip.'

Becky nodded her head.

Jake opened the door and waved Dolly back inside to her daughter. Then he trudged down the hall to the room where Seth O'Hara waited. He wasn't quite sure how to approach Seth. Was the man before him biased against gay men? Or was it worse – did he harbor hatred toward homosexuals? Or did Dylan shortchange his dad? Was Seth just a father who would, no matter how he felt about the issue, continue to love and support his son?

'Am I going to be arrested on an assault charge?' Seth asked.

'Only if Todd Childress files a complaint. I am going to talk to him and his father after I talk to you. Depending on how things go in here, it's possible that those charges will be dropped.'

Seth shook his head. 'What do you mean "depending on how things go in here?" What's happening?'

Jake laid one hand on the back of the other and leaned over the table. 'Seth, I know why and how your son died.'

'Did Todd confess?'

'In a manner of speaking, yes. But he did not confess to murder. He told me what happened between him and your son Dylan – an encounter that led to your son's suicide.'

'There you go again – just like the rest of them.'

'No, Mr O'Hara, that's where you are wrong. The rest of them told you it was suicide but could offer no reason. I know exactly what drove Dylan to that ultimate act – but I'm not sure how you're going to take it.'

'Are you going to tell me the truth?'

'Yes, sir.'

'Then I'll take it just fine. Shoot,' Seth said as he folded his arms across his chest and stared straight on at Jake.

'Mr O'Hara, did you have any suspicions that Dylan was gay?'

'My son, gay? Of course not. I'm not gay. My son's not gay. End of story.'

'You know, sir, that it doesn't work that way. Heterosexual couples do have homosexual children.'

'Not my son,' Seth insisted, shaking his head in denial.

'Yes, Mr O'Hara. I have it from a very reliable source.'

'Oh, the deputy's brat. The little Childress faggot. He told you my son was gay, didn't he? And you bought it.'

Jake closed his eyes and took a deep breath. 'Todd Childress did tell me of an incident in the shower in the locker room . . .'

'Nothing but a sexual fantasy by the Childress boy. It has nothing to do with my Dylan.'

'It was confirmed by someone close to Dylan, Mr O'Hara. Someone who did not want to tell me because of a promise made to your son. She swore she'd never tell his secret.'

Jake and Seth were interrupted by a knock on the door. 'Agent Lovett, sorry to interrupt but Mrs O'Hara insisted that I let you know she's here.'

'Why don't you escort her down here?' Jake said. A moment later, Martha sat by her husband and took one of his hands in her own. She listened carefully as Jake repeated what he'd told Seth.

'I see,' she said and sat quietly for a moment. 'Becky Carpenter must have been who told you.'

Jake didn't respond.

'It had to be,' she said. 'He wasn't close to anyone else.' She turned to her husband. 'Seth, you never suspected?'

'That our son was gay? Of course not,' he said, pulling back his hand.

'I've thought about it many times. His only close friend was a girl, but there didn't seem to be any fire between them. He never dated. I never wanted to say anything – what if I was wrong? It could be traumatic for him. I thought he'd tell me when he was ready.'

'Are you serious, Martha?'

She nodded. 'Yes, Seth. But it wouldn't have mattered, would it? He would have still been our son. I know I would have still loved him. Wouldn't you, Seth? Wouldn't you?'

'He was my son, Martha. I can't believe you needed to ask.'

'Well, Seth, sometimes your language about gay people . . .'

'I didn't mean anything by it, Martha. I wouldn't have said anything if I'd known or even ever had a question in my mind.'

Martha turned to Jake. 'May we go now, Agent Lovett?'

'Yes,' he said. 'I may need to arrest your husband on assault charges at some point – but maybe not. In the meantime, there is no reason why you two can't go home.'

'Thank you. I'm going to try to arrange the funeral for the day after tomorrow. I'll let you know when it's definite.'

'Thank you, Mrs O'Hara, Mr O'Hara.' Jake stood in the hall and watched as the slumped and defeated couple made their way down the hall. Now he needed to use all his powers of persuasion to get Seth out of the mess he'd created.

FORTY-TWO

Back at the justice center, Lucinda made a beeline to the research office, where she found Lara working at her computer. 'Quivey, I need your help.'

'That's why I'm here,' Lara said with a smile.

'I need you to look back at 1977 to 1978 for any crimes involving anyone who attended or worked at Livingston High School.'

'Any crime? Even shoplifting or traffic violations?'

'No. Not now. Look for felonies. Suspected felonies. Anything that could possibly have any connection to Teresa "Tess" Scott Middleton.'

'You got it. I'll send you a report as soon as I have anything.'

'Thank you, Lara. I owe you.'

'Yes, ma'am,' Lara said with a chuckle. 'You sure do.'

Lucinda stopped next at the lab where she was intercepted by Dr Audrey Ringo. Her bright orange-red hair battled for dominance with her turquoise outfit. With her white lab coat hanging on the peg, she was a solid blue-green from the neckline of her dress to the shoes on her feet. Without anything to break up the color, Audrey looked as straight up and down as one of those foam pool noodles people play with when they're swimming.

'Lieutenant,' Audrey said. 'When are you going back under the knife to take care of those scars on your face?'

'Soon, Audrey,' she said with a sigh.

'As I am sure you know, I had surgery last year,' Audrey said, referring to her mastectomy. 'I tried to keep it secret but this place is like a harem of old gossiping women.'

'I would think, Audrey, that you would understand my desire to keep the matter of my facial reconstruction private.'

'Not the same, Lieutenant. The results of my procedure are hidden. Yours are out there for everyone to see. They talk about it constantly, wondering about it obsessively. I suspect there's even a pool betting on when you'll take the plunge again.'

'Audrey, you and I both know that is not true. No one – but you – cares. My medical procedures are too boring for anyone else to contemplate. So cut the crap.' Lucinda gritted her teeth. She knew that Audrey was a brilliant forensic scientist but realized that she was a miserable human being at times, seeming to thrive by creating discomfort in the people around her.

Before Audrey could spit out another venomous comment, Beth Ann Coynes popped out into the hallway. 'Lieutenant, I thought I heard your voice. Did you get my message?'

'No. I haven't been to my desk.'

'We got a hit on the DNA profile from under Candace Eagleton's fingernails. Come look.'

Lucinda followed Beth Ann to her workstation and peered at the image on the computer screen. A mugshot of a man wearing a gray suit and a prominent smirk stared back at her. 'Who is he?'

'Julius Trappatino of Trenton, New Jersey. Suspected hit man.'

'The mob?'

'Occasionally he does hits for The Family. But he's not on payroll; he's strictly freelance and expensive. Suspected in a dozen or more murders, but nothing ever proven.'

'His age?'

'Thirty-four.'

'That makes him too young to be in the same graduating class with the others,' Lucinda mused.

'Excuse me?' Beth asked.

'Never mind. Just trying to fit him into the current cast of characters,' she said. 'You're sure about this ID?'

'Oh, yes. Absolutely. It's a statistically perfect match for one of the DNA profiles.'

'There's another?' Lucinda asked.

'Two others, actually. Three in all: Trappatino, the victim and an unknown.'

'Unknown?'

'Male is the best we can do. Any luck on getting a sample from the husband?'

'No. Would you like to call him to schedule an appointment with serology?'

Beth Ann gave her a puzzled look and then said, 'Oh, right. You have to go through his attorney now.'

'Don't let him know that you know about that when you call.'

'You got it.'

'Thanks. Later,' Lucinda said as she went back down the hall and evaded another conversation with Audrey Ringo.

When she arrived at her desk there was already a message from Lara containing news story attachments. She read them through with a mounting frustration – a litany of dropped charges, compromised evidence and crafty evasion. She would need as much help as she could get to bring Julius Trappatino to heel. She could hardly believe she was thinking it, but she knew she needed the resources of the FBI.

She called the field office and asked for Jake even though she knew he wasn't there. 'This is Lieutenant Pierce.'

'Oh, Lieutenant, Special Agent Lovett is on a leave of absence.'

'I need his assistance on an investigation.'

'Didn't he tell you he's desk-bound now?'

'Yes. But I need him to be reactivated.'

'That's way above my pay grade, Lieutenant. In fact, no one here in this office can make that happen.'

'Give me a phone number for the wicked witch of the north, then.'

Lucinda was rewarded with a chuckle and the number to Sandra Goodman's direct line. She introduced herself when Goodman answered.

'And what can I do for you today, Lieutenant?'

'I need FBI assistance and I want to work with Special Agent in Charge Jake Lovett.'

'That is not possible at this time, but I can connect with another agent from that field office.'

'I do not want another agent. I want Agent Lovett.'

'Special Agent in Charge Lovett is not engaging in field work at this time. I can strongly recommend . . .'

'I don't care who you might recommend. I've worked with Lovett in the past and I trust his judgment and his analysis.'

'It is simply not possible at this time. The same resources and commitment are available to you with any agent.'

'Listen, Director Goodman. That does not matter. I am sitting here with a homicide case that appears to be connected to a hit man whom I believe you have had under investigation.'

'His name?'

'I'll tell that to Special Agent Lovett.'

'I do not understand your attitude.'

'Let's just say I have trust issues.'

'I'm sorry. That's not good enough.'

'How about this, Goodman? I'll call my mayor and tell him to go ahead and contact his friend at the Justice Department and schedule the news conference about Julius Trappatino.' Each word of Lucinda's bluff bit into her tongue as she spoke it.

'The mayor has friends at the Justice Department?'

'Who doesn't?' Lucinda quipped. She loathed the politics of inter-agency dancing even though she played it well.

'It may take me some time to locate Special Agent in Charge Lovett. But when I do, I'll give him your number and have him call. In the meantime, can someone else help you?'

'No. But please bear in mind, with every passing moment my lead grows colder.'

'Of course, Lieutenant,' she said and slammed down the receiver.

Lucinda smiled. She didn't like the lies or game-playing but still could not help feeling smug and satisfied when she won. Maybe Coynes will have luck with that phone call to Eagleton.

FORTY-THREE

J ake walked back to the on-duty room, hoping to find Deputy Childress in the house. He spotted him at a keyboard working on a report. 'Deputy Childress, have you got a moment?'

'Sure. You still got my boy?'

'Yes, I do, Deputy. I'd like you to come with me to talk something over with him.'

In the interrogation room Todd wouldn't look his father in the eye. 'Can you look at me, son?'

Todd just shook his head.

'What's the matter with you, boy?'

'We'll get to that in due time, Deputy,' Jake said. 'Todd, I know you were assaulted and threatened by Mr O'Hara. I know it was a very frightening experience. The question that remains is: do you want to press charges?'

'Damned right we'll press charges,' the deputy bellowed.

'No. No, Dad, I don't want to press charges.'

'Don't want to press charges? That man held a gun to your head. I know he's grieving but for cripe's sake, that is no excuse.'

'Agent Lovett,' Todd said. 'Since I'm eighteen years old, doesn't that mean that the decision is all mine to make?'

'I can't believe you're saying that, boy. After all I've done for—'

'Deputy Childress, please,' Jake said, holding up a hand. 'Yes, Todd, it is your decision. I do think, though, it would be a good idea if you'd share with your father what happened the afternoon Dylan took his life.'

'You tell him.'

Jake shook his head. 'No, Todd, it should come from you.'

Todd sighed.

The deputy was now on his feet, pacing the room. He threw his hands up in the air and said, 'Well, somebody tell me.'

'Todd . . .' Jake said.

Todd kept his eyes focused on the surface of the table as he told his dad about the incident in the locker room. He ended by pleading his case. 'Dad, I swear to God Almighty – I had no idea he'd commit suicide. I was going to make it easy for him. Just get him to give me something to keep quiet.'

'Give you something? Son, you crept right close to blackmail – extortion. And that's a crime – a felony. I can understand why you got a little prickly with the O'Hara boy but Lord have mercy, boy, what were you thinking? You shoulda just told him to cut it out, you weren't interested. Since when did you become a holy crusader?'

'Dad, I just didn't think . . .'

'That's right, Todd. You just didn't think. Agent, can he go home now?'

'If the matter of pressing charges is settled,' Jake answered.

The deputy turned to his son. 'Go on. Get out of here. You might want to talk to your mother before I get home from work. If I have to explain all this to her, you might not like what I say.'

Todd rose, slump-shouldered from the table and plodded across the room. At the doorway, he turned back and began, 'Dad . . .'

'Later, son. We'll talk about this at home.' Once Todd disappeared from view, the deputy turned his attention to Jake. 'No, Agent. We won't be pressing any charges against Seth O'Hara. You just tell him to stay away from Todd.'

'I don't think you'll have a problem with Mr O'Hara, Deputy.'

'Good. I've got my hands full with my boy.'

FORTY-FOUR

'Lieutenant.'

Lucinda looked up to find Lara Quivey in her doorway with papers in both hands. 'Whatcha got?' she asked.

'Tracked down Bonnie Louise Upchurch of Livingston High School to Texas where she legally changed her name to "Olivia Louise Cartwright" nineteen years ago.'

'Is she still in Texas?'

'No. Tracked her to Reno, then to San Diego and finally to Seattle. I'm still looking for where she went from there.'

'What's in the other hand?'

Lara looked down as if she'd forgotten she was holding that sheaf of papers. 'Oh, right. I found six possible crimes that met the parameters you described. The one that really stood out was the discovery of a body buried just inside the Thomas Jefferson National Forest off an old logging road.'

'How does a body found in the woods in Virginia connect to Livingston High School in New Jersey?'

'Amazing, isn't it? The body was that of seventeen-year-old Lindsey Barnaby, Class of '78, Livingston High School, Trenton, New Jersey. No one could ever figure out how she got from there to Virginia. The state guys thought that a serial killer operating in the area was responsible. It looked like his work – death by a blow to the head and found buried in the same five-mile radius of where his other victims were found. But if it was, it had to have been his first killing and she doesn't match the profile of all of his other victims. They were runaways and prostitutes. He pled guilty to many of the murders but insisted that Lindsey was not his victim. So the case is still cold – as in liquid nitrogen cold.'

Lucinda opened up the yearbook and flipped through the pages until she found a photograph of Lindsey Barnaby. She was a cheerleader and in the same choral group as Candace Eagleton. 'Lara, can you find out where she lived when she was in high school – see if, by chance, it was in the same neighborhood as any of the others?'

'I'll get right on it,' she said.

Lucinda watched her dart away and wondered again how she ever could have made headway in many of her cases without Lara's assistance. She thought she probably should polish up her own computer research skills and do some of the work herself. But when would she find the time? And how long would it take her to have as much faith in her own abilities as she did in Lara's?

She only had a moment to contemplate that thought before she was jerked out of her reverie by the bark-like voice of Captain Holland. 'My office, Pierce. Now.'

What now? she wondered as she followed him down the hall.

Inside his office, Holland pointed to a chair and said, 'Sit.'

Lucinda knew from his tone that soon she'd have to beg – with or with out his command.

Holland stared at her. The red bristles of his close-cut hair seemed to undulate on his head. The veins in both of his temples throbbed. Hard knots rose at the locus of his jaw joints. 'Here's the chain of command in action. A campaign contributor calls the mayor and chews on his ass. The mayor calls the police chief and gnaws on his butt. The police chief calls me and kicks my ass to Kingdom Come. Now it's your turn.'

Oh, shit, Lucinda thought. Whose toes have I stepped on now?

'Any pleas for mercy? Any wild excuses?'

'No, sir.'

The captain shot to his feet and placed both palms flat on his desk as he leaned forward. 'What the hell is wrong with you?'

'Sir?' Give me a clue, Lucinda thought.

As if on cue, Holland picked up a document and slapped it on the desk in front of her. 'A restraining order, Pierce? A restraining order? You're not a rookie. You should know when someone says that you need to communicate through their attorney that you leave that damned person alone.'

Lucinda scanned the document. Frank Eagleton. Oh, shit. Bad news travels way too fast.

'Not only did you violate that policy, you embroiled someone else in your little plot. Not satisfied with adding black marks to your record, you have to drag someone else down with you.'

'That was not my intent, sir.'

'Intent be damned. To make matters worse, I had to call Doctor Ringo and explain it all to her. You know how I don't like to talk to that woman. She chewed on the tattered remains of my ass for ten minutes before she took a breath. You've ruined my day – hell, my week – maybe my month. What do you have to say for yourself, Pierce?'

'Beth Ann Coynes is blameless. This is all on me.'

'Oh, really. Interesting. That's not what Miss Coynes told Doctor Ringo.'

'Honestly, Captain, Coynes is not responsible. I am.'

'Really? Well, she told Doctor Ringo that she was aware of your frustration in not being able to get a DNA sample from Frank Eagleton. She thought she could alleviate it by calling him herself. She said that you were unaware of her actions.'

'I don't know why she would do that, sir. It is not what happened.'

'I agree with you on that, Pierce. But I think you were both complicit in this conspiracy to violate policy. Doctor Ringo, however, has chosen to place all the blame on you and view Coynes as a victim of your manipulation.'

'Glad to hear it, sir. I wouldn't want to compromise Coynes' employment.'

'Glad to hear you say that, Pierce. 'Cause right now, you are going to haul your defaced ass down to the lab. You are going to apologize to Doctor Ringo for dragging one of her staff into your irresponsible mess.'

'Yes, sir.'

'And for God's sake, do not call her "Audrey." It's Doctor Ringo and ma'am and nothing else.'

'Yes, sir.'

'And if she calls and tells me otherwise or that your apology was not abject, your ass is mine.'

'Yes, sir.'

'Well, don't just sit there. Go!'

Lucinda rose and stepped toward the door, coming to a dead stop when Captain Holland said, 'One more thing, Pierce.'

She turned around and said, 'Yes, sir?'

'Cut this shit out.'

Lucinda nodded, turned and went out the door. She took the stairs down to the lab where she asked for Dr Ringo at the front desk.

Audrey Ringo stalked down the hall towards her, leaning forward as if fighting a headwind. 'What do you want now?' she shouted.

'I'd like a few minutes of your time, Doctor Ringo.'

'Don't you think you've already wasted enough of it?'

Behind Audrey, Beth Ann poked her head out of a doorway. Her face was pained. Her arms bent at the elbows with her palms facing upward. She mouthed, *Sorry*.

Lucinda's eye darted back to Audrey. 'I want to apologize, Doctor Ringo.'

'And offer up some lame excuse?'

'No, ma'am. I want to accept full responsibility. I was irresponsible, reckless and untrustworthy.'

'Let's not forget arrogant.'

'Yes, ma'am. I was arrogant and I truly regret my behavior.'

'Do you realize you could have destroyed the promising career of a young forensic scientist?'

'Yes, ma'am, I do.'

'Well, there's someone else who deserves an apology,' Audrey said, pinching the fabric of Lucinda's sleeve and tugging her towards the back. She led Lucinda to Beth Ann Coynes' work station. 'There. Do it.'

'Miss Coynes, I apologize for dragging you into a mess of my making. I regret involving you and hope that it will have no negative impact on your career.'

'But . . .' Beth Ann began.

Lucinda gave her a tight shake of her head.

Beth Ann bit her lower lip, darted her eyes over to Audrey and back to Lucinda. She closed her eyes and inhaled. When she opened them, she said, 'Thank you, Lieutenant. I forgive you completely. I hope this won't happen again.'

'Thank you for accepting my apology, Ms Coynes.'

Released by Dr Ringo, Lucinda scurried back to her desk. An email from Beth Ann was waiting in her inbox. 'Just in case we aren't clear: when I said I hope this won't happen again, I meant I hope we never get caught again.'

Lucinda smiled. Would she do it again? Damned right. If she thought there was even a modest possibility of success, she'd do it without hesitation. Now how would she get that DNA sample? Maybe Sergeant Colter would be willing to follow Frank Eagleton around. Maybe she could snatch up a discarded cup or soda can. She'd tell Colter the whole story and let her decide if she wanted to help. If she did and got reprimanded, Lucinda would shoulder that blame, too. Captain Holland's words – 'Cut this shit out' – reverberated in her head. She knew she would – just as soon as she had Candace's killer behind bars.

FORTY-FIVE

J ake pulled his phone out of his pocket to call Lucinda and give her a rundown on how it all ended. He saw several missed calls and vaguely remembered the vibrations on his thigh as he shuttled from one interrogation room to the other.

He was not surprised to see more than one from Lucinda. He hadn't gotten back to her in too long. The messages from the regional director and the one from the office took him by surprise. He thought they were ignoring him.

The office call came from the agent acting in his position during his absence. 'Jake, the wicked witch of the north wants you back in the field. Have no idea why. But call me.'

The acerbic sound of the regional director's voice made him wince. 'You just got lucky. Something bigger than you has intervened. You need to contact a Lieutenant Lucinda Pierce in the local PD. She has a lead on Julius Trappatino. Nail the bastard. Don't screw this up.'

Lucinda's message made him smile. 'I need you. I told the wicked witch I need you. I hope she's contacted you. If she calls my bluff, I'm screwed.'

Jake called Lucinda first. 'You know every man likes to be needed. Your place or mine?'

'Very funny, Jake. But seriously, I've stumbled across a suspect who apparently is in the FBI's gunsights.'

'Julius Trappatino.'

'You knew?'

'Got a message from the old wicked witch herself. I'll call my office and have them email you everything we have about him. And I'll be back just as soon as I can pick up my stuff at your brother's house and get down the highway.'

'Are things still up in the air?'

'Nope. It's suicide. Dylan killed himself rather than come out of the closet.'

'You're kidding me.'

'Wish I were. He didn't want to face his dad and thought that Todd was going to expose him.'

'What a waste – what a horrible waste,' Lucinda said with a sigh.

'Amen to that. The funeral will be soon. I feel as if I should come back up here for that.'

'Me, too.'

'You want to go up together if my murder investigation doesn't get in the way?'

'Let's do that. I need to find out if Frank Eagleton knows Trappatino but Eagleton took out a restraining order on me.'

'He doesn't have one on me,' Jake said. 'And this is now FBI business. I'll swing by and talk to him before I meet you in the office – you'll be there?'

'If I have to leave, I'll give you a call.'

'If you get any information on a possible location for Trappatino, give me a call right away – no matter where it is. I can get an agent on it right away.'

She disconnected the call and pondered the whereabouts of Julius Trappatino. What if he was also looking for Bonnie Upchurch? If he was not as far along in his search as they were, perhaps he was in one of the cities along her continental progress. She punched Jake's number in her cell.

'Something already?' he said as he answered.

'Nothing solid. But remember the Bonnie on Rowland's list?'

'Yeah.'

'I think it's Bonnie Upchurch. She was a year behind the others at Livingston High. We tracked her to Dallas where she changed her name to Olivia Cartwright. We then trailed her to Reno, San Diego and Seattle. If Trappatino is following that trail, he might be in any of those cities.'

'I'll alert those field offices to be on the look-out for him. Do you know where Bonnie or Olivia is now?'

'No. We do know that she left Seattle.'

'Can you email all her addresses over to my office to Special Agent Cameron Harper?'

'Sure, that's not a problem.'

'Harper can attach them to the alert so that the agents in those cities have a place to start looking for Trappatino.'

'Later, Jake.'

'Hey, Lucy, when this is wrapped up, you want to run away from home together?'

Lucinda grimaced. He made it so hard to compartmentalize her relationship with him. She wanted professional in one box and possible personal entanglements in another. Jake did not make that easy. 'No time for this now, Jake.'

'Aw, Lucy . . .'

'Goodbye, Jake.' She wanted to pack that personal side up in a box and set it on the shelf – or maybe behind the shelf – for the time being. That thought brought an Emily Dickinson poem to mind:

> *I cannot live with you,*
> *It would be life,*
> *And life is over there*
> *Behind the shelf.*

Damn, she thought. Why is literature a required college course? And why does that useless crap lodge so firmly in my brain?

FORTY-SIX

She snatched up her disposable cell on the first ring. 'Where have you been? I thought I would have heard from you before now.'

'I'm sitting across the street and down three doors from Bonnie's rowhouse,' Julius Trappatino said.

'Does that mean she's reverted to her original name?'

'It doesn't mean anything. Bonnie or Olivia, does it really matter once she's dead?'

'Is it time?'

'Not yet. I need to know more about her habits and patterns first.'

'Don't dawdle. The cops are looking at me now. I need this over,'
she said.

'Dawdle? You think I dawdle?'

'Bad choice of word.'

'No kidding. My price just went up.'

'You can't do that.'

'Oh, yes I can. If you want the job done, I can.'

'Whatever. I told you cost was not an issue. But we did have an
agreement.'

'Yes. And you violated our unwritten contract. Respect at all
times.'

'What contract?'

'See, the benefit of my contract being unwritten is that I can say
it contains whatever I want it to contain. And you just violated a
key provision. That calls for a contract penalty.'

'Just do the job. I'll pay you. And do it quick.'

'I can do quick. I can run her down on the road without any
trouble – but we've done that before and we don't want links, do
we?'

'No. We don't. You know that.'

'Quick could be a suicide . . .'

'Stop jerking me around,' she said. 'How are you planning to do
it?'

'Do you really want to know?'

'Yes.'

'What about credible deniability?' Julius asked.

'You let me worry about that.'

'I was thinking of a gas leak leading to an explosion in the middle
of the night.'

'Can you contain that to her unit?'

'Do you really care? What's a little collateral damage in comparison to the damage Bonnie can do?'

The woman didn't respond.

'Well, come on. If you don't have the stomach for this, tell me
now and I'll pack up and go home. You'll still owe me, though, if
you pull the plug.'

'I'm not pulling the plug. Go for it. Call me when it's done.'

FORTY-SEVEN

Lucinda smiled as she looked down at the screen. Charley was calling. 'Hello, girlfriend. How are you today?'

'Are you at work?' Charley asked.

'Yes, ma'am.'

'You shouldn't have to work on the weekend.'

'Bad guys don't take time off, Charley. Now, you didn't call to give me a hard time about that, did you?'

'No, Lucy. I called to ask you a favor.'

'What kind of favor?'

'Mr Bryson's funeral is on Tuesday. I want to go. But Kara can't go with me because Ruby is too young to go. And Daddy isn't here.'

'I don't know if your dad would want you to go, sweetie.'

'He said he'd take me if he was here but he's not coming home until Wednesday or Thursday. But he did say if I found a responsible adult to take me, I could go.'

'Do I qualify?' Lucinda asked.

'Lucy, you are more responsible than Daddy.'

'I doubt that.'

'You never give yourself enough credit, Lucy. And besides, I asked him and he said you would be his first choice.'

'Charley, I can't promise right now. I'm in the middle of a fast-moving murder investigation. If I can get away, I do promise that I will. Pick out what you plan to wear so you'll be able to get ready quickly.'

'I already know what to wear, Lucy,' Charley said.

Lucinda heard the pain in her voice and felt certain she knew what the young girl was thinking. She said nothing, waiting to hear what Charley would add.

'I'll wear the black dress I wore to my mom's funeral.'

Tears came to Lucinda's eyes. She wanted to wrap her arms around Charley and hold her tight. She swallowed the lump in her throat and said, 'That would be very appropriate, Charley.'

'I know Mr Bryson wasn't murdered like my mom but I don't think she'd mind.'

'I'm sure she won't.'

'Do you think she can look down and see me, Lucy?'

'Do you want your mom to be able to look down on you?' Lucinda responded.

'Yes, I do. When I think she is, I feel safe. When I doubt it, I'm scared.'

Lucinda closed her eyes and let the tears flow down her cheeks. 'Yes, Charley. I am certain she looks down on you and keeps you safe.' Lucinda wished she really was sure. If she were certain, then she'd know her own mother was watching over her. It would be such a comfort.

The computer on her desk dinged to indicate incoming email. It was from Jake's office. She clicked on the attachment and perused the FBI file on Julius Trappatino. She was midway through her review of the details of his suspected crimes when she heard a rustle of paper at her doorway. She looked up to see Lara Quivey quivering with excitement. 'Yes, you found something?'

'Yes. I located Bonnie Upchurch, aka Olivia Cartwright.'

'Where?'

'In a rowhouse on Taylor Street in the Mill Hill Section of Trenton, New Jersey.'

'She went back home?'

'Yes, indeed.'

'One moment,' Lucinda said, raising an index finger in the air. She jerked her cell out of her pocket and called Jake. Before he could say a word, she said, 'I've got an address for our Bonnie. Here's Ms Quivey.' She handed her phone to Lara, who read off the address to Jake and then handed the cell back to Lucinda.

'She needs protection,' Lucinda said.

'I'll call the field office up there immediately. I'll be at Eagleton's place in ten minutes or so,' Jake said and ended the call.

'Now, Ms Quivey, it's the weekend. What are you doing here?'

'Well, on Friday, I had hold of this small thread and I just had to keep tugging on it. I had to know if it led somewhere and it did.'

'You're the best. I won't forget this. You may have saved a woman's life – at the very least, you've given us an opportunity to make that happen. Now, go home. Have a life.'

Lara smiled. 'I'll poke around a bit more and see if any more threads pop up before calling it a day. Can't leave while I'm on a roll, can I?'

FORTY-EIGHT

Trappatino spent a quiet afternoon in his car watching the old neighborhood. The block began with brick and ended with brick – typical post-World War Two construction. One rowhouse up against the other, people packed tightly together. It was a nice way to live, he thought, if you liked being surrounded by people. He didn't.

He definitely preferred his hideaway out near the cranberry bogs. His cabin set well off the road on a long, straight drive. He could see cars coming even before they took the turn. He had a telescope trained on the road where it passed his home. No one would take him by surprise.

Where he sat now was a far more dangerous place. He felt exposed and vulnerable. In his world, there were only two types of people: those who paid him to kill and those whom he killed. All others were irrelevant and a constant source of irritation and often an inadvertent threat.

He watched the dog walkers, the joggers, the postman and a flock of casual strollers moving up and down the street. The sun was starting to set when he saw a light flash on inside the target home. He realized he was at a real disadvantage parked here in front of the house but there was no way he could park in the alley without blocking the traffic.

He got out of his car and went around the block. Counting, he located Olivia's driveway. She hadn't closed the gate after pulling onto the property. Like every other house, the backyard was surrounded by a tall fence. He peered into the backyard. Old landscaping was now full of weeds. A barbecue grill rusted from the weather and lack of use. A broken lawn chair sat in the grass beside it. It didn't appear as if she spent any time at all out there. A steep set of wooden stairs led to a small platform by the back door.

He thought about creeping up the steps to look in the window on that door but the fading light was still strong enough to make him stand out if she happened to be in the room on the other side.

It would have to wait. He knew that further exploration should be delayed until full dark.

He went back around to his car and slid behind the wheel to wait. He paid little attention to the slouched figure coming his way a few minutes later. Looked like a loser to him: backward baseball cap, baggy pants, one foot on, one foot off of a skateboard, scooting up the sidewalk.

After a quick glimpse in his rear-view mirror to make sure the person was still moving down the street, he ignored him. He didn't watch him reach the end of the block and turn the corner. He couldn't see him pull out a phone and call Jake.

FORTY-NINE

Jake listened as the voice on the other end of the line said, 'He's here – parked a couple of doors down from the target home.'

'You're certain it's him?'

'Absolutely.'

'Are you going to take him now?'

'No.'

'What?' Jake asked.

'We have to catch him in a criminal act. Too many times he has weaseled out of charges. We can't screw up this time.'

'I'm on my way and I'm bringing a local homicide detective with me.'

'Fine,' the voice said. 'But we have to move when we have to move. We can't risk that woman's life to wait for you.'

'Understood,' Jake said.

He ended the call and placed another to Lucinda.

'Hi, Jake.'

'Go home. Pack an overnight bag. A change of clothes, toothbrush, whatever else you need but make it quick. I'll meet you there in forty-five minutes.'

'Where are we going, Jake? What's going on?'

'The address you gave me for Olivia Cartwright?'

'Yes.'

'It's confirmed and Julius Trappatino is in a car parked in front of it.'

'See you in forty-five minutes,' Lucinda said and ended the call.

She used her lights and a whoop of her siren to get through a bottleneck downtown and reached her apartment building in record time. Entering her front door, she brushed aside the excited welcome from her cat Chester as she hurried to the bedroom. Chester stood in the doorway, wailing for her attention.

She extracted a rolling duffle bag from her closet and stuffed a pair of jeans, T-shirt, a charcoal-gray suit and off-white blouse into the bag. She rammed a pair of tennis shoes and a pair of gray heels into the side pockets and grabbed a toiletry bag that she speed-packed before dumping it into the duffle.

Lucinda then turned to Chester. 'Oh, itty bitty kitty boy, I'm going away for a while. Come on. Let's go fill your bowls.' She scooped him up in her arms and his wails turned to purrs. He pressed the side of his face against her chin and rubbed.

Setting him down in the kitchen, she filled one bowl with a full can of his favorite tuna with cheddar canned food. While he ate, she piled another bowl high with dry cat food and a third with water, then checked on his litter box and was pleased to find it in good condition.

She then took care of her food, slapping a slice of turkey and a slice of havarti cheese and a leaf of romaine on a single piece of buttered five-grain bread. She didn't realize how hungry she was until she took her first bite. She forced herself not to gobble.

She had a few minutes to snuggle with Chester before her cell rang. 'Pulling into your parking garage.'

'Stop in front of the elevators on level one. I'll be there in a flash.'

When she stepped out of the elevator, rolling her bag behind her, Jake popped the trunk and jumped out of the car. He grabbed her bag and tossed it into the trunk.

'That wasn't necessary but thank you.'

'My mom taught me to be a gentleman.'

'And she did an excellent job.'

'I've arranged for an FBI plane to pick us up and transport us to the Robbinsville airport near Trenton. A special agent from that field office will be waiting to pick us up and take us to the scene or to the office if they've already picked him up. And that will probably be the case. I don't think they'll put off his arrest much longer unless he just sits in his car and does nothing.'

'I guess that means we won't know what's happening until we're back on the ground.'

'Not unless something extreme happens. Like if they shot and killed Trappatino, I imagine they'd get a message to our pilot. Short of that, I imagine we'll be clueless until we get there.'

As they boarded the plane, Lucinda was surprised. She expected something basic and worn. Instead she saw leather seats for eight and a conversation area with a table in the back.

Jake poked his head into the cockpit and said, 'Hey, how did we rate this plane?'

'You just got lucky. I was in the area and hadn't flown since yesterday.'

'Hope our luck holds on the ground,' Jake said before sliding into a seat and snapping his seat belt. Turning to Lucinda, he said, 'This baby is normally used to flying VIPs around. Can't believe we got it.'

'I can't believe how comfortable this seat is,' Lucinda said. 'It's hard to believe I'm on an airplane and I can actually stretch out my legs.'

'And we both need to do that and try to get some sleep. This is going to be a long night.'

Neither one of them actually thought sleep was possible but they woke up suddenly when the wheels hit the ground. As the plane taxied to a stop, both experienced an adrenaline jolt that catapulted them into alertness and prepared them for any challenge ahead.

FIFTY

Trappatino's original plan called for him to wait until the middle of the night – 2 a.m. or 3 a.m. to enter the house and set the right conditions for a gas explosion. When he saw the last light on the second floor turn off at 9:30 p.m., he decided to make his entrance in half an hour.

He doubled checked his equipment bag. He had the wrench he needed to unscrew the natural gas drip cap. He had a can of lubricant in case it proved stubborn. He had the exquisitely crafted glass cutter, one of his favorite tools, to breech a window and access the home. And he had what he liked to call his romantic touch – an eight-inch high, champagne-pink pillar candle and a disposable lighter.

He started his car and circumscribed the block, pulling into a parking space as far from the house as he could get and still have a view of it. If the explosion occurred quicker than he anticipated, he didn't want the vehicle caught under flying debris or blocked in by emergency vehicles. He'd rather be a bit further away but that would mean lurking on the street to keep an eye on the house before he made his move. The street was too quiet for him to remain inconspicuous loitering in the vicinity.

He looked up and down the street, taking care to determine if shadows behind windows indicated that anyone was peering out into the darkness. The coast was clear. He turned off the interior light in his car and slipped out of the vehicle with a sports bag in his hand. He casually walked to the end of the block, turned a corner and approached the alley.

He looked up the narrow passageway for any sign of movement. He heard no one in their backyards and only saw the light from one back porch and it was well past his target house. Street lights illuminated the alleyway, making him stick to the shadows by the fences as he made his way to the middle of the block. Ducking into the drive where the gate remained open, he quickly crossed the open space to the stairway.

He grasped the banister and felt the sharp pokes of peeling paint against his palm. He crept up the stairs, ready to duck and freeze in place if any sound or movement alarmed him.

On the small landing by the door, he leaned his back against the wall. He slowed his breath and listened for any sound emanating from the house. In less than two minutes, he was ready to move again. He attached the suction cups of his tool to the window in the door and scribed a circle on the glass at dead-bolt level. Pulling it loose, he carefully set it down in the corner of the porch and put away his cutting tool.

Reaching in through the window, he flipped the dead bolt then reached down further to turn the lock on the door knob. He paused to listen again before easing open the door. He was in a small galley kitchen. At the end of it, a door led to the basement. To the right, an archway led to the dining room.

He set the candle in the middle of the dining-room table and lit the wick. Returning to the kitchen, he turned on two burners on the gas stove. He then went down the rickety wooden stairs to the basement.

In less than a minute, he located the natural gas drip cap. Using the wrench, he turned it open without any difficulty. He hurried back up the steps. Leaving the basement door open, he checked the burners on the stove and saw that the flames had flickered out. Gas was no longer getting to the stove. He set the knobs to the automatic pilot setting, knowing that when the fumes reached the stove, the explosion would rip the house apart.

He looked at the burning candle on the dining-room table and smiled. Odds were the stove would ignite the fumes first but he knew the airflow patterns could be unexpected. That the old-fashioned simplicity of the candle might do the trick pleased him, bringing a soft smile to his face.

He opened the back door to make his exit but when he did, he found the barrel of an AK47 pointed right at his heart. A man dressed in black held the weapon steady.

Before Trappatino could react, he heard the front door burst open and the sound of feet moving rapidly in his direction. Before he could analyze his situation, he felt a barrel in his back and hands pulling his arms behind him and slapping cuffs around his wrists.

Trappatino heard feet pounding up the stairway to the second floor as he was jerked out of the house and dragged, stumbling down the steps. He hoped that they wouldn't figure out what he had done until it was too late. He hoped the explosion killed not only his target but as many law enforcement personnel as possible.

FIFTY-ONE

Jake threw open the door on the plane and waited impatiently for the steps rolling in their direction.

'You're not going to take a flying leap, are you?' Lucinda asked.

'I know you think highly of my abilities but I doubt I can make the jump to the ground without damaging one body part or another.'

'Good. Men don't always employ common sense in these situations.'

'Don't start with the stereotypes, Lucinda, or I'll make you squirm with a few of my own.'

Lucinda chuckled as the steps clicked into place. Jake snapped the locks and began his descent. A suited man took the steps two at a time as he raced up to meet them. He stuck out his hand and said, 'Special Agent Racanelli. They've got him in custody and are transporting him to the field office right now.'

Jake introduced Lucinda as they traversed the parking lot to the waiting black SUV. Racanelli ran down the events of the evening including the discovery of the gas leak, the evacuation of the neighborhood and securing the scene from explosion.

'What about Bonnie? Or Olivia? Is she OK?' Lucinda asked.

'We don't know,' Racanelli said.

'What?' both Lucinda and Jake said in unison.

'Well, we found a woman in the residence but it wasn't Olivia Cartwright.'

'Who was it?' Jake asked.

'Selma Upchurch Boone, Olivia's sister.'

'Where is Olivia?' Lucinda asked.

'No one knows. Selma lives in Knoxville, Tennessee, and is up here to visit her sister. On her last trip up, Olivia had given Selma a key so when she arrived she went into the house and made herself at home. A little after eight o'clock, Selma got a frantic call from her sister telling her that someone was watching the house and she needed to leave immediately.'

'Why didn't she go?' Jake asked.

'For years, she's gotten one paranoid call after another from her sister. They were all false alarms. Selma said that she was tired from her travels and decided to ignore this one, figuring when the morning came, her sister would show up, a little embarrassed by yet another senseless round of fear, but doing fine.'

'Oh, yikes, what a bad time to ignore her warnings,' Lucinda said.

'Well, Selma was sort of philosophical about it. She said that it must not be her time to go and something about her sister crying wolf too often. I was rather shocked at her cavalier attitude considering how close she came to being blown to pieces. When I pointed that out to her, she just shrugged.'

'We need to find her sister,' Lucinda said.

'Yes, Lieutenant, we're working on that,' Racanelli said in a voice more appropriate in *Mister Roger's Neighborhood*. 'We've issued a BOLO – that's Be On the Look-Out – for Ms Cartwright.'

'Jeez, Racanelli, the lieutenant here is a homicide cop. She knows the lingo,' Jake said.

Racanelli shrugged. 'Hey, you know, she's not FBI. You know what I mean?'

'You see, Jake, that's just what I've been talking about for years. Arrogance. It's as natural to an FBI agent as breathing. That's what's behind that special agent crap. You all think you are so special. So above us ordinary cops,' Lucinda ranted.

'Aw, jeez, Racanelli. Look what you started,' Jake moaned.

Racanelli laughed. 'Yeah, what did I always say, Jake? They're all pissy and oversensitive. It all has its root in their jealousy and feelings of comparative incompetence.'

'Shut up, Racanelli. Just shut up,' Jake ordered.

Racanelli chuckled in amusement. Lucinda folded her arms across her chest. Jake placed a hand on her arm. She shrugged it away and looked out the window away from both of them.

Lucinda wondered why many people felt the need to put someone else down in order to feel good about themselves. She knew that Racanelli's comments said far more about him than they did about her but she doubted he was even aware of that fact. Yet, still, it rankled. There is nothing more debilitating than belittling by another professional in your field. It felt like betrayal. And it often seemed so short-sighted. No matter what your profession was, an attack on one member of that group brought down the public perception of all of your peers. In this case, the comments were all in-house, so to speak. But she was certain Racanelli did not hesitate to put down any and all non-FBI law enforcement members over dinner, on an elevator or in a million other places where it could be overheard.

Lucinda sighed deeply but was not aware she had done so until Jake gave her hand a squeeze. She turned toward him and flashed a weak, tight smile. She certainly would be glad when she saw the back of Special Agent Racanelli.

When they reached the field office, Racanelli led them into the strategy room. Photos of Trappatino spanning a decade were fastened to the wall with crime scene photos taped beneath each one. On the long conference table were stacks of murder books – the suspected homicide history of the man they now had in custody. Jake and Lucinda started at opposite ends of the table, absorbing as much as they could in preparation for taking part in the questioning of Julius Trappatino.

They hadn't met in the middle yet when an agent burst into the room. 'Selma Boone just got a call from her sister.'

Lucinda and Jake followed the agent down the hall to the room where Selma sat in a stark wooden chair in front of an aged wooden table. She was a tiny, thin woman who looked younger than her years with a heart-shaped face, cupid-bow mouth, smooth, youthful skin and short brown hair streaked with gray – the only telltale sign that she was past forty. She wore an ecru, cotton, short-sleeved sweater hanging over a pair of jeans. Lucinda instinctively knew that the lack of jewelry and make-up was not Selma's usual look but only the by-product of being awakened suddenly and hustled out of the house without any time to tend to her appearance.

'Ms Boone,' Lucinda said, 'I understand your sister called.'

'Yes, ma'am.'

'What did she say?'

'She was in a bit of a tizzy because she drove by the house to check on me and saw all the police cars and yellow tape outside her townhouse. She wanted my reassurance that I had gotten away before anything bad had happened. I told her that nothing bad had happened except for being rushed out of the house by men dressed in black with no idea of where they were taking me.'

'How did she respond to that?' Jake asked.

'She got angry and started yelling at me for not heeding her warning.'

'Did you tell her we wanted to talk to her?'

'Yes, sir. She told me that if she pulled into the parking lot, she'd be shot dead before she could get inside the doors. She said she knew that's what happened to some guy named Rowland. She said he went to the FBI and all it got him was dead.'

Jake winced at that assessment but accepted that it was true. 'Listen, Ms Boone, Lieutenant Pierce here is not FBI. You think she might talk to her if you called her back?'

'Maybe. But now that her paranoia has been reinforced by what just happened, I can't say for sure.'

When they were set up to record and trace, Selma followed Jake's directions, placing the cell on the table and turning on the speaker phone. Olivia answered with a curt, 'Yes, Selma.'

'Olivia, I have a homicide detective here. She's not FBI but she thinks she can get you in here safely. Will you talk to her?'

Olivia let the silence hang in the air for a long thirty seconds. Then she said, 'Is she local law enforcement?'

'Yes, but not here – she came up from Virginia.'

'Virginia?' she said. 'Has she connected me to anyone in Virginia?'

'I don't know,' Selma began.

Lucinda joined the conversation. 'Ms Cartwright, yes we have. We have connected you in some way to three different individuals currently in the state.'

'Are any of them alive?' Olivia asked.

'One of them,' Lucinda said.

'Probably Tess.'

Lucinda felt her heart beat harder. 'What is Tess's last name?'

'I don't feel comfortable doing that on a cell phone – as I'm sure you know, they are very vulnerable to security hacks.'

'Let me pick you up and bring you in.'

'No. I won't make it to the door.'

'Yes, you will, Olivia. I'll drive you through the manned gate and into the secure garage. We'll take the elevator up. You'll never be outside and exposed for a moment.'

After another moment of silence, she said, 'There's a chiropractic center in the twelve hundred block of Chambers Street. Pull up in front of it, open the passenger door and I'll come out and jump in your car.'

'OK,' Lucinda said, jotting down the address.

'And don't come in a marked car or in one of those black monstrosities that look like they belong to the FBI or a gangster.'

'OK.'

'And come alone. If I see anyone else in the car, I won't come out. If I see any cars following you, I won't come out.'

'All right, Ms Cartwright. When do you want me there?'

'Twenty minutes. It's less than a ten minute drive so you should have no problem getting here on time. If you're more than five minutes late, I'll be gone. And it won't be easy to find me again.' Olivia terminated the call.

'All I need now is a non-threatening vehicle to drive,' Lucinda said.

'I can take you in my personal car,' Agent Racanelli said.

'Weren't you listening, Agent?' Lucinda snapped. 'I need to be alone when I pick her up.'

Without responding to Lucinda, Racanelli turned to Jake. 'You are not going to let her go out there alone, are you? If it needs to be a solitary person, we do have a female agent who could do it. Cartwright won't know it's not the woman she talked to.'

'Shut up, Racanelli,' Jake said, 'and give the lieutenant your damn car keys.'

'How can I trust her with my car? How can we trust her not to screw this up?'

Jake stepped forward into Racanelli's space, his chest nearly bumping the short man in the chin. 'Because she is twice as smart as you, has at least double your experience and because I trust her a hell of a lot more than I trust you.'

'Fidelity, Bravery and Integrity stand for something, Lovett. Or have you forgotten?'

'Do I need to call your SAC or will you accept my order and turn over your keys?'

Racanelli opened his mouth but thought better of making another comment. He pulled his car keys out of his pocket, tossed them on the table and left the room.

'Good riddance,' Lucinda said as she scooped up the keys.

'I'm sorry, Lucinda,' Jake said.

'Not your fault, Jake. It looks like he drives a Ford. I'll go down and click the door button and find the car that responds.'

'I can ask him what he's driving and where it's parked,' Jake offered.

'Oh, please, don't give him that satisfaction.'

In the garage, Lucinda had to roam around, following the sound of the unknown vehicle. It took three presses of the remote before she found a light tan Ford Focus with a Rutgers University sticker in the rear window.

With instructions from the GPS, it was easy to find the address. She did it in less than eight minutes. She pulled up in front of the building, got out, opened the passenger door and slid back in behind the steering wheel. She focused on the chiropractic office entrance, looking for Olivia Cartwright. Then, suddenly, a woman with a size and facial features similar to Selma's slipped into the car and pulled the door shut.

'Where did you come from?' Lucinda asked.

'You don't need to know,' she said and proceeded to ball up her small body in the foot well of the front passenger seat.

'What are you doing?'

'I don't want anyone to see me. Just drive.'

Lucinda pulled away from the curb and said, 'OK, now, tell me Tess's last name.'

'Don't talk to me. Someone will see you. Someone will guess I'm in here and then we're both dead.'

Lucinda rolled her eyes. 'Just answer that one question.'

'No. Stop talking to me or I'll jump out of this car whether you stop or not.'

Lucinda glanced to her left and was delighted to find a child lock. She engaged it but didn't call Olivia's bluff. 'I will look straight ahead. I will keep my lip movement to a minimum. Just answer the damned question because I won't shut up until you do.'

Olivia glared up at her, then said, 'Scott. Tess Scott. Oh, wait, it's Tess Middleton now. Now, please, no more questions until we reach safety.' Olivia bent her head down and wrapped her arms over it like a little school child in a 1950s filmstrip demonstrating the duck and cover position during an air-raid drill.

Lucinda wanted to clap her hands with delight over the connection to Tess Middleton but kept them firmly on the steering wheel. She was certain that Bonnie/Olivia possessed all the information needed to make sense of all the disparate puzzle pieces strewn around in her head.

FIFTY-TWO

'Hey, Lovett,' Racanelli said as he walked in the room. Pointing a finger at the agent, Jake said, 'Don't start.'

'Hey!' Racanelli said, throwing out his hands and pulling his neck down into his shoulders. 'Just wanted you to know we found two phones in Trappatino's car. One is connected to a regular AT&T cell account listed in the name of Joseph Trevor, the other is a prepaid disposable with no record of any calls and only one phone number in the contact list.'

'Any name with that number?'

'Nope. It leads to another disposable.'

'Interesting,' Jake said. 'I guess we'll have to call that number and see what we can find out.'

Racanelli left the room and returned with the phone, handing it to Jake.

Jake placed it on the table, dialed the number and turned on the speaker. The call was picked up in the middle of the first ring. 'Is it done?' a female voice asked.

Jake did not know what to say so he remained silent.

'Trap. Answer me.'

'What?' Jake said.

'Stop toying with me. Is it done?'

'Is what done?'

'Stop jerking me around.'

'May I ask who this is, please?' Jake asked.

The woman gasped and disconnected the call.

Jake turned to Racanelli. 'Trap as in Trappatino?'

'Maybe.'

'I think I'll go see what Mr Trappatino has to say about that.'

'OK, let's go,' Racanelli said.

'I don't think so – I'll talk to him one-on-one.'

'You're shutting me out?'

'Yeah, Racanelli.'

'You've got to be kidding.'

'No. Not at all. I don't trust your judgment and because of that, I will not be comfortable with you in the room. I don't mind, though, if you watch the live video in the control room.'

'You son of a bitch.'

'I'd prefer, if you call me names, you to pick something that does not reflect negatively on my mother,' Jake said and walked down the hall, listening to Racanelli grumble behind him.

Jake studied the killer in the control room before going in to question him. His body was lanky but well developed. Muscles strained against the sleeves and shoulders of his shirt. His hair was black and medium length. Stubble darkened his face. His mouth was set in a look of disdain. His eyes were devoid of any expression – they sat in his sockets, obviously alert, but cold under half-elevated lids.

Jake flipped the chair around and straddled it backwards. 'Well, Mr Trappatino – or should I call you Trap?'

Trappatino did not respond – he stared straight ahead at Jake's face.

'We found a cell phone in your car. It only had one number on it so we called it. What do you think we heard?'

Trappatino languidly closed his eyes and opened them again.

'Well, I'll tell you. A woman answered. And she said: "Is it done?" Now, I was wondering what she was talking about. What did that woman want you to do?'

'You're in the FBI. You figure it out.'

'I imagine I will. At this point, I'd say it was connected to your little escapade that we interrupted. I imagine you were hired to kill Bonnie Upchurch, now known as Olivia Cartwright – is that right?'

Trappatino blinked but did not say a word.

'Well, I hate to tell you this, Trap, but even if you had succeeded with that explosion, you would have failed in your mission. Sure people would be dead, but the one you were hired to kill wasn't in the house.'

Trappatino's eyelids lowered further until he peered out of narrow slits. 'Bullshit. I saw her.'

'Oh, you saw a dark-haired, petite woman who looks an awful lot like the old Bonnie Upchurch but it wasn't her. It was her sister.'

'You're lying.'

'I can't wait until the lieutenant brings Olivia Cartwright back here. I'll let you have a glimpse of her and her sister together. I'll bet you won't be able to tell which woman you saw go into the house. In the meantime, why don't you fill me in on who hired you to kill that woman?'

Trappatino laughed. 'Just like that, hunh?'

'It would save us both a lot of time.'

'Right now, time is not my big concern.'

'I can't argue with that,' Jake said.

'Wouldn't do you much good if you tried.'

'You know, Trap, I understand why you never rolled on one of your clients. That wouldn't be good for business. But now, the situation has shifted. You have no future in the killing business.'

'People just like you have said that to me before.'

'But see, Trap, here's where this case is different. We caught you red-handed in that rowhouse. You're not going to be able to wriggle and slip away laughing at all of us. This time, the evidence is there and you were there. And at this moment in history, post 9/11, we can slap terrorism charges on you on top of the breaking and entry, attempted arson and attempted murder charges. All the prosecutor has to do is whisper "terrorism" and you're toast. Life in prison at the minimum.'

Trappatino shrugged.

'We're going to find out who hired you, Trap,' Jake continued. 'And when we do, that person will want a lawyer and that attorney will advise the client to claim that you acted on your own. And that person will pretend to be in shock. If it's a woman, she'll dress in black, cry and point a well-manicured finger in your direction – making sure her hand shakes, just a little bit, when she does to add credence to her testimony. You stay on this ship, Trap, and you're going to sink beneath the waves all by your lonesome.'

Trappatino turned his face a little to the left and stared into the space over Jake's shoulder.

'Yeah, well, just saying, Trap. You think about it. I've gotta run right now. But I'll be back.'

Jake walked out of the room, shut the door behind him and leaned against the wall. He was very pleased with that interview. He'd got nothing from Trappatino but he'd planted the seeds. After the killer had a bit of time to think it over, he may decide to cooperate. Then again, it could all backfire. The thrill of not knowing surged through Jake's veins.

FIFTY-THREE

Arriving at the FBI field office, Lucinda escorted Olivia Cartwright inside. She allowed her to spend a moment with her sister Selma. She watched as they embraced and shed tears over their reunion. Lucinda was shocked by how much they looked alike. The hairstyles were similar but one was highlighted, the other unaltered; it was the only way she thought that she could tell them apart. She knew, though, if they dressed alike and both colored and brushed their hair the same, she wouldn't be able to tell which one was which.

The sisters didn't want to separate. Lucinda gently parted them and put each woman in a different room. She sat down with Olivia

Cartwright, waiting patiently while the woman composed herself. 'Ms Cartwright, could you please tell me how you know Tess Middleton?'

Olivia patted a tissue to her eyes and said, 'She was Tess Scott when I knew her back at high school.'

'Did you know her well?'

'Not really. She was the most popular girl. Sometimes she noticed me. I was just a hanger-on who waited on the sideline wanting to be acknowledged.'

'Did you also know Charles Rowland?'

'Chuck? Yeah. What a loser. But he would do anything Tess asked. I got the impression that she allowed him close to her because she liked having a lap dog.'

'Candace Eagleton?'

Olivia furrowed her brow and shook her head.

'Sorry,' Lucinda said. 'She would have been Candace Monroe.'

A smile flashed across Olivia's face, lightening her grim expression. 'I liked Candace. She was very nice to me. She was one of Tess's close friends but she wasn't at all like Tess. She seemed to really like people in general and me in particular. She called me 'Upgirl.' Definitely a better nickname than the one I got most often.'

'And that was?'

Olivia rolled her eyes. 'Upchuck, of course.'

'Oh, I should have known.' Lucinda winced as she thought about how dreadful that had to be for any kid.

'How did you feel about Tess?'

'At first, I was in awe of her. I know that she acted like a queen bee most of the time and was incredibly condescending to me. But I so desperately wanted to be part of the in crowd that I overlooked that and became one of her worshipers.'

'Did that change?' Lucinda asked.

'Oh, yes, most definitely.'

'When did that change?'

'When she started threatening me. That's when I realized that she might be dangerous. That's when I began to fear her.'

'Is that fear what made you move so many times?'

'Yes. I moved to Dallas. And she found me. I couldn't believe it. So that's why I changed my name legally and moved to Reno without leaving a forwarding address. But I have to admit, I'm not sure if I can directly blame her for my subsequent moves. I grew fearful that she'd find me in each place. It all made sense to me at the time but when you talk to my sister, I'm sure she'll tell you I just grew paranoid over meaningless incidents. Selma's put up with a lot from me over the years.'

'If you are so afraid of Tess, why did you move back to Trenton?'

'For one, I knew she no longer lived there. And I thought enough time had passed that I really had no grounds to continue to worry and fret over that woman. I thought my new name would protect me. And I had that soul-deep urge to return to my roots as I got a little older.'

'Let's go back to the threats. Why did Tess threaten you?'

'Because I knew her secret. Because she wanted to make sure I did not reveal it.'

'What secret, Ms Cartwright?'

Olivia opened her mouth, shut it and looked down at the table while she fiddled aimlessly with her fingers.

Lucinda bent her head down towards the table and looked up at the silent woman. 'Ms Cartwright.'

Olivia turned her face away but not quite quick enough – Lucinda saw the tears welling in her eyes.

Placing her hand on Olivia's hands, Lucinda said, 'Tell me. You've been keeping this secret a long time. It will do you good to let it go.'

Olivia shook her head and raised it to look at Lucinda. 'I'm sure, for a moment, I will feel better; but, in the long run, it will entangle my life in the sordid actions of Tess Middleton. I could go to jail.'

Lucinda sat up straight and studied the woman in front of her. 'Tell me, Ms Cartwright: whatever happened, did you take an active role in it?'

Olivia furrowed her brow and moved her mouth from one side to another. 'I did show up. But I had no idea of what would happen when I did.'

'Then you shouldn't have to worry about being charged.'

'I think you're wrong. All I did was observe but I should have reported what happened to the police and I didn't. I think they call that accessory after the fact. A person can be charged with that, can't they?'

'Yes, but how old were you when this event happened?' Lucinda asked.

'I was sixteen. Old enough to know better.'

'I don't know about that, Ms Cartwright. I promise you that I will run interference for you. I can make a strong case to the district attorney that you were living in a state of fear and have continued to do so for decades. And if worse comes to worst, I would testify at your trial – but I don't think it will come to that.'

'Lieutenant, I apologize in advance because I don't mean to offend you. But I have to say this.'

Lucinda nodded. 'Understood.'

'You see stories all the time about how cops can lie to you, can promise you things and then are never held accountable. How can I trust what you are saying?'

Lucinda reached out for her water bottle and took a sip. She was pleased to see Olivia lift her water bottle to her lips, mirroring her actions. That told her the rapport was built – Olivia was on the edge of talking. All she needed was a little reassurance. 'I won't lie to you, Ms Cartwright – that does happen. In fact, it is something I have done from time to time. But I'm not doing it now. All I can do to convince you is offer to put it in writing, sign it, date it and give it to you. And if that's what you need to feel safe, I will do it.'

Olivia studied the surface of the table for a long minute. When she lifted her head and looked at Lucinda, she said, 'That won't be necessary, Lieutenant.'

'You'll tell me Tess's secret?'

'It's my secret, too,' she said.

Lucinda nodded. 'I understand.'

Olivia inhaled deeply. 'Tess was dating the high school quarterback – actually, they were going steady. They'd had a big fight because he told Tess he needed to study but someone reported back to her that he'd been out that night and there was another girl in his car.

'Tess confronted her boyfriend and he admitted that he'd gone out with Lindsey Barnaby and said that he screwed her in his back seat. When Tess ordered him to come with her to confront Lindsey, the quarterback refused. That's when she called me and Candace.' Olivia paused and took a gulp out of her water bottle.

'What did you do then?'

'Candace and I met Tess at her house. Tess said that Lindsey needed to be told in no uncertain terms to leave her boyfriend alone. She wanted us to be with her so that Lindsey would realize she was serious. Then, Tess instructed Candace on what to say and had her call Lindsey.'

'What did Candace tell her?' Lucinda asked.

'She said, "Lindsey, I really, really need to talk to you. It's really important. And I need you to keep it secret. I know I can trust you. Please, please, meet me on the Field Hockey playing field at the school." Lindsey agreed and we three piled into Tess's car and went to the field to wait for her to arrive.

'Lindsey was surprised when three of us piled out of the car. She said, "Candace, what's going on? I thought you wanted to talk to me alone." And Tess said, "No, bitch, I'm the one who wants to talk to you." Lindsey asked why and Tess shoved her, knocking her to the ground. Tess stood over Lindsey and yelled at her, telling her to leave her boyfriend alone. That's when Lindsey made her mistake,' Olivia said, and now her tears flowed freely. For a moment, her whole body racked with sobs.

Lucinda waited for the emotions to run their course and then quietly asked, 'What did Lindsey do?'

'She jumped to her feet, walked up into Tess's face and shouted, "If you can't keep your boyfriend, it's not my fault. Maybe, like he said, you're always on the rag and smell like it, too." Tess backed away from Lindsey. I thought she was intimidated by Lindsey's response. I thought she was just trying to get away from her. I didn't realize what was going to happen. But, suddenly, the trunk of Tess's car was open and when she spun around, she had a baseball bat in her hand. She raised it up and swung it at Lindsey's head.' Olivia's body lurched and a hand flew up to cover her mouth.

Lucinda was certain she was about to vomit. She grabbed the trash can in the corner and brought it to Olivia's side of the table. 'Here, if you have to, you can let it go in here.'

Olivia made tight shakes of her head, swallowed hard and said, 'I'll be OK. Just give me a minute.' She swallowed a few more times, wiped her lips with a tissue and took several quick sips of her water.

She inhaled deeply and continued. 'I can still hear the sound of the bat hitting Lindsey's head. It was a sickening thud that made my stomach flip and form a hard knot. I hear that sound in my dreams still. I don't think I'll ever forget it.'

'What happened then, Olivia?'

'Candace ran forward and placed herself between Tess and

Lindsey even though Tess had raised the bat up again and seemed ready to swing it one more time. Candace yelled at Tess and Tess dropped the bat on the ground. Candace knelt down by Lindsey and grabbed her wrist, dropped it and put a few fingers on Lindsey's throat. She turned towards us and shook her head. That's when I doubled over and threw up.

'I was down on all fours heaving when Candace said, "We have to call the police." Tess grabbed the bat again. I stumbled to my feet and threw my body at her. Tess stepped back out of my way and I fell to the ground at her feet. Tess said, "You two just better keep your mouths shut. My dad has lots and lots of money and lots of influence. He can get me the best lawyer in the country. And I'll tell him that the two of you tricked me. That you brought me out here under false pretenses. That you killed Lindsey. I will be believed, my dad will see to that, and you will go to jail." Candace said, "You can't be serious."

'That's when Tess laughed and laughed. When she stopped, she said, "Don't worry. You won't go to jail. I'll eliminate you just like her unless you swear to never say a word." Candace and I looked at each other, then over at Tess. She made us come over to Lindsey's body and place our left hands on it, raise our right hands in the air and swear that we would never say a word.'

'Then what did you do? Did you help her dispose of the body?'

Olivia's hand flew to her mouth and she shook her head back and forth. 'Oh, no. Omigod, no! Charles Rowland did that.'

'How do you know?' Lucinda asked.

'When we started to walk away – neither one of us was more than a mile from home – she grabbed me by the hair – I wore it quite long then – and she jerked me back. She said, "Tell Chuck to get his ass over here now. Don't tell him why. Just tell him I said so." I called him when I got home.'

'Do you know if he went?'

'I didn't know for a couple of weeks. Candace and I kept reassuring each other that Lindsey was alive – just badly hurt – and recuperating at a hospital. But we had our doubts and we needed to know for sure. So when Chuck got stink-face drunk at a party, Candace and I cornered him outside where he'd gone to take a leak.' Olivia laughed weakly. 'Best way to disarm a guy: catch him drunk with his fly down. Anyway, he admitted that he went with Tess that night and helped bury Lindsey's body.'

Lucinda knew the next question she would ask could possibly confirm Olivia's credibility or destroy it. 'Did he tell you where?'

'Sort of. He said that they drove most of the night – down to Virginia and into the mountains. He said he remembered seeing a sign for the Thomas Jefferson National Forest but wasn't sure if he was actually in the national park or not. But that's where they left Lindsey and then they drove back home. He said that Tess was grounded for staying out all night but his parents had more of a boys-will-be-boys attitude.'

'Thank you, Olivia. Here is a statement form,' she said, passing a piece of paper across the table. 'Would you please write down everything you told me and sign it on the line at the bottom?'

Olivia nodded.

'You can use the back if you need more space. I'll return as soon as I can.' Lucinda's heart pounded a tattoo in her chest. She raced down the hall in search of Jake.

She spotted him pouring a cup of burnt-smelling coffee in the break room. 'Tess Middleton is at the bottom of this,' she said, and related all she'd learned from Olivia.

'I need to confront Trappatino with this information,' Jake said, 'but I'm not sure if he's had enough time to marinate on my last words to him.'

'So why don't we go talk to Selma and see if she can confirm anything I learned from Olivia, first?'

When they did, they learned that Selma really had no details. She just knew that Olivia believed she was being threatened because she knew someone's secret. She knew that was why Olivia changed her name and kept moving across the country and back. 'I kind of hoped that now that she'd moved back to Trenton and was living in our family home, all this would be over. For a long time, I thought it was all senseless paranoia – a symptom of my sister's mental illness. I'm ashamed that I was so dismissive of her fear.'

Back in the hallway, Jake said, 'Are you ready to throw Tess Middleton into Trappatino's face?'

'Let me make a call and have someone pick her up and bring her in.'

'Can't that wait?'

'She's a powerful and wealthy woman, Jake. I'd hate to learn she heard we had Trappatino in custody and decided to make herself scarce.'

FIFTY-FOUR

J ake and Lucinda entered the room where Trappatino sat with a sneer embedded in his face. 'Hey, Trap,' Jake said. 'I'd like to toss a few names in your direction.'

Trappatino shrugged. 'What's with the scarred woman?'

'Where are my manners?' Jake laughed. 'I'd like to introduce you to your new worst enemy, Lieutenant Lucinda Pierce.'

'She a local cop?' he said with a chuckle of derision.

'I'm right here, Trap,' Lucinda said. 'You can direct any questions about me to me.'

'She thinks she's the shits, doesn't she?'

'And she is,' Jake said.

'OK, Lady Lieutenant, why don't you stand up and walk back to the door so I can check out your legs again? It seemed like they were long, lean and shapely.'

Lucinda's arm flashed across the table and her hand gripped Trappatino's collar and pulled him up out of his seat. 'Excuse me?' she said and then shoved him back into the chair.

'She's got a bit of a temper, hasn't she?' Trap said, rubbing a hand on his throat.

'As I was saying,' Jake began, 'we've already established your awareness of Olivia Cartwright, formerly known as Bonnie Upchurch – we caught you in a criminal act in her home. How about Charles Rowland? Know him?'

Trappatino stared straight ahead.

'Candace Eagleton?'

Still no response.

'How about Lindsey Barnaby?'

For a second, a furrow flashed across his brow and was gone. Jake looked at Lucinda, who gave him a slight nod. They both realized there was something different about the murdered girl's name and wondered if he had ever heard it before.

'Surely, you must know Tess Middleton.'

Trappatino gave them a cold, disinterested look.

'Well, you see, Trap,' Lucinda said, 'we think that she's the woman who hired you to kill Olivia, Charles and Candace. And she's probably going to be pretty pissed off when she learns you blew it this time.'

Jake said, 'In fact, once we pick her up, she'll probably give you up in a heartbeat.'

'She's a powerful woman, Trap,' Lucinda said. 'She has a major corporation and a political career to protect. She's going to try to pin everything on you. And she'll probably get away with it.'

'So here's your chance, Trap,' Jake said. 'Throw her under the bus before she runs you down like roadkill.'

Trappatino looked at Jake, running his eyes over the agent's face as if trying to memorize his features. He turned his gaze to Lucinda and repeated the study on her face.

'So what is it? Jake asked. 'Are you going to take the fall for a rich woman who can buy and sell you a hundred times over?'

'Or are you going to save your own ass?' Lucinda asked. 'We have two homicides in Virginia. Throw in how you terrorized your victims before they died and you'll be looking at lethal injection.'

Trappatino stared at her with a look of disdain.

'We don't kill as many as they do in Texas or Florida, but we really want to play a more prominent role in death penalty statistics. It's a matter of pride for the Commonwealth of Virginia.'

'I want to call my lawyer,' Trappatino said.

'Really? You disappoint me, Trap,' Jake responded. 'I thought you were smarter than that.'

'I bet you say that to all the girls,' Trappatino retorted. 'I'm not stupid. I want my lawyer.'

Jake and Lucinda looked at each other and rose to their feet. Both acting as if it didn't matter, they walked to the door. 'Someone will be in with a telephone shortly,' Jake said as he opened the door and they walked out of the room.

'Dammit,' Lucinda said once they were out of Trappatino's hearing. 'We blew it.'

'Not necessarily. His lawyer might steer him in the right direction. Terrorism charges are federal charges and a smart attorney will latch onto the significance of that very quickly. I'll have the agent who goes in with the phone remind him that he needs to inform his lawyer of those charges and see what happens.'

'I don't know, Jake. Trappatino has been in tight corners before and he's always walked. He has no experience with failure in the courtroom and because of that has no fear of the process. He probably believes he can sail on this one, too.'

'We'll have to make sure his lawyer sees how airtight the terrorism charge is. We'll have to make sure he understands his client could easily spend the rest of his life in jail.'

'But we foiled his attempt, Jake. Juries want to punish the successful killers far more than the screw-ups. And what do we have to tie him to the murders in Virginia?'

'We have DNA evidence for Candace and we'll find what we need for Roland. We may not get a death penalty but his lawyer will have to see that when we're done with his client, he will never see the outside of a prison again.'

'I hope you're right.'

Jake's cell rang and he looked at the screen. When he saw it was from an agent in his field office, he pulled Lucinda into an empty interrogation room, shut the door and put the call on speaker phone.

'Middleton is not at home, Jake. In fact, we've been told she's left the country.'

FIFTY-FIVE

'Where?' Jake asked.

'The guy didn't know.'

'What guy?'

'The guy that was at the house when we arrived.'

'Start at the beginning.'

'We got to the house and were greeted by a man and his dog. He invited us inside. At the dining-room table, there was another man with a pile of papers; apparently he was a real-estate agent.'

'And who's the guy with the dog?'

'He claims to be Middleton's fiancé. He said that she left him here to make arrangements for the sale of the house. She's taking a month-long sabbatical from her work at the corporation to raise the media's interest and plan her election campaign. He said that he'd be joining her in the next couple of days.'

'Where will he join her?'

'He doesn't know. He said it was a surprise. He said that when she arrived at her destination, she would have a courier deliver his flight tickets to him. He thought that was very romantic.'

'He's got no clue that he's probably just been dumped?' Jake asked.

'Not one little clue.'

'You believe him?'

'Yeah, he's as bright as a busted light bulb.'

'Keep him under surveillance just in case and flood the airport with agents. Check out any other mode of transportation out of the city, too. Is her car gone?'

'Nope. Her brilliant, self-proclaimed fiancé said that he put her in a cab to the airport earlier today.'

'OK, get busy. I'll get back there as soon as I can,' Jake said and disconnected the call.

'We need to get back there right away,' Lucinda said.

'Just as soon as I can locate the pilot – I'll get on that now.' Jake left Lucinda alone with her thoughts.

Has she already flown out of their grasp? Lucinda wondered. If so, where did she go? She suspected a fleeing Middleton would know enough to pick a destination that did not have an extradition treaty with the United States. And with her money, she could be comfortable in the most backward third world country. Would she elude justice? Would her absence make it impossible to get homicide convictions for the murders of Candace and Charles? And what about Lindsey Barnaby? Would those three cases remain open forever?

No matter how hard she thought about it, she could not envision a scenario that had a happy ending for herself or for the victims. She couldn't figure out how she was going to make Middleton pay.

An hour later when she boarded the plane with Jake, she still had no answers. And the agents from Jake's field office found no sign of Tess Middleton anywhere. Both she and Jake tried to sleep on the flight back but every time either one of them drifted off, they startled awake with one question in their minds: have the agents found Tess Middleton?

Every time the pilot responded that he'd received no updates from the ground. Lucinda felt she was drowning in helplessness. Nothing she could do while trapped in the air in that fancy tin can. She breathed a sigh of relief when they touched down in Virginia.

A car waited for them on the tarmac, dropping Lucinda off at her office. There were a few people present when she arrived that Monday morning but it was still early and many were not yet in for the day. At her desk, she logged into her email, hoping for reports with more information.

She clicked on an email from Lara Quivey. Lindsey Barnaby grew up just around the corner and four houses up from where Candace lived when she was in high school and on the same street as Bonnie Upchurch/Olivia Cartwright. It was pretty much a moot point now that she'd interviewed Olivia.

She sighed and noticed an email from the medical examiner's office. Attached to it was a toxicology report of the excised area around what appeared to be an intra-muscular injection site. The lab found the presence of Promethazine. The body of the message explained the significance of this discovery.

The investigator for the office contacted Candace Eagleton's primary physician, who informed them that the victim had a prescription for the injectable form of the drug because of severe anaphylactic reactions to bee stings. Further, the doctor said that she always had a sufficient supply for six injections and had not reported having to use any of them since the prescription was refilled. It was her normal operating procedure to do so.

Coordination with the forensic team revealed that the drug had not been found in the search of the home. That, combined with the presence of the drug in the excised area, led to the conclusion that some, if not all of the injections, were administered to the victim before her death.

'Promethazine is an antihistamine. Its side effects include drowsiness, blurred vision, involuntary muscle movements and spasms, a weakening of muscles and severe dizziness. In sufficient dosage, it could render a person incapable of defending themselves against an attack.'

Lucinda leaned back in her chair. The drug explained the lack of violent struggle – Candace would be incapable of anything but a weak defense. But, how, she wondered, would Trappatino be aware of her prescription? How would he know where to find it? Is it possible that Trappatino had nothing to do with her murder?

FIFTY-SIX

Tess Middleton directed the cab to the Hilton Hotel near the airport. She trusted Dufus the dog not to betray her plans but she knew the two-legged dufus she left at her home was not as bright as his pet. If he knew anything, there was a good chance he'd let it slip out to the first person who asked him.

If that happened, a search for Tess at the airport that night would be fruitless. By the time she flew out the next afternoon, anyone looking for her would have given up. She pulled out and examined her tickets. A non-stop flight to San Francisco in the name of Lindsey Barnaby – and the return ticket that she would never use. Passage on a different airline to Singapore. And tickets for a third airline to fly her to the Hulhole airport in the Maldives. She smiled. Paradise would be an excellent place to rebuild her life.

She double-checked to make sure she had the right passport. Opening up the blue booklet she saw her face staring back at her and the words that identified her as Lindsey Barnaby. She'd shredded her own passport and dropped the pieces of cross-cut paper into the James River to wash to the sea.

She had a fortune tucked away in overseas bank accounts and her lawyer had instructions to deposit any further earnings in a segregated account. Even if federal authorities managed to block her access to those newer funds, she still had sufficient assets to live very comfortably – luxuriously – for more than one lifetime.

Tess pushed down her anger at Trappatino's screw-up. Rage could only cloud her judgment. She needed to remain sharp and on top of everything until she reached safety. From there, she could plan her revenge. She'd dumped her disposable cell into the river, too, one piece at a time.

She'd booked the adjoining room next to hers, creating an imaginary lover to occupy it. Unlocking the connecting door, she went down the hall and entered the other room, opening it on that side as well. She made sure the bolt was thrown and the chain engaged on both doors leading to the hallway. She then unplugged a floor lamp on each side and placed it by those entrances to give her an extra warning should anyone try to enter.

Tess wanted to take a long, luxuriant soak in the whirlpool tub but feared it would make her too vulnerable in case the unexpected happened. She settled for a quick shower and then redressed completely before stretching out on the bed to get what sleep she could.

Anxiety over the next afternoon's events made sleep elusive. She assured herself that all she needed was rest. She could catch up on her sleep on board the plane – she had many hours of flying ahead. Knowing that, she drifted off but maintained the alertness of a cat, ready to jump at a moment's notice.

FIFTY-SEVEN

Lucinda called Jake and relayed her new reservations about the guilt of Julius Trappatino in the death of Candace Eagleton. 'I just can't put the pieces together in any scenario that makes sense. He couldn't have known about her prescription for the allergy drug.'

Jake was quiet for a minute and then said, 'Unless someone told him.'

'Who? If we go with the theory that Tess Middleton hired him, how would she know?'

'But it's the only thing that makes sense,' Jake said.

'Not with the administering of the Promethazine,' Lucinda insisted. 'That shoots holes in that scenario.'

'So what are you saying? That someone else killed Candace for some other reason and it coincidentally happened at the same time that attempts were made on the lives of the other two people who knew Tess Middleton's secret?'

Lucinda shuddered. 'Coincidence. I hate that word.'

'Yeah, but what are we left with?'

'Frank Eagleton,' Lucinda said.

'He has an alibi,' Jake said.

'Yes, but if you know something is going to happen, you can make sure you have an alibi.'

'Now you sound like a conspiracy nut.'

'I'm going to pretend you didn't say that, Jake,' Lucinda said. 'Now tell me: where is Tess Middleton?'

'Don't know. She was not spotted at the airport. No one using identification with that name passed through security yesterday.'

'Does that mean she lied to her fiancé? Does that mean she did not intend to fly out today?'

'Maybe. Or maybe she slipped past us using an alias.'

The silence stretched out as they both lapsed into thought. Then it hit her.

'Jake, don't a lot of people with false IDs use the identity of dead people?'

'Yeah. They get birth certificates. And social security cards. And then a passport.'

'She is using the name of one of her victims.'

'The murders are too recent. She wouldn't have time to get a passport in Candace's name and heaven knows, she'd never pass as Charles,' Jake argued.

'But she had plenty of time – thirty years, in fact – to assume an identity in Lindsey Barnaby's name.'

'Crap. I should have thought of that. I gotta run and get that name out to everyone.'

Lucinda hung up and wondered what she could do now. She wanted to talk to Frank Eagleton about his wife's prescription medication but knew she had to go through his attorney. She placed a call and was told he was in court. She left a message and fretted over her current state of inaction. She began perusing all the background materials provided to her by the research department, looking for something she might have missed or anything that might prompt a new line of inquiry.

Engrossed in her review, she grabbed her cell when it rang without looking at the screen.

'Lieutenant Pierce?'

The voice sounded familiar. 'Yes. Is this Mr Eagleton?'

'I was informed you called my attorney this morning.'

'Yes, I did. I told him I needed to speak to you.'

'He's going to be tied up in court all day today and I didn't want to leave you hanging. What do you need to know?'

Lucinda was perplexed. He was so adamant that everything go through his attorney. What game was he playing now? Has he had a change of heart about the investigation? Or is he playing me? Does he want to be helpful or is he feeling cocky? 'Mr Eagleton, I wanted to ask you about the emergency supply of Promethazine your wife had.'

'What about it?'

'Could you come to the justice center or could I come by your office so that we can talk?'

'No. Don't have time for that today. But if you have questions, I'll be glad to answer them right now.'

Lucinda thought about waiting until she could meet with him face-to-face. But when would that be? She decided to get what information she could while Frank was amenable to talking. 'Do you know if she had to use any of it since she got the prescription refilled?'

'I don't believe so. She had two doses left when she got it filled again and I don't think she used it once. Unless maybe she needed to inject the morning before she died.'

'Where are the remaining doses?'

'In the medicine cabinet in her bathroom.'

'You sure about that?'

'Yes. Even though we were sleeping in separate rooms, she always wanted me to know where to find her medication in case she was too incapacitated to inject herself.'

'It wasn't there, Mr Eagleton. Where else do you suppose it might be?'

'Not there? That makes no sense.'

'I didn't think so either.'

'I can look again when I get home. There should be eight doses remaining or at least seven.'

'And you know how to administer it?'

'Yes. I haven't done it more than two or three times in all the years we were married but I know exactly what to do.'

'Did you inject your wife on the morning of her death?'

'No. I did not. What's this all about?'

'I received toxicology results from the area around an injection site on your wife's body.'

'She must have gone out in the garden that morning and gotten stung.'

How convenient, Lucinda thought. He certainly had a quick response for that one. 'Does she spend a lot of time in the garden?'

'More than she should. She loved the flowers – and is especially fond of the scent of the roses. I've warned her about how dangerous it is for her to smell them but she never would listen.'

'I'm sure you did,' Lucinda said, trying to make her tone of voice believable. 'Thank you for your time, Mr Eagleton.'

'I'll call you tonight if I find her medicine.'

'You do that, sir.' Lucinda disconnected the call. She was certain she'd hear back that night – positive that he would find the Promethazine, one way or the other. She immediately picked up the landline and hit the extension number for the head of the forensics unit, Marguerite Spellman.

'No, Lieutenant,' she said, 'there was nothing of the sort in the medicine cabinet. In fact, there was nothing in there when we left. I removed every drug – prescription and over-the-counter – for possible testing. That cupboard was bare when we left the scene.'

'Look through the recovered contents again – just to be certain. I know that sounds lame, but please indulge me.' Lucinda's cell was ringing as she ended the call. 'Pierce.'

'Lindsey Barnaby has had an active passport for the last twenty-two years.'

'The same Lindsey Barnaby?'

'Same birth date. Same city of birth. Same social security number.'

'It's got to be Middleton.'

'That or a coincidence – someone heard of her death . . .'

'Don't start with that crap, Jake. It's just too connected to be unconnected.'

'Do you realize that makes next to no sense?'

'Don't be picky – you know what I mean.'

'Yeah, I do. We're checking now to see if that passport went through security. So far, it doesn't appear so.'

'Why aren't we at the airport?'

'I'm on my way to pick you up right now.'

Before she could insist that she do the driving, Jake was gone. She hated the way he drove – but she did love his car. She gathered her things and took the stairs down to the first floor.

When Jake's car pulled up, she noticed its usually immaculate exterior was covered with dust, and beneath that outer layer it was riddled with dings and scratches. 'What happened to your car?' she asked as she climbed in.

'The dirt and gravel roads of Albemarle County happened.'

'You've got to let me pay for the bodywork you need.'

'Only if it's a wedding present.'

'Wedding present? Who's the lucky girl?'

'Ha, ha, ha, Lucy.'

'You actually thought I'd accept that?'

'I was hoping.'

'That was the lamest excuse for a proposal I've ever heard.'

'What's a guy to do? When I'm direct, you blow me off.'

'You won't get commitment from me with trickery, Jake.'

'What will it take, Lucy?'

'Shut up and drive, Jake.'

'No. What will it take?'

'I told you that I wouldn't consider it until I'd finished with my surgical procedures on my face.'

'And yet, you keep putting them off.'

'Cut it out. I don't have the time right now.'

'You won't make the time because it's a handy excuse to avoid commitment.'

'We're working, Jake. Keep focused on the job at hand.'

'So why do I think that when all the surgery is over you'll put me off saying that you can't make a commitment until you can see out of both eyes.'

'They can't do that, Jake. They can't transplant an eye to replace the one I lost.'

'Exactly. Now you get my point?'

'Just drive, Jake. And don't miss the turn-off to the airport.'

Entering the airport, Jake stopped at several people who appeared to be innocuous travelers – some in business suits, others in casual wear. If Jake hadn't pointed them out she would have never suspected that they were part of the team searching for Tess Middleton.

Jake's cell rang. He listened without saying a word. Turning to Lucinda, he said, 'Lindsey Barnaby is booked on an American Airlines flight to San Francisco. Terminal C, gate twelve.'

They power walked over toward the security line for the terminal and scanned the waiting faces. Commotion erupted at one of the desks where TSA checked identification. A woman argued with the man at the podium and tried to jerk her passport out of his hand. Another uniformed man moved quickly in that direction. Suddenly, the woman broke free, turning toward Lucinda and Jake, revealing her identity: Tess Middleton.

She loped off back into the terminal with the pair hot on her heels. Lucinda's height helped her see above the mass of moving bodies. She shoved them to the side as she fought against the crowd moving straight at her. She thought she lost Tess then spotted her again, slipping into the ladies' restroom.

She signaled to Jake and dashed in after her. She looked around the room. No one in the open was Tess. She looked under the door of the first cubicle. She saw two pairs of legs – one adult, the other a child. The child jabbered away at someone she called 'Mommy.' Behind the next door, she saw a pair of legs with jeans draped around the ankles and moved on to the third one.

She saw no sign of occupancy. She pulled gently on the handle. Locked. Her heart pounded in her chest. Outside the restroom, she heard the sound of voices. Someone – probably Jake and maybe others – were blocking entry. Women's raised voices whined and objected. She moved to the fourth door. She saw a pair of legs and high-heeled shoes that could belong to Tess. The fifth cubicle appeared empty. She pulled on the door. It opened revealing nothing more than a vacant space with a toilet. The sixth space was occupied by a woman with dark legs. Not Tess.

She had two doors to consider. One was harmless. The other was her quarry. Her quarry was cornered. Could she be dangerous? Possibly. She would have to wait until everyone else left the room. She placed her hand on her gun but didn't pull it out – she didn't want to alarm anyone knowing their reaction could give an edge to Middleton.

The woman and a little girl exited their stall. The child looked at Lucinda and stopped chattering. Her mouth fell open and she stared at Lucinda's face. Lucinda smiled.

'Becca,' the woman said. 'It is not polite to stare. Come wash your hands.' She gave Lucinda an apologetic smile.

Lucinda shrugged in response. A teenager wearing jeans walked out of the second door and a woman of color left the sixth space – now only the two suspicious stalls remained. Lucinda wanted to pull her gun but still she waited. She heard the sharp clatter of the door latch being jerked back. Lucinda held her breath. The fourth cubicle door opened slowly. Lucinda grasped the handle of her gun and flipped off the safety.

Emerging, the woman recoiled at the intensity of Lucinda's stare. She sidled past the booths and left without washing her hands.

Lucinda pulled her gun. What now? She suspected whoever was in cubicle three would see her feet wherever she moved. Sneaking into the adjacent booth and aiming over the transom at her was not a reasonable option. She got into shooter's stance with the barrel of her gun pointing at the door and the occupant beyond it. 'Tess Middleton, I know you are in that booth. Come out with your hands on top of your head.'

No word was spoken. No movement made.

'If you don't come out of that cubicle, I am coming in. You may be hurt when I kick in the door. Please come out now.'

Still no response.

'There are FBI agents and police officers outside of the restroom door. You have no options left, Middleton.'

When silence filled Lucinda's pause, she raised up her leg and slammed the sole of her foot into the center of the door. Metal screeched, the door slammed backward and a woman screamed.

'How dare you? Do you know who I am? I have a right to privacy. What do you think you're doing?'

Lucinda grabbed Tess by the back of the collar, spun her around and pressed her face against the cubicle wall.

'You will regret this. You let me go immediately or I am pressing charges.'

'You do that, Middleton,' Lucinda said as she snapped a cuff around one wrist and jerked Tess's other arm behind her back.

'Unhand me. I am a candidate for the United States Senate.'

Lucinda clicked the other cuff home and jerked on the chain between to pull her out of the booth.

'I am the head of a major corporation. You can't abuse me and get away with it. I will sue and you will lose your job.'

'Oh, really, are you accepting applications at Scott Technologies?' Lucinda said as she pulled open the door to the hall and shoved Tess out in front of her.

Tess spotted a man in a TSA uniform. 'Officer, arrest this woman! She assaulted me in the restroom stall.'

The man looked away from her.

'I've got your badge number,' she shrieked at him. 'When I'm senator, you're toast.' Tess continued to bellow, threaten and cajole anyone who would listen all the way outside to a waiting marked police vehicle.

'Damn, I wish that woman would shut up,' Jake said.
'I'm sure she will right after she asks for a lawyer.'

FIFTY-EIGHT

L ucinda and Jake entered the interrogation room where Tess
Middleton waited with a scowl on her face. Lucinda stifled a
laugh thinking about how much Tess's political opposition
would love to get their hands on a photograph of Middleton with
that sour expression on her face.

'Ms Middleton . . .' Lucinda began.

Tess held up a hand. 'You can stop right there. You do not need
to read me my Miranda Rights. I will tell you right now that I want
my attorney and will not answer your questions until he is here
with me.'

'Nonetheless, ma'am,' Jake said, 'we need to go through the
proper steps in the process.' He read from a sheet of paper as Tess
looked away from him.

When he finished she turned back and glared. 'You will be sued
for false arrest, police brutality and defamation of character.'

'Ms Middleton,' Jake said, 'we are holding you on charges related
to the counterfeit passport you attempted to use at the airport.'

'You didn't find that alleged counterfeit passport in my posses-
sion. I want to call my attorney now.'

Jake and Lucinda looked at each other and rose to their feet.
'The deputies will arrange for your call as soon as you're transferred
to the county jail.'

'I want to speak with him right here.'

'This is not your corporation and we are not your employees,'
Lucinda said. 'You are under arrest and will be treated like any
other prisoner in the system. You are not special here, Ms Middleton.
And until you appear before a judge to argue about bail, you will
remain behind bars – and I imagine that the judge won't be too
keen about letting you out since you have already proven your
willingness to flee the jurisdiction.'

'You can't stand it, can you?' Tess asked.

Lucinda stared at her without saying a word.

'You are a lowly public servant and here I am, another woman who has succeeded beyond your wildest dreams. And on top of that, I am beautiful, my face is flawless – unfortunately you can't say the same. I wonder who you ticked off to get that damage to your face and I wonder something else, too: which one of my opponents paid you to have me arrested?'

'I thought you'd invoked your right to remain silent.'

'Only in response to your questions, Lieutenant. I will find out who bribed you. And I will take my revenge. Once I'm in the United States Senate, you'll never work in law enforcement again.' She darted her eyes over to Jake. 'Nor will you, Mr FBI agent.'

'That's Special Agent to you,' Lucinda snapped. 'In fact, it's Special Agent in Charge. You'd best heed that 'in Charge' part – your wealth and your political connections carry no weight here. And after your performance this afternoon, only your mother would vote for you.'

'When I am through with you, not only will they vote for me, they'll erect a statue in my honor and name their babies Tess.'

'Let's go,' Jake said, grabbing Lucinda's elbow and steering her towards the door.

Back in the hallway, Jake said, 'You can't fight her in a bitch-fest. She was never going to stop.'

'I know but she so infuriates me.'

'Me, too. Let's go nail her ass.'

They went into Jake's office and made a series of calls to anyone who'd been assigned by them to find information about Tess Middleton. The subpoena served on her banking records was the first thing to produce solid results.

An agent from the white-collar crime division of the FBI asked, 'Lovett, has she denied knowing Julius Trappatino?'

'We can't ask her questions until her lawyer is present.'

'She probably will deny knowing him, don't you think?'

'I suspect so,' Jake said.

'I've got what you need to impeach that statement. Lindsey Barnaby arranged for $20,000 to be transferred from her account to a bank in San Diego in the name of Junior Tavertino. We discovered that she'd received a deposit of that same amount from the account of Theresa Scott Middleton.'

'Middleton even had a bank account in the name of the woman she murdered?'

'Hard to believe, isn't it? Some people's arrogance knows no bounds. It's a common thing with white-collar criminals.'

'How do we prove that Junior is Julius Trappatino?'

'We've taken care of that; I wired a photo to the San Diego field office. They went by the bank and the teller who handed out the cash identified Trappatino as the man who collected the money.'

'Bingo!' Jake said.

'It gets better,' the agent said. 'Junior Tavertino paid cash for a ticket from San Diego to Seattle. A few days later, he paid cash for a ticket to New Jersey.'

'Good job. Nail it all down tight. We'll go see what we can weasel out of that Middleton woman. Even if she doesn't talk, we can get her on conspiracy charges.'

'What?' Lucinda said as he hung up the phone.

'We got her! Let's head over to the jail – I'll fill you in on the way.'

On the way over, Jake and Lucinda tamped down their excitement. They did not want to show their hand – or even let Tess or her attorney know they had one to play – until the moment was right.

Looking into the interrogation room, Lucinda groaned when she saw Stephen Theismann sitting next to Tess Middleton.

'What's wrong?' Jake asked.

'My very least favorite attorney.'

'Do you like any lawyers?' Jake asked with a chuckle.

'There is no "like" list for them – only a "tolerable" list and Theismann is not on it.'

'That will make taking him by surprise even more enjoyable,' Jake said and pushed open the door.

Theismann cut off Jake before he could introduce Lucinda. 'Lieutenant Pierce and I have a history.'

'Don't forget, Theismann, when your client Evan Spencer ignored your advice and told me the truth, I was able to eliminate him as a suspect.' As she spoke, Lucinda cut her eye over to Tess. She saw the woman's right eyebrow jerk upward for a second before settling back in place.

'Yes, Lieutenant, I am sure on rare occasions you are capable of playing fair.'

'Well, OK,' Jake said. 'Let's focus on the present situation. Your client handed a false passport to a TSA official at the airport. That is a federal offense. We also have reason to believe that she was involved in the death of the woman whose name was on that passport.'

'Agent Lovett, my client is a successful and influential CEO and a candidate in the race for the United States Senate. Your imagination is working overtime if you think she had anything to do with anyone's death.'

'I'd like to ask your client a few questions to see if we can clear this up, then,' Jake said.

Theismann nodded.

'Ms Middleton, do you know a man named Julius Trappatino?'

Tess furrowed her brow and shook her head. 'No, I don't think so – but I meet so many people in the course of my work and campaign that it's possible.'

'Do you know a man named Junior Tavertino?'

Tess smiled and shook her head. 'I don't think so – with the same caveat, Agent.'

'Surely if you sent that man twenty thousand dollars he would stick in your memory, wouldn't he?'

'Twenty thousand dollars? I don't know what you are talking about.'

'That's not what Trappatino says.'

Theismann placed a hand on Tess's forearm. 'Agent, could I have a moment with my client, please?'

'Certainly,' Jake said. He rose and left the room with Lucinda. In the hallway, they grinned at each other.

'He suspects we can prove that money transfer,' Lucinda said with glee.

'Suspects? I'd bet he's pretty damned sure of it.'

'I hope you're right,' Lucinda said. 'I'm going to go get a bottle of water; you need anything?'

'Yeah. A Dr Pepper.'

'Gag,' Lucinda said, wrinkling her nose. 'I forget you liked that carbonated prune juice.'

'Hey, I don't make fun of your secret passion for salted pumpkin seeds.'

'Jake, how you can even compare the two is beyond me.' She went down to the break room and returned with the two plastic bottles, handing the soft drink to Jake.

'Here,' he said, holding the can out to her, 'just taste it. It's really good.'

'I have tasted it. And I don't want to taste it again as long as I live.'

Theismann stuck his head out of the door of the interrogation room. 'Agent Lovett, my client has a statement to make to you.'

Jake and Lucinda walked through the doorway.

'Excuse me, Agent,' Theismann said. 'My client would like to speak to you – just you.'

'I can get your client taken back to her cell now, if she'd prefer.'

Tess widened her eyes and jerked her head towards her attorney. Theismann's nostrils flared and a small spot on his throat throbbed. Jake and Lucinda stood just inside the door with their arms folded across their chests.

Finally, Theismann broke the silence. 'Very well. But I want my client released as soon as she delivers her statement.'

'Well, Theismann, I guess that depends on what she has to say in her statement,' Jake said.

'Please, have a seat,' Theismann said.

Tess began when Jake and Lucinda settled into the chairs across from her. 'I do know Julius Trappatino. And I know the name Junior Tavertino. I admit they are the same person. I admit that I sent those funds to Trappatino under his alias. But no matter what he says, I did not pay him to try to cause harm to anyone. I paid him to find people for me. I wanted to talk to my old classmates. I knew I needed to tell the truth about Candace Monroe Eagleton's responsibility for the death of Lindsey Barnaby. I just wanted to give them all a fair warning first. I am a victim of Trappatino as much as any of them. I have been terrified that he was going to come after me next. That's why I was trying to leave the country. I was afraid.' Tess made a choking sound and pulled out a tissue to blot her eyes.

'Will your client be willing to write and sign a statement to that affect, counselor?'

'If she does, will you release her?'

'If and when we can verify the content of her statement,' Jake said.

Theismann looked at his client. Tess nodded. Jake pulled a form out of the drawer on his side of the table and slid it over to Tess.

'We'll wait outside while you prepare this,' Jake said. He and Lucinda left the room again.

Outside the room, Lucinda said, 'Creative. Very creative.'

'Naming a dead person as the killer of Lindsey Barnaby was a nice touch.'

'Doesn't get any better,' Lucinda said with a laugh.

'Listen, as soon as we have that statement in our hands and look it over for consistency with what she said, I want you to confront her with the information we got from Bonnie Upchurch/Olivia Cartwright.'

'What about Trappatino? Shouldn't he be confronted with what Middleton said?'

'Yes, I'll call the Trenton field office and get that done.'

Lucinda leaned against the wall, wondering where this would all go. She still had her doubts about Trappatino. The injection was troubling. How would he or Tess know about Candace's prescription? Something was missing. She wanted to close the case but only if the right people were facing charges. A conviction is no good if it's wrongfully obtained and the real killer continues to walk free.

Then again, how else could all these deaths and the attempted murder in Trenton hang together if not for a plan by Middleton and Trappatino? She didn't know and she didn't have a clue about how to answer the question about the injection that gnawed on the back of her brain.

Theismann interrupted her thoughts to tell her that the statement was completed. She told him that she and Agent Lovett would be with them in a moment. When Jake returned they stepped inside. They read over what Tess had written and slid it back across the table for her signature. Jake and Lucinda signed off on it and tucked it away in the drawer.

'Ms Middleton . . .' Lucinda began.

'Agent, I thought we were through here,' Theismann said.

'The lieutenant has a few questions for your client, first.'

'Do you remember Bonnie Upchurch from high school, Ms Middleton?' Lucinda asked.

'Vaguely.'

'Vaguely? Are you aware that she changed her name to Olivia Cartwright?'

A faint rosiness colored her cheeks. 'Yes. I learned about that when you arrested Mr Trappatino.'

'Not before.'

'No.'

'Are you aware of her claim that she changed her name because she was afraid of you?'

Tess snorted.

'I would advise you not to answer that question,' Theismann said.

'Oh, please, Stephen – they should know the kind of person they are talking to. Poor little Bonnie. Always afraid of her shadow. Given to paranoid delusions as long as I knew her. It does not surprise me at all. There was no reason for her to fear me but she feared everyone – it is meaningless.'

'Did you know that Bonnie claimed that you killed Lindsey Barnaby thirty years ago?'

'Oh, my. She worshipped Candace. She had to transfer her memory somewhere else. Tag, I'm it. It's really sad. I hope you will be able to get some help for that poor, tormented woman.'

'She also said that you and Chuck Rowland transported Lindsey's body down to Virginia and disposed of it in or near the Thomas Jefferson National Forest where her body was found.'

'Oh my, this is so terribly sad. I knew Candace had to have someone's help to dispose of the body. I suppose Bonnie must have been the one who helped her and now that poor woman can't face the truth of her involvement.' Tess shook her head. 'It's so sad. Is there anything I can do for her? I can afford the best mental institution, psychologists and psychiatrists. I want to help her in any way I can.'

'So that's why you paid Julius Trappatino to kill her?' Lucinda asked.

Theismann rose to his feet. 'Agent, that is enough. This reckless police officer is violating our agreement.'

'What agreement, counselor? Do you know of any agreement, Lieutenant?'

'Well, we did promise we would attempt to verify Ms Middleton's statement, didn't we, Agent Lovett?'

'Yes, we did. And counselor, that is what we are doing here.'

'This interview is over,' Theismann said.

'Certainly, Mr Theismann,' Lucinda said with a smile. 'Would you like to have a few words with your client before the deputy takes her back to her cell?'

'Agent Lovett,' Theismann said, 'before you send in a deputy, could I have a few minutes with my client?'

'Ask the lieutenant. I'm outta of here,' Jake said as he walked out the door.

Lucinda saw the muscles along Theismann's jaw tighten as he inhaled deeply. 'Yes, Lieutenant, I will take advantage of your offer. I'll let you know when we have finished.'

'Five minutes, Theismann. Five minutes and not a second more,' Lucinda said, then turned and exited the room.

FIFTY-NINE

After seeing that Middleton was returned to her cell and her attorney sent on his way, Jake and Lucinda headed back to the FBI field office. On the way, Jake received a request to fax Tess Middleton's written statement to an agent in Trenton.

It was the first thing Jake did when they arrived. He and Lucinda both got busy writing their reports about the interview with Tess Middleton for their respective agencies, both fearing that the powers-that-be would come pounding down on their heads on Tuesday. Arresting a prominent individual, no matter how guilty, always brought pressure to bear on the individual investigator.

After half an hour in the office, the phone on Jake's desk rang. Lucinda watched as the excitement in Jake's face escalated throughout the call. Jake was saying nothing more to his caller than yes or no or excellent, piquing Lucinda's interest.

He hung up the receiver and flashed a big smile at her.

'Well, what was it?' she asked.

'Trappatino has indicated his willingness to make a deal. Your district attorney is flying up to Trenton right now to meet with the federal prosecutor. After they coordinate their approach, they will meet with Trappatino and his attorney.'

'He has a lawyer now?'

'Apparently, until he saw Middleton's statement, he was not willing to make a deal. And until then, he didn't want an attorney.'

'I've seen federal and state prosecutors get together and make a deal with a killer before. I haven't been very pleased with the result,' she said, recalling the deal offered to a man she'd arrested two years earlier.

'I was assured by the field office that testimony against Tess Middleton is the prerequisite of any plea bargain.'

'I don't want him walking the street any time soon.'

'Nor do I but don't worry. They've filed the terrorism charges. There is no way that they're going to let him walk on that; it would cost the federal prosecutor his job.'

'That's some comfort, but I still don't trust him.'

'No matter what deal goes down, Lucinda, we will make things right, just as we did the last time. Just as we did before.'

'We got lucky.'

'No, we were smart. We caught the lie and avoided an unfair plea bargain. I'll be by your side, fighting with you for justice for Candace Eagleton and Charles Rowland. I'll be there for you with that, just as I am for everything – both professionally and person-ally. I understand your apprehension, Lucy, but I will never abandon you, not on any level.'

Tears burned in Lucinda's eye. She hated her emotional reaction – it felt weak and helpless. She turned her head and surreptitiously swept the moisture away with the back of a hand. She cleared her throat. 'Jake, we are in the middle of an important case. This is not the time and place for personal matters.'

'It never is, Lucinda. You can't hold me at a distance forever. We need to talk this through.'

'Later, Jake.'

'As soon as we wrap up this case?'

Lucinda didn't even want to commit to that but said, 'Yes,' anyway.

'Promise?'

'Jake, is that really necessary?'

'Yes.'

'Yes. Are you satisfied?'

'Yes. Yes, I am.'

'Good. Now, what's next?'

'The meeting with Trappatino and his attorney is supposed to happen at ten a.m. tomorrow morning.'

'Why aren't we there?'

'Because they don't want us there.'

'Of course they don't,' Lucinda said, her anxiety about the upcoming interview raised another notch.

'After we finish up these reports, we should get some rest. And tomorrow morning I can't see a reason why you won't be able to take Charley to the funeral.'

'I suppose not. The service starts at the same time as the meeting in Trenton.'

'I'll follow it closely and let you know if anything develops.'

'Yeah. It's too late to call Charley tonight but I imagine Kara's still up. I'll let her know not to send her off to school in the morning.'

'Are we good, Lucy?'

Lucinda smiled. Jake's unexpected flashes of vulnerability raised feelings of tenderness. 'Yes, Jake, we are good.'

The next morning, Lucinda donned a simple black dress and heels. She accessorized with the gold and onyx jewelry that one of her mother's friends had given her to wear to the funeral service of her parents so long ago. Fastening the clasp on the necklace, memories rushed back. She'd been angry back then that the adults arranged a service for two. Her father shouldn't have been there. He killed her mother then took his own life. She wished that no one had even claimed his body. She wanted him in an unmarked pauper's grave, not resting for all eternity by her mother's side. They said they did that for us – but why didn't they ask us if that was what we wanted?

That was why Lucinda no longer visited her mother's grave. Seeing the stone with both of their names, side by side, always made her angry – rage towards her father, irritation with her mother for marrying him and guilt-fueled disappointment in herself for not stopping her father from pulling the trigger the first time. She had no regrets for not intervening in the second shot – the one he put through his own head. She wished she'd spoken up and told him just to kill himself and leave her mother alone. If she had, would he have listened? That was a question that would never have an answer and it ate at Lucinda every time it crossed her mind.

She placed her gun and her badge in a black purse and walked out of her apartment. She stopped at her office to make sure no developments had broken in the night and then drove to the Spencer condominium.

When she walked in their front door she saw Charley standing still in the middle of the living room. She wore a black dress with off-white lace on the collar sleeves and the hem. It wasn't the same dress she'd worn to her mother's funeral service. Much to Charley's dismay, she'd outgrown that one.

Nonetheless, it still triggered an emotional memory of a little motherless child looking helpless and vulnerable, yet somehow strong – an incredible, somber child with a maturity beyond her years and a very adult way of demanding justice for her murdered mother. Lucinda crouched down in front of her and spread her arms wide.

Charley fell into her embrace and cried. 'It's just not fair, Lucy.'

'No, it's not, Charley. But, remember this, Mr Bryson is at peace now. All the demons that haunted him are gone.'

Charley pulled back and looked straight in Lucinda's face. 'Do you believe that? Do you really believe that?'

'Yes, I do. Are you ready to go?'

Charley nodded.

'Do you have some tissues?'

'Yes.'

'It's not too late to change your mind. You really don't have an obligation . . .'

'Yes, I do,' Charley said, sticking out her chin. 'He was my friend.'

'Yes, he was, Charley. Let's go, then.'

As they walked into the hushed sanctuary of the church, Charley wiggled her hand into Lucinda's. Lucinda looked down at her and smiled and gave her hand a squeeze. They walked up the aisle and took a seat in the fourth pew from the front. Lucinda noticed that Charley's legs still weren't long enough for her feet to touch the floor.

A closed coffin sat like a lone sentinel in front of the meager congregation. A huddled group of mourners sat close together on the front pew – Lucinda suspected they were members of Jim Bryson's family. Little clusters of two and three spotted the room. She hoped Charley did not ask why there weren't more people present.

The pounding, dirge-like sound of an organ announced the beginning of the service. In a moment, everyone joined in an anemic singing of 'Amazing Grace.' The only voice that rang loud and clear was Charley's bright melody. She seemed to know the words to all the verses which struck Lucinda as odd for the child of a Jewish mother and a lapsed Protestant. She was staring at the girl when the song ended.

When they sat back down, Charley whispered, 'Kara told me they usually sing that song at funerals. So I looked it up and memorized it for Mr Bryson.'

A lump rose in Lucinda's throat. Charley continued to surprise her all the time. Lucinda's mind drifted off as the minister spoke. She doubted he knew the deceased well. She planned on tuning in again when someone who did rose to speak. For the moment, she contemplated what was happening in Trenton. She slipped out her cell – she'd turned off sound and vibration but left the phone on so that she could check the screen. No calls. The minister's last sentence jolted her out of her reverie.

'Miss Charley Spencer would like to say a few words about her friend, Jim Bryson.'

Charley pulled a folded piece of paper out of a patent leather handbag. She rose, smoothed her skirt and walked up the aisle. Lucinda had no clue this was coming. Charley never said a word.

A man in a black suit slipped a set of portable wooden steps behind the podium and Charley walked up them and opened her paper, flattening it with her hands. The same man lowered the boom on the microphone and then faded backwards.

Charley looked over the people in front of her and then her eyes went to the shining coffin. 'Mr Jim Bryson was my friend. I will miss him every day when I come home from school. He used to meet me in the lobby every day after school. He'd ask me about school and most days he brought a bag of M&Ms. We'd sit on the sofa and talk. He smiled a lot. I thought he was happy. He never burdened me with his problems.' Charley choked on her words and tears streamed down her face. 'I wish he had. I wish I could have helped him. Goodbye, Mr Bryson.'

She walked down the steps and to the casket. She placed both palms flat on the highly polished wood and rested one cheek on its cool surface. Then she walked with the dignity of a grieving widow on the silver screen and resumed her seat.

Others said brief words about the deceased but none of them moved the audience like Charley had. After the service, she was embraced by nearly everyone in attendance.

While Charley was the center of attention, Lucinda pulled out her cell again. This time, she had a text message from Jake: Deal done. Middleton implicated. Meet with her & lawyer at 1. Be there?

Yes, Lucinda typed back and hit send.

Charley, satiated by the hugs and sympathetic words, stepped over to Lucinda and said, 'Thank you, Lucy.'

'Thank you, Charley. I am so proud of you. And I am proud to have been here with you.'

'I'm hungry,' Charley said.

Lucinda laughed. 'We do have time to stop for lunch before I take you home but then I have to get to work.'

'Another bad guy?'

'Jake and I have a couple of them this time.'

'Nail them to the wall, Lucy,' Charley said with unyielding seriousness.

Lucinda wanted to laugh at that phrase coming from the young girl's mouth. She wondered what movie or television show put those words into her mouth. She gave no indication of her merriment, though, when she responded. 'You know we'll do our best to accomplish just that.'

'Do you have any DNA evidence?'

'For one of them we do.'

'That sucker's dog meat,' she said.

Lucinda squeezed her lips tightly together to keep the threatened laugh inside.

SIXTY

S ergeant Robin Colter sat at a table near the door to the kitchen in the elegant Casa Barcelona, keeping a close eye on Frank Eagleton. She'd never been in a totally a la carte restaurant before and was alarmed at the prices. She knew she had to order or be escorted outside. Although she thought she'd be reimbursed, she didn't want to risk a high bill.

She asked for water for frugality's sake and was appalled when a bottle of Evian was delivered with a crystal goblet. When she demurred and requested tap water instead, the haughty waiter looked down his nose with a sneer and said, 'Madam, we do not serve tap water at Casa Barcelona.'

She smiled as she choked on the listed price: seventeen dollars. 'I don't particularly care for Evian, but I'll make do,' she said. She hoped the department would cover the expense.

'What else can I get for madam?'

Robin knew she had to order something. 'I'm not terribly hungry but a small salad would do.'

'And for your dressing, madam?'

She looked the list and saw there was an additional charge for all the dressings. She ordered the cheapest one: oil and vinegar. The small bowl of mixed greens and its simple accompaniment came to forty-five dollars – with the water, the cost of her Spartan meal was over sixty dollars. Robin was horrified.

She also noticed that her service was far slower than that at the table for four where Frank Eagleton held court. She'd come in right behind him and yet he'd been seated half an hour before her even though she could see a number of vacant tables waiting for diners. By the time her salad was set before her, Eagleton and his guests had finished their entrées and were having aperitifs or dessert.

She saw Frank raise his hand ever so slightly. The appearance of the waiter with the small portfolio containing the bill was instantaneous. Frank pulled cash from his pocket, loosened his money clip and stuffed the bills inside. The waiter bowed to him as he accepted the payment.

The four rose and walked toward the front door. Robin looked at her half-eaten salad and the expensive water and then stood and approached Eagleton's table. She grabbed the coffee mug he'd used, noting with dismay that there was still at least a half-inch of the liquid remaining in it. She carefully slipped it into the paper bag in her large handbag. She put one hand underneath her purse, hoping she could keep the cup upright.

Before she could return to the table to settle her bill, the waiter loomed over her. 'Madam, you have not paid for your repast.'

Thinking fast, she said, 'But Mr Eagleton said he was taking care of it.'

He looked down at her with an expression that said he knew she was a liar. 'Alas, madam, there must have been a communication gaffe. Mr Eagleton did not cover your bill. I apologize for that and will allow you to make good on your charges.'

'Of course,' she said, wondering how she was going to extract her credit card without upturning the cup. 'One moment,' she said and rested her bag carefully on the surface of the abandoned table. She stuck both hands inside, using one to steady the cup and another to manipulate her credit card out of her billfold.

As she struggled, the waiter tapped his foot impatiently. The maitre d' approached and asked, 'Is there a problem?'

Robin's hand emerged with her card and, handing it to the waiter, she said, 'Oh, no, not at all. Thank you for asking. I had a tiny difficulty locating my card, that's all.'

When the waiter returned with her card and receipt, she signed the bottom, added a fifty cent tip and extracted her copy of the bill. Walking out of the restaurant, she said a little prayer: 'Please let them find the DNA they need and please let me be reimbursed for that meagerly meal.'

SIXTY-ONE

B ack at the county jail, Lucinda and Jake nodded to each other before walking through the door to face Tess Middleton and her attorney. Each had a copy of Trappatino's statement in hand. They sat down at the table and slid both copies of the document across to lawyer and client.

Stephen Theismann looked at the paper in front of him, glanced over at the other copy and, realizing they were identical, began to read. Tess, on the other hand, looked all around the room at anything but the piece of paper or the faces of the investigators directly across from her. She wore a bland expression of disinterest and boredom. She clicked her fingernails on the table surface.

Theismann looked over at his client when he finished reading, and covered her busy hand with his. 'Agent, I need to confer with my client.'

'Certainly,' Jake said. 'But you should know, we are preparing arrest warrants charging your client with two charges of homicide, one of attempted murder and one of attempted flight to avoid prosecution. I suspect there will be additional charges before it's over.' The two investigators rose and left the room.

In the hallway, Lucinda asked, 'Did anyone ask Trappatino how he knew about the availability of the Promethazine in Candace's home? It's not in his statement.'

'Do you think he's lying about Middleton's involvement?'

'Not particularly. But what if someone else is involved and he didn't mention it?'

'Covering up for someone who hasn't thrown him under the bus?'

'Yes. He referred to Middleton as his contact and employer. But something in his statement makes me feel he's leaving out a detail or two.'

'What?'

'Frank Eagleton was a major donor to her campaign.'

'So were a lot of people. She has more than enough funding to buy her senate seat.'

'Oh, my,' Lucinda said through twitching lips, 'who's the cynic now?'

'Yeah, you got me. But here's my hang-up: two people dead, one survived a murder attempt. All knew about the murder of Lindsey Barnaby. That gives her clear motive, particularly if she'd been subject to extortion by one or more of them. But what does Eagleton have against the others? Have you found any connection between him and them?'

'No,' Lucinda said, shaking her head.

The door opened and Theismann invited them back into the room.

'One moment,' Jake said, pulling the door shut again. 'I want you to take the lead in there. It unsettles Theismann and I want him unsettled.'

Lucinda nodded and they went inside and resumed their seats. 'Ms Middleton, what do you have to say about Mr Trappatino's statement?' Lucinda asked.

'It's crap. Nothing but pure, unadulterated bullshit. All you have is a story created by a consummate liar who thinks he can play you to get a deal for the charges he's facing,' Tess said.

'OK, Ms Middleton, let's go through his statement and focus on his particular accusations. But first, do you have any proof that Mr Trappatino knew any of these three victims?'

'Of course not. I hardly know the man. And I haven't seen any of my classmates in ages.'

'But you have had correspondence with at least one of them a short time ago.'

'Exactly. A crazy, whacked-out email from Candace. That was one of the reasons I hired Mr Trappatino to find Bonnie – or I guess I should say Olivia. I wanted to arrange a meeting with her and me and Candace to put those crazy ideas to rest.'

'Why did you hire a man who is a known assassin?'

'I certainly didn't know that. I thought he was a private detective. If he's a hired killer, why haven't you arrested him long before this?'

'I'd like to know that, too, Ms Middleton. But I suspect you knew exactly who you were hiring, because you wanted the people who possessed your secret to die.'

Theismann interrupted. 'Agent, that is inflammatory speech. Can you please keep the cop under control or ask her to leave?'

Jake stared at him and then nodded to Lucinda.

'Well, Ms Middleton?'

'It's absurd. I am the CEO of a major corporation and a candidate for the United States Senate. The very idea that I would be hiring killers is ridiculous. You have nothing but the word of this known criminal.'

'You keep saying that, Ms Middleton. But you should know that we have someone who has made a corroborating statement.'

'That bastard. It was his idea. And when I turned him down, he went behind my back and contacted Mr Trappatino and subverted my purpose in hiring him.'

'What bastard, Ms Middleton?'

'You know very well who I am talking about.'

'Agent,' Theismann interrupted again, 'the cop is baiting my client.'

'Really? Well, let's nip that in the bud,' Jake said, leaning forward on the table and starring at Tess. 'What bastard, Ms Middleton?'

She slapped a palm on the table. 'That Frank Eagleton bastard.'

A charge of electricity surged across Lucinda's scalp and ran down her arms. The picture was now whole. 'What did he ask you to do?'

'I told you that I refused his request.'

'What was his request?'

'Ms Middleton, I think we ought to stop this right here,' Theismann objected.

'And have me delivered to that dingy cell again? If you could have gotten me out on bail, as you should have done, I wouldn't be in a position where I needed to prove myself.'

'We discussed this. The forged passport proved your intent and ability to flee.'

'And I told you that I just wanted to get away from all those crazy people.'

'Still, Ms Middleton, I am advising you of your right to remain silent.'

'I do not believe that is in my best interests,' she said, turning away from her attorney. 'Lieutenant, I hate to – what is the word – rat out? Squeal? Whatever. I hate to do that to another human but you have left me no choice. Frank Eagleton approached me. He said that he knew his wife was attempting to blackmail me. He assured me that he thought that was wrong of her. He said that she had been causing problems for him, too. She was holding some tax issue over his head, using it as leverage to get more from him in a divorce settlement. He said we could be partners because we both would benefit if Candace was dead.'

'And you sent him away?'

'Of course. Killing is wrong. There's always a better solution. Certainly, my life would be easier if Candace just disappeared. But wanting her dead, that was another story.'

'What did Frank Eagleton have against the other two victims?'

'I have no earthly idea. I don't think he even knew them. You know what I think?'

'No, what is that?' Lucinda asked.

'Well, for starters, that Trappatino man enjoys killing people – I'm sure you've met others like him. And Frank Eagleton wanted to get rid of his wife. The two got together and found a way they could both get satisfaction and frame me for these murders at the same time.'

'Really? How diabolical!' Lucinda said as she thought about the ludicrousness of Tess's conspiracy story.

'And you know what else? I am certain that my political enemies helped them. Those operatives have no scruples. They'll do anything to get a win for their candidate. They don't care if they destroy me. They don't care that I'm the best candidate for the Senate or that I could do a world of good for the Commonwealth of Virginia and this great nation or ours.'

Middleton's arrogance curdled in Lucinda's stomach but she was grateful for it – it was that characteristic that drove the woman to talk when she should remain silent. Lucinda hid her visceral reaction and spoke in a reassuring voice. 'For now, we'll have to send you back to your cell, Ms Middleton, at least until we talk to Mr Eagleton.'

'He's going to lie,' she sputtered.

'I don't doubt that. But trust me, we will find the truth – the whole truth.'

Tess Middleton blanched, recovered and said, 'Well, see that you do.'

SIXTY-TWO

'You knew it, Lucinda!' Jake crowed when they were alone.

'That does not make proving it any easier.'

'But you knew someone had inside information on Candace – someone had to tell him about the Promethazine. You nailed it.'

'Yes, but Eagleton has already lawyered up. Another round of his I-told-you-so bragging that he knew his wife did not commit suicide. Another tiresome blather about how that proves his innocence. We need to talk to Trappatino before we talk to Eagleton again. In fact, I'd rather not speak to Eagleton until we have him under arrest.'

'I'll call the Trenton field office and get someone over there right away.'

'No, Jake, we need to do this.'

'But Lucinda, they got the original statement without a hitch. Surely they are capable of the follow-up questions.'

'Jake, look at me.'

'What?' he said, glancing in her direction.

'Look at me. Really look at me.'

Jake stared at her, scanning her features in search of meaning. 'What, Lucy?'

'I,' she said, patting on her chest with the flat of her palm, 'need to be there, Jake. I need to look into his face when he tells me what I want to hear about Frank Eagleton. I need to do this, Jake.'

Jake nodded.

'Can you make this happen? Now?'

'I'll do what I can – but I can't make any promises.'

'Do it,' Lucinda said.

An hour and a half later, they were up in the air northward bound. Although they both were exhausted neither could get any sleep. Somewhere over the Washington DC area, the pilot turned around and tapped on his ear piece. Lucinda shrugged, not understanding what he wanted. He mimed pulling the headset over his head. Lucinda nodded and smiled and reached for her phones by her seat.

Once she had them in place he said, 'Received an urgent message from the forensics lab. Lab Tech Coynes wants you to know that Sergeant Colter turned in an abundant DNA sample for Frank Eagleton. Coynes is running the profile now.'

Lucinda said, 'Thank you,' and threw a victory fist in the air. She leaned over and spoke loudly into Jake's ear, explaining the message to him.

Down on the ground, a car with lights flashing delivered them to the jail in record time. Entering the interrogation room, a lawyer who, judging by the obvious expense of the cut and fabric of his suit, was far beyond the economic feasibility of your average criminal, sat next to Julius Trappatino, who was now wearing that hideous orange prisoner jumpsuit.

'Well, if it isn't the Beauty Boy and the Beast.'

The attorney laid a cautioning hand on his client's forearm. 'Agent, Lieutenant, I must inform you that I have advised my client that he does not – and should not – speak with you at this time. We have struck a deal with federal and local prosecutors. You have his full statement.'

'Really?' Lucinda said. 'Trap is afraid to speak to us?'

'No,' Trappatino's voice boomed. 'You flatter yourself.'

The attorney placed a hand on his arm again. 'My client has expressed a curiosity about the reason for your visit. I have advised him that satisfying that curiosity is not in his best interests. Nonetheless, he has insisted. But I warn you, I will terminate this interview if you do anything to compromise his plea bargain.'

'Yes, I am sure you will,' Jake said. 'Trap, do you know a man named Frank Eagleton?'

'Why would I?'

'I don't have the answer to that, Trap. Do you?'

'I suppose by his name, he is related to Candace Eagleton?'

'You know that, don't you, Trap?' Lucinda said.

'I might. What about him?'

'Your employer Tess Middleton has indicated that it was Frank Eagleton who plotted with you to frame her.'

Trappatino smiled. 'She did, did she? Convenient way to wiggle out of her own guilt, don't you think?'

'Perhaps,' Jake said. 'But unless you contradict her and provide additional information about the death of Candace Eagleton, our hands are tied. And without a trial for her complicity in these crimes, you will not have the opportunity to testify. And there goes your deal.'

Trappatino turned to his attorney, who said, 'There is a measure of optimism in their outlook; nonetheless it is a fairly accurate and unfortunate assessment of the situation.'

Trappatino looked across the table. 'I don't like this.'

'I can't say that we do either,' Jake said. 'We'd rather leave you to face lethal injection alone.'

'You are asking me to roll on someone who has never done me any harm.'

'Only because he hasn't given his statement yet,' Lucinda said.

Trappatino spread his hands flat on the surface of the table and stared at them. When he raised his head, he said, 'What do you want to know?'

'How does Frank Eagleton fit into this picture?'

Trappatino sighed. 'He did not make the arrangements with me. He did not pay me. However, he did talk to me. He told me he could help me by injecting his wife with a few doses of her allergy medicine to make her compliant.'

'And you did that?'

'No, I did not inject her. When I arrived at the Eagletons' home, Frank let me in the front door. He had a syringe in his hand. He said that he'd given her four times her normal dosage and she could no longer lift her head off of the pillow. I looked at his arms and saw scratch marks. I told him to keep his arms covered until they healed.'

'Was that the extent of your conversation?'

'No. I recommended Neosporin to accelerate the healing,' he said with a smile.

A flash of anger raced through Lucinda, making her clench her jaw. 'And then?'

'He said that he wanted to remove what remained of the drug from the home and we argued. I thought that since she had a prescription, it needed to stay where it was. But he was insistent. Knowing that pointed to him, rather than me, I let it go.'

'And then the two of you hung her from the railing.'

'Hah. You must be kidding. When I suggested that we go get her, he protested. He said he would have no part in the murder of his wife. I told him he already did when he stuck that needle in her arm. But he was not willing to witness the result of his desire to eliminate her. By that time, he disgusted me. I just wanted him gone. He told me to wait while he retrieved the medication. I asked him about a suicide note. He said that he'd found a note she had written that would suffice nicely. I watched him leave and go to work.'

'Details, Trap. We need details,' Lucinda said.

Trappatino's chest expanded and he forced out a long exhale. 'I grabbed her by the ankles and dragged her from the bed. She didn't resist when she hit the floor. She moaned a bit but made no attempt to stop me. Then, when we reached the threshold of the door, she jerked and grabbed onto the wooden trim on the inside of the door. For a moment, I regretted not insisting on keeping a dose of the prescription as a precaution. I tugged on her, forcing her to lose her grip. Then she went limp again. She had no more struggle left. I throttled her with the rope a few times hoping to get some useful information. When that failed, I hung her and walked out of the home.'

'You will sign a statement to that effect?'

'Yes,' Trappatino said with a nod.

'We'll be back in a moment then,' Lucinda said.

She located a computer she could use and sat down at the keyboard. Jake hung over her shoulder, offering editing suggestions as she worked. When she finished the summary of the interview and hit print, she said, 'I want a transcript of the complete interview and I want him to sign it.'

'You think that's necessary?' Jake asked.

'I do not want to take any chances.'

'OK, then, you've got it.'

'I want him to initial every page.'

'No problem.'

'OK, let's go.'

Trappatino read over the statement and wrote his name on the bottom of the page. He looked up and said, 'I suppose this means I'll have to testify against him, too.'

His lawyer interrupted. 'That is not part of our agreement with the prosecution.'

'In light of this new evidence – previously withheld by your client – I am certain that the prosecutors will demand a revision.'

'That does not mean we will have to accept it,' the lawyer said.

'Oh, no, not at all,' Jake said. 'If your client prefers the death penalty, you can ignore the new offer.'

'With that cheery thought,' Lucinda said, 'we'll bid you adieu for now.'

SIXTY-THREE

Out in the hallway, Lucinda and Jake high-fived and grinned uncontrollably.

'We nailed that bastard,' Lucinda crowed.

'A few husbands might get away with the murder of their wives,' Jake said. 'But we get most of them – most of the time. They're such likely suspects; I don't know how they think they'll get away with it.'

'But they do – over and over. Unfortunately, putting them in jail does not resurrect their wives. Now, that would be justice,' Lucinda said with a sigh.

'Shall we have someone pick up Frank Eagleton?'

'Oh, no. We'll get them busy on the arrest warrant – I'll fax this new signed statement, but I want the pleasure of arresting Frank Eagleton myself. I want to hear those cufflinks click shut as I wish him well in his new cell.'

'I sure won't be the one to deprive you of going in for the kill. But maybe we ought to put him under surveillance. I'd hate to find out he fled before we could effect the arrest.'

'Good idea. I'll take care of it – and the preparation of the arrest warrant. You take care of getting a copy of the tape and having the transcription made.'

They handled the details, got a ride back to the airport and set off for home. As they touched down in Virginia, Lucinda activated her cell. A voice message from Beth Ann Coynes waited for her. She pressed the playback button and listened.

'Lieutenant, Beth Ann Coynes here. The preliminary test results indicate that Frank Eagleton's DNA is consistent with the second male profile found beneath Candace Eagleton's fingernails. I am proceeding with confirmatory testing.'

Jake, too, had a message waiting. He listened and disconnected with a sour look on his face. 'Hope you had good news,' he said.

She told him about the DNA testing and asked, 'Your news was bad?'

'The wicked witch is demanding my presence in her office in DC.'

'That's bad news?'

'I'm sure she wants me there for a personal shin-kicking or worse – that's how she operates.'

'But Jake, you stopped a man attempting to blow up a city block, you apprehended a paid assassin that the FBI has wanted to arrest for years and your contribution to two murder cases was invaluable. How could she call you on the carpet?'

'Because that's what she does best.'

'Maybe this time, it's in her political self-interest to embrace your accomplishments and bask in the glory of your work.'

'I can only hope. You'll have to handle Frank Eagleton on your own. Sure you don't want to call his attorney and give him the opportunity to turn himself in at the station?'

'Are you trying to kill all my fun? No, I want to go in with a sea of blue behind me. That way when we arrive at the station, there's bound to be a lot of media cameras laying in wait for his perp walk. I certainly wouldn't want to deprive Eagleton of that moment in the spotlight.'

They separated as they reached the security exit – Lucinda going out of the airport, Jake headed to the gate as instructed by the regional director's administrative assistant.

Lucinda felt a sense of jubilation tempered by sadness at the tragic turn of events that turned Candace into a victim of her husband. What compelled him? Greed? Anger that she was leaving? Some unknown factor? Or a combination of the three?

Candace was not totally blameless. She should have never tried to extort money from Tess Middleton. She should never have informed her husband she was leaving – she should have just left and concealed her new location. It's a sad fact that the most dangerous time in a woman's life begins when she announces her departure and continues for two years.

But even though Candace was involved in a blackmail scheme, she'd committed no capital crime. She did not deserve the death penalty. Certainly, she had set herself up to be in this vulnerable situation but still, she did not deserve to die because of it.

Now she was going to hold Frank Eagleton accountable for his role in his wife's death. And she was going to enjoy it because she hated when someone lied to her – despised it when someone tried to manipulate her and play her like a fool.

Back at the justice center, Lucinda added the finishing touches to the arrest warrant request and appeared before a judge for approval. Once the document was signed, she gathered up the uniforms and asked Sergeant Robin Colter to accompany her on the arrest. Colter deserved to share the moment, Lucinda thought. She had gotten the DNA that provided the last bit of evidence needed to make the murder charge stick.

Jake paced in the vestibule of Sandra Goodman's office. She kept him waiting over ten minutes before telling her secretary to send him in to see her. When he entered she stood in front of her desk, her arms akimbo, venom in her eyes.

'Once I learned that your flight left on time, I arranged for a press conference. It begins in five minutes. When it does, I will tell the media about the wonderful job you have done – saving lives, capturing a dangerous criminal, solving a murder case. I am doing this not because I think you deserve accolades for your performance – you and I both know you forced your way back into active duty. I do it for one reason only: it is in my best interest. It will make me choke. But I will do it.

'When the press conference is over, you will immediately go on vacation and please go far away – preferably out of the country – for at least two weeks. I do not want you to have any additional press opportunities because I don't want to see your face looming at me when I open the newspaper at breakfast and I don't want to see you on television staring into my living room as I attempt to unwind from my day. In fact, I want a brief period of time to forget you exist. Do you understand?'

Jake looked down at the toe of his turquoise Chucks, as he ground down into the floor. He fantasized that Goodman's nose lay beneath his foot. A vacation would be nice if he could take Lucinda with him. Still, it galled him to be ordered away as if what he had done was a source of shame for the department. He knew it wasn't. He knew it was the wicked witch's ego and envy at work. Nonetheless, he resented the position she was making him occupy.

He looked up after a minute and said, 'Whatever you want, Director.'

'Well, then, let's go.'

When the mediafest was over, Goodman walked away without a word to Jake, leaving him standing before a roomful of hungry reporters all alone. They moved in for the kill. Most of the questions were typical follow-ups on these types of occasions: how did he feel about his role in these investigations; what did he plan to do now and how did it feel to be a hero.

One astute reporter asked something decidedly different: 'What's the bug up Goodman's ass, Agent Lovett? She doesn't like you much, does she?'

Jake turned to the middle-aged man with the perception of a smart, seasoned journalist. He wanted to answer the question but knew he should not. He simply said, 'No comment' and left the room.

SIXTY-FOUR

Lucinda ordered no lights and no sirens as the caravan of law enforcement set out for Frank Eagleton's home. She had Robin call his office first to make sure he had left for the day.

The cars glided into place outside of the house. Lucinda sent a handful of uniforms around to the back of the house and she and Robin approached the front door with a comforting contingent of officers at their backs.

She stepped up on the front step and a gunshot rang out. Lucinda turned to order a battering ram to break down the heavy front door. She ignored the sound of knuckles on glass until Robin shouted, 'Lieutenant!'

She spun back around and followed Robin's pointed finger. Eagleton stood in front of one of the tall, narrow windows that flanked the door. One of his arms was wrapped around the throat of a young blonde woman. The other held a revolver up against her head.

'Damn,' she exclaimed. A man who killed the mother of his

children would not hesitate to shoot the woman he held tightly against his chest. She pulled out her cell and called Eagleton's landline. She was close enough to hear the ring echo inside the house. Again, Frank shook his head. She stared at him and he smirked. He mouthed, *Check.*

She turned around and yelled for a bullhorn. A young uniformed officer sprinted up the walkway and handed her the equipment. 'Frank Eagleton,' she bellowed and swallowed hard. She hated this part. She knew she was going to sound like a refugee from a cheesy crime show. 'Frank Eagleton, your house is surrounded. Let the hostage go. Drop the gun on the porch and walk out with your hands folded on top of your head.'

On the other side of the glass, Frank laughed.

'Bullshit,' she said, her voice amplified through the megaphone. She winced, hoping none of the neighbors heard. At least no media had arrived yet. She turned to Robin and whispered, 'Get the roadway blocked to keep out the media and any returning residents. And clear out the occupants of all the homes on this side of the block.'

She turned her gaze back to the window and lifted the bullhorn again. 'Eagleton, there is no way out if you won't speak to me. If I call again, will you answer?'

Eagleton shook his head.

'Don't make us come in after you.'

Eagleton laughed again. He pulled back the revolver six inches and jammed it hard into the side of the woman's head. She flinched from the blow and trembled all over.

'So you want to play charades, Eagleton?'

Frank bent forward and appeared to be whispering in the woman's ear. She looked up, held her hands to her mouth and shouted, 'He says, "Look, Ma! No hands!"'

'Who are you?' she asked the woman.

She opened her mouth to answer and Frank shoved the end of the revolver between her teeth.

Shit, Lucinda thought as Robin returned to her side. She whispered into Lucinda's ear, 'Don't look but a sniper accessed the roof of the house across the street. He's lying flat and says he's got a bead on Eagleton. He says he feels fairly certain that he can deliver a round into Eagleton's right ear but it will be tight and there is a risk of hitting the hostage.'

'Tell him to hold fire for now,' Lucinda said. 'Frank, you're not a stupid man. This is no time for games.'

Eagleton nodded. Beside him, the hostage's tears mingled with mascara, leaving a dirty black trail on her cheeks.

Lucinda wanted to smash the glass and snatch her away but knew it was an unrealistic impulse. But how to get the woman safely away? She didn't really care if Frank emerged from the house dead or alive. She turned to Robin and whispered, 'I need a chair – are there any in the back of the house?'

'I'll see,' she said and took off. She returned in a moment with a canvas director chair. 'Will this work?'

'Perfect,' Lucinda said. 'See if you can get Frank's son and daughter over here.' She unfolded the chair on the broad walkway at the edge of the porch, set the bullhorn down beside it within reach and settled down, staring straight at the window. She hoped her message was clear – she was seated and comfortable and ready to wait him out for as long as it took.

An hour later, she could tell Frank was tiring. He shifted his weight from one foot to the other often. The hostage continued to tremble, hard enough, it seemed, to make body parts loosen. She heard a commotion behind her and saw an arriving car battling its way through the media mob on the perimeter of the secure area. She turned back to see Frank looking away from her toward the hubbub. She picked up the bullhorn. 'We have visitors, Eagleton.'

Frank responded with a shrug and gave his hostage a squeeze. The sharp pitch of her yip reverberated on the glass. A scowl formed on Frank's face. Lucinda gathered that he was not pleased to see his son and daughter coming up the sidewalk. Lucinda rose from her chair and greeted them behind a large, portable sheet of bullet-resistant glass on wheels. It reminded Lucinda of a transparent version of a supplemental classroom blackboard.

The eyes of Frank's daughter Molly blazed and her cheeks burned. She snatched the bullhorn from Lucinda. 'I've prayed to God for your soul for many years. I see my prayers have gone unanswered. You killed my mother and now you are willing to forfeit the life of your hostage. But the game's over. The only way you will save your sorry skin is to let her go. I cast you out of my life for now and for all eternity. I'd ask for God to have mercy on your soul but you do not deserve it.' She shoved the bullhorn back at Lucinda, turned and walked away.

In contrast, Frank's son, Mark, had tears in his eyes as he accepted the megaphone from the detective. He raised it to his mouth and then dropped it to his side. His head hung down as he fought to control his emotions. He shuddered, straightened up and brought the sound amplifying device to his lips. 'I am so sorry, Dad. I should have been there for you. I know everything was difficult with mother. I should have been more supportive. I should have been there.'

Mark paused and studied his father's face for a moment. 'Dad, please, let that woman go. I am not going to leave until this is over and I do not want it to end with you lying dead at my feet. Please, Dad. These people don't understand. They will stop at nothing. On the way in, I saw a sniper on the roof across the street . . .'

Lucinda jerked the bullhorn from Mark's hands, furious that he revealed that bit of information. She looked at Frank's eyes going back and forth across the neighbor's slate tiles until his eyes settled on one spot.

'Eagleton, listen to your children. Let the woman go. Or pick up a phone and talk to me. Don't make this end with your death.'

For the first time since the stand-off started, Frank stepped back away from the window, dragging his hostage with him. Lucinda could no longer see him. Was he going to let her go? Was he going to call? Or, God forbid, was he going to shoot her and then himself? Should she send in the entry team? Or would that set off a situation that ended with a dead hostage? Was it the only way to save her life? She jumped to a decision then reversed it. Everything was unknown. Every move would be a gamble. Her cell rang. She snatched it out of her pocket and looked at the screen. Jake? Ohmigod! She disconnected the call and waited.

Finally, the phone rang again.

She recognized Frank's cell number and pressed the connect button. 'Mr Eagleton?'

'You are responsible for this, Lieutenant. If you'd done the right thing and called my attorney instead of barging onto my property, this woman would not be in this situation.'

Lucinda's breath caught in her throat. Stay calm, she urged herself. 'Yes, Mr Eagleton, I made a big mistake. Please don't make her pay for my wrongdoing. I can't take it back but if you let her go, I will extricate you from this situation without any bloodshed. Where are you now?'

'Wouldn't you like to know? All you need to know, though, is that I am still in the house. She's got a bicycle chain wrapped around her thigh and she's fastened to an immovable object. I've got one hand on my cell; the other is still holding the gun to her head.'

'May I speak to her, Mr Eagleton?'

A moment of silence preceded his answer. 'No.'

'OK. This is an overwrought situation. Only you can defuse it, Mr Eagleton.'

'On the contrary, Lieutenant, you can defuse it. Just walk away – and take your goons with you.'

'You know I can't do that.'

'Call off the sniper.'

'Mr Eagleton, would you like to speak to your son?'

'You leave him out of it! Send him away now.'

Lucinda walked over to Mark and handed him the phone, hoping he would not make the situation worse.

'Dad,' Mark said.

'Go home, son. Go home, now. That cop should have not gotten you involved.'

'No, Dad, I can't. Please can I come inside with you?'

'Just leave, Mark. We'll talk later.'

Mark dropped the cell on the ground and sprinted to the front porch. Lucinda shouted an expletive and launched her body into the air, tackling him before he could reach the door. She shouted and officers came running. They slapped on cuffs and escorted Mark back to a waiting patrol car.

Lucinda retrieved the phone and said, 'Mr Eagleton?'

'What's happening? What did you do to my son?'

Lucinda's mind raced. Should she tell him the truth? Or would that make him do something rash? 'Your son is OK. Please don't make this day any more difficult for him. Release the hostage. Please.'

'Let me speak to Mark.'

'That's no longer possible, sir.'

'That's where you're wrong, Lieutenant. I'm in the catbird seat. And you've now really pissed me off.'

'Mr Eagleton, let's wrap this up now. Send her out . . .'

A shrill, sharp scream echoed in the house and made the hair up and down Lucinda's arms stand at attention.

SIXTY-FIVE

J ake, standing near a gate at the Ronald Reagan Washington National Airport, looked down at his phone in surprise. His call to Lucinda didn't go to voicemail, it just cut off. He contemplated the possible reasons and decided she must be interviewing Frank Eagleton. Still, he wondered, why hadn't she simply shut off her phone before she started?

His eyes drifted to a television monitor mounted on the ceiling. He saw an aerial view of a house surrounded by police vehicles, amid a large crowd of media. He walked closer to hear the commentary. Before the audio came into range, he realized he recognized the house. It took him a moment to identify it but when he did, it hit him hard. Frank Eagleton's house.

When he could hear, he went numb. A hostage situation going into its third hour. He got as close to the screen as he could, searching the crowd out front for a glimpse of Lucinda. No one's features were distinct but one figure reminded him of her.

He was mesmerized by the stagnant situation before his eyes. The commentator spoke of a stand-off. Boarding for his flight was announced. He looked over his shoulder at the line forming by the Jetway but could not tear himself away from the screen.

A figure broke away and ran toward the front door. Another soared through the air and brought the first one down. That had to be Lucinda. He knew it. He was torn between wanting to know more and catching his flight to get down there and lend his assistance. He dashed for the plane when he heard the intercom announce last call.

Walking down the aisle, Jake felt claustrophobic. He'd flown thousands of times but never before had he felt imprisoned. He wondered if that was how the prisoners he'd transported felt when he'd executed an extradition treaty and forced them onto a plane.

Jake sat in his seat, overflowing with restless impatience. The plane could not take off soon enough. It could not fly fast enough. He did not know how he would contain his anxiety until he arrived at the scene.

He began second-guessing what he saw. Was that Lucinda who hit the ground? If so, was it really a tackle, as he first thought, or was she shot? Bile rose in his throat. He squeezed the arms of his seat.

Seated next to him, a white-haired woman, who appeared to be in her eighties, patted the back of his hand. 'It'll be all right. We'll be back on the ground before you know it.'

Agitated, Jake almost snapped at her but stopped himself before he did. 'Thank you, ma'am,' he said. 'I'll be all right.'

'I know you will, dear. If you need to squeeze my hand, please feel free.'

Much closer to the scene of the hostage situation, another pair of eyes focused on the developing situation on the television. Charley Spencer picked up her cell phone and sent a text message to Lucinda. 'Lucy. Watching TV breaking news. Are you there? Is that you near the house?'

Charley sat back to watch the unfolding news but kept an eye on her phone, waiting for the pinging glass sound that heralded the arrival of a response. When she hadn't received one for ten minutes, she leaned forward toward the television and chewed on her thumbnail.

SIXTY-SIX

Lucinda shouted into the bullhorn: 'Eagleton! What just happened in there? Send out your hostage now!'

She gave him two seconds to respond and when she heard nothing she ordered everyone inside. 'Go. Go. Go.'

An officer approached the front door and heaved a battering ram into it again and again. Lucinda heard the sound of broken glass as the officers in the rear of the house breached the French doors. The second the ram splintered the wood surrounding the lock, she pushed inside. 'Eagleton! Hands on your head. Down on your knees.'

'Here, Lieutenant!' an unknown voice shouted from deeper in the house. Lucinda raced toward the sound. In the kitchen, Frank Eagleton was lying on his side, curled into a ball on the tile floor, moaning. Doubled over but still on her feet, the hostage was tethered to the interior framing of a lower cabinet, a bloody butcher knife clutched in her fist. Her face was ashen, her legs trembling, her lips moving without a sound.

'Cut her loose. Get the paramedics.' While an officer used a saw to free the woman, Lucinda put an arm around her to keep her knees from buckling and dumping her on the floor.

'Hush, hush,' she said. 'Everything is going to be all right. You're safe now. Let me have the knife.' Lucinda wrapped her fingers around the hand holding the knife. The hostage startled, jerked back and stabbed Lucinda in the thigh.

'Holy shit!' she yelled and jumped back. 'Drop the damn knife, lady.'

She let go of the weapon and it clattered on the tile. 'I'm sorry, I'm sorry, I'm sorry,' she sobbed. 'I'm so sorry. Please forgive me. I'm so sorry.'

Uniforms surrounded her in a flash.

'Easy, easy,' Lucinda urged. 'Don't hurt her; just get her out of here. She needs medical attention.'

'Colter!' Lucinda yelled.

Robin stepped into the kitchen and rushed toward Lucinda with outstretched arms.

'Not me. The knife. Bag the damn knife.'

'Lieutenant, you're bleeding.'

'Later, Colter,' Lucinda said and grabbed a kitchen towel off a nearby hook. She pressed it into her wound and watched as it slowly bloomed red. She lowered herself to the floor next to Frank Eagleton, keeping the pressure on the cut.

'Lieutenant?' Colter said.

'It looks worse than it is, Colter. Get me something to prop up my leg.'

'But, Lieutenant . . .'

'Do it, Colter.'

Robin's eyes darted around the kitchen, then she dashed into the living room. She grabbed a sofa cushion and returned to Lucinda, tucking it under her injured leg.

'Eagleton,' Lucinda said.

Frank whimpered and moaned.

'Man up, Eagleton. You weren't hurt that badly or you'd be in a pool of blood by now.'

'I'm going to die,' he wailed.

'Not unless I kill you.'

Frank moaned louder.

A paramedic kneeled beside him and gently rolled him on his back to examine his wound. He pulled back his shirt and used scissors to release the waistband of his pants.

'What does it look like?' Lucinda asked.

'I'd guess that the knife deflected off his iliac crest – the top of his hip bone – and didn't go any deeper. Doesn't appear to have hit any internal organs but we'll have to get him to the hospital to check it out.' The paramedic cleaned the cut and called for a stretcher.

'Wait,' Lucinda said. 'I need to talk to him.'

'Ma'am, I need to get him to the hospital – and you, too, for that matter.'

'It can wait. Eagleton, stop moaning and look at me.'

Eagleton whimpered and said, 'Oh, please, let me die in peace.'

'Don't be such a wuss, Eagleton. Look at me, dammit!'

Eagleton slowly turned his head to the side.

'Why the hell did you pull this stunt?'

'Because I'm being framed, Lieutenant. And now I'm going to die.'

'Shut up with the dying crap. You're going to be fine. What do you mean you're being framed?'

'I went to that woman just to warn her. I knew Candace was up to no good. I knew she planned to blackmail her.'

'What woman?'

'Tess Middleton. I told her that Candace was doing it only because I contributed to Middleton's senatorial campaign. I never thought she'd kill my wife. Now she's trying to pin it on me.'

Lucinda rolled her eyes. 'Right. What about the other guy?'

'What other guy?' Frank asked.

'Oh jeez, you know what other guy. The one you let into the house. The one you helped murder your wife, you lying son of a bitch.'

'Lieutenant,' Robin interrupted. 'If you are going to continue in this vein, we need to read Mr Eagleton his rights.'

'Screw that,' Lucinda snapped.

'Lieutenant, you're injured and you're in pain. But you know I'm right.'

'Of course you are. That doesn't mean I have to like it.'

Robin suppressed a laugh. 'No, Lieutenant, you don't have to like it one little bit.'

The stretcher arrived and two emergency techs loaded Frank onto it and rolled him outside. The paramedic knelt beside Lucinda and said, 'Your turn, Lieutenant.'

'I'm fine. I'll drive down to the emergency room when I finish here.'

'Don't mind me, Lieutenant. I'm used to dealing with hysterical victims at both crime and accident scenes. I know how to ignore them very well,' he said as he cut up the side of the skirt of her navy suit with a pair of scissors.

'I am not hysterical.'

'Patients after trauma are often hysterical, in denial or in shock. Whatever it is, I just ignore them and continue with what needs to be done.'

'Whatever, but I have a job to do.'

'I'm sure you do, Lieutenant, but so do I. You've got a nasty little puncture wound here but it's not too deep at all. We'll need to have a doctor double-check it, maybe put in a couple of stitches and get you a tetanus shot. But then you'll be good to go.'

'I don't need to go in an ambulance.'

'You want me to lose my job?'

'Let's not be ridiculous,' Lucinda said.

'I could say the same to you, Lieutenant. Let us take proper care of you and then you can go on your way. If you resist, I'll have to call your captain.'

Lucinda exhaled. 'Fine.' She kept her mouth shut as she was loaded onto a stretcher and rolled to an ambulance. She hated not standing on her own two feet but she certainly didn't want to drag her captain into it.

Twenty minutes later, she lay in a bed in a bay of the treatment area of the emergency room with curtains drawn around her. She heard the metal hangers rattle on the ceiling track as the curtain pulled back to reveal Jake.

'Lucinda,' he said, grabbing her hand and placing a gentle kiss on her forehead.

'I won't break, Jake.'

He lowered his mouth to hers, sucking her lower lip in between his teeth. Pulling back, he said, 'Oh, that was nice.'

'Get me out of here and you can have more of them.'

A white jacketed arm poked in through the curtain and shoved it back on its rails. 'Good evening, Lieutenant,' a young doctor said as he looked down at the metal clipboard in his hand. 'Looks like you've had a bad day.' Turning to Jake, he said, 'You're going to have to leave for a bit while I examine my patient.'

'A word, Doctor?' Jake asked.

The doctor nodded and stepped outside the curtains.

'She's going to be fine?'

'It appears that way – unless I find something unexpected.'

'Then she can travel?'

'Not right now but I don't anticipate any problems an hour from now.'

Jake faked a punch to the doctor's upper arm. 'Thanks, Doc.'

EPILOGUE

J ake returned to the hospital and entered Lucinda's examination area sporting a huge grin. A nurse followed him pushing a wheelchair.

'What are you smiling about, Jake?' Lucinda asked.

'It's time to go.'

Lucinda made a dismissive gesture in the direction of the wheelchair. 'That is not necessary,' she said.

'But it is hospital policy,' the nurse said.

'Oh, please . . .'

'C'mon, Lucinda, I know you don't like rules and you prefer not to follow established procedures. But we'll get you out of here more quickly if you don't argue with this poor, beleaguered nurse who's just trying to do her job.'

The nurse laughed.

Lucinda rolled her eyes and slid into the chair. As she rolled down the hall, she asked, 'And just why do we need to get out of here quickly?'

'What?' Jake said. 'You like hospitals?'

'You know that's not true.'

'Just the same, when are you coming back for more facial reconstruction surgery?'

Lucinda sighed. 'Dr Burns came to visit me this morning. He denied it but I'm sure you or Charley put him up to it.'

'You think I would admit to that if I had? If I say I did, you'll be angry with me. If I say I didn't, I'd be implicating Charley – and you'd never forgive me for that. I lose either way. No comment – although thoroughly unsatisfactory – is my only option.'

Lucinda gave him a baleful look. 'You did, didn't you?'

Jake shrugged.

'Anyway. Dr Burns called his appointments secretary and set it all up this morning.'

'What's he going to do?'

'He said he would eliminate the puckering caused over here by scar tissue,' she said, touching the damaged side of the face. 'Then he badgered me about coming back before the end of the year to smooth out the skin on my upper cheek.'

'Did you set that up, too?'

'Are you kidding me, Jake?'

Jake snickered. 'When did you schedule the next procedure?'

'Next month.'

'Perfect timing,' Jake said.

'What does that mean?'

'Everything is taken care of. You are now on a two-week vacation. We'll swing by your place and pack up what you need. Then we'll stay at my place – it's closer to the airport. Our flight leaves at seven fifteen in the morning.'

'What flight? What vacation?'

'You and I are going to Negril Beach.'

'Jamaica?'

'Yep. Seven miles of unspoiled white sand beach. Lounge chairs by the water tucked under thatched umbrellas. Hammocks swinging beneath the palms. Fruity rum drinks with umbrellas and hunks of pineapple. Long walks by the lapping water in so many incredible shades of blue it's enough to make you cry. Dining under the stars. Snorkeling among the fish. And pure unadulterated relaxation.'

'I can't just do that.'

'I know you find it difficult to relax. But a couple of days in Negril will suck the type A even out of you.'

'I didn't mean I couldn't relax. I mean, I just can't up and run away from home. I have a job, responsibilities . . .'

'Oh, yes, you can. Your captain approved your leave. I've lined up a babysitter for beloved cat and confidante Chester. And Charley made me promise to take pictures. All you need to do is tell Chester goodbye.'

'But there's still one loose end in the case,' Lucinda objected.

'A loose end? Middleton was the brains. She hired Trappatino. She used Eagleton since he fit in with her plans. All three are under arrest. Rowland and Candace are dead. Bonnie is found. Sounds wrapped up to me.'

'Who is "unknown?"'

'Unknown?'

'You know. It was written on that note you found in Rowland's apartment.'

Jake shrugged. 'Who knows? Rowland was just wondering about the possibility there was someone else, I'd say. There's no indication that there was.'

'But what if there is someone else involved?' Lucinda asked.

'See – that's exactly why you need to get away from here and relax.'

'Why are you doing this?'

'Because you deserve it. Because I want to spend time with you. Because the beach is incredible. Because it will give us some time without other distractions to talk about our future.'

'I've never said we had a future, Jake. And besides, I still have at least two more surgeries.'

'And that is what we will talk about. No pressure. Just a clear understanding of each other and our expectations.'

'What else are you plotting, Jake?'

'I'll admit. I thought of arranging to get married on the beach . . .'

'I knew it.'

'But I thought better of it,' Jake added. 'It is just my little fantasy. I do not expect it to happen on this trip.'

The nurse stopped the wheelchair beside Jake's waiting car. He put a hand on each of the arms and leaned towards her. 'I need to know what goes on in that complicated head of yours.'

'And you think I know?' Lucinda said with a laugh.

The next afternoon, Lucinda and Jake arrived in the airport at Montego Bay and Jake led her to the Tim Air counter.

Lucinda whispered, 'Tim Air? What kind of name is that for an airline?'

'When an airline transports you to paradise, does it matter what it's called? You're going to love it. Trust me.'

'Dangerous words, Special Agent Lovett. You better hope you can deliver.'

And he did. The small plane followed the emerald-green coast high above the multiple hues of turquoise and deep blue. The beauty below her was a jolting shift from everyday reality. It almost seemed too much to absorb. The aerial view filled Lucinda's chest with intense emotion. A thin white strand wrapped the coastline as they neared Negril, separating the vibrancy of the sea from the lushness of the tropical growth and pastel-colored resorts. She squeezed Jake's hand.

There was no place she'd rather be than on a green island surrounded by water. And she had to admit, she could not think of anyone she'd rather have by her side than Jake. She could hardly wait to land. She wanted to smell the salty air, wriggle her toes in the sand like an unabashed tourist, listen to the lapping water and the cries of the seabirds.

The plane turned inland and began its descent. Lucinda gasped. Below were tall grasses, boggy patches of muck and one thin dirt strip of dry ground running down the middle. A safe landing appeared impossible. She tightened her grip on Jake's hand and didn't let go until the wheels hit the ground and the plane slowed to a crawl. She hadn't realized she was holding her breath until she released a huge exhalation of relief.

Jake smiled at her with total satisfaction. He'd taken a risk whisking her away like he had. But he was so afraid that if the current state of limbo continued he was going to lose her. He was determined to whittle away at her protective shell, prove his trust-worthiness and find out what really lay deep within her heart.